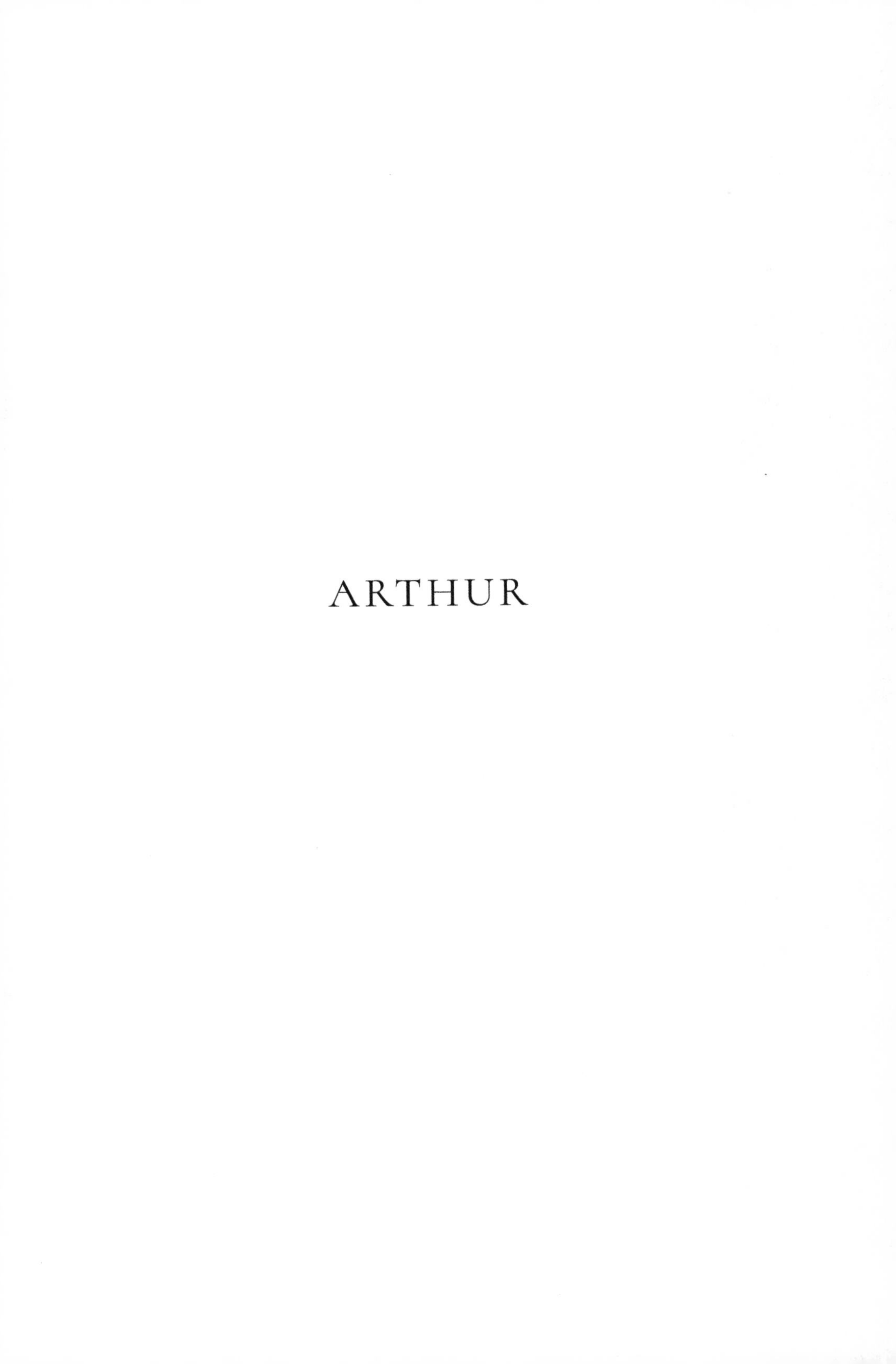

ARTHUR

ARTHUR

BRETT F. BRALEY-PALKO

Thane & Prose New York, London

Contents

Dedication

This book is a love letter to my dogs: Murphy, Elsa and Milo. You three are my soulmates, and so I dedicate this book to you.

Prologue

I have been aboard the *Mathilde* for three days now, which has given me more time to think than I have had in years. While I am currently sharing an interior portside room with my ex-best friend, Horace, and four dogs, I spend most evenings in silence.

I do my best thinking in silence. It's a habit of mine now to find a lonesome space and stare into the ocean at night. I believe it was Homer who described the sea as wine-dark. I can't think of any Cabernet that's as dark as the Atlantic appears right now. I must remember to ask Horace if they had Cabernets in ancient Greece.

I must also remember that I am still mad at Horace, so I will disregard the above.

I have one special spot I like more than any other on this ship. I learned about it two nights ago when I was eavesdropping on the Captain's table. It seems there is an old Romanian count onboard who is wheelchair-bound, but has the vessel's best suite—with a balcony and a dressing room. He is too nervous to go on the balcony, or even the ship's deck, for that matter, afraid a bump will send him rolling off into the water. Being a cripple, he can't swim. Being a count, he is too proud to ask for another room. Being a Romanian, he is content to sit in his room and play cards with his nurse all day.

The Captain was gossiping about this Romanian count whose neighbors complain night and day of his cigarette smoke. He will not open the balcony door even a crack—even a sliver!—to let some fresh air into his room.

By this time, I had to take my leave from eavesdropping. I am smuggling four dogs and myself into America and it was our dinner time. I have sewn extra pockets into my dinner jacket to nick food from the buffet table to my modest room. The dogs yip and bounce and tap-dance on their hind legs when I wear my dinner jacket, as they know a meal is coming. I have learned that half of them like seafood and half do not. That night's meal was steak tips in Bordelaise, so all snoozed contentedly, bellies full and legs twitching happily. I had a little steak left over in my breast pocket. I saved this aside for Horace—who was gambling, if I recall correctly—to have as a midnight snack. (I was not mad at Horace two nights ago.)

As the dogs snored, I changed quickly into flannels and wet my face. I had lost my hat the very first night onboard. A wind blew and off it went. I did not grow up near water. Horace said this was a rookie mistake. I was annoyed when he said this. Horace grew up in Derbyshire.

I was curious to catch a glimpse of this count. I have met countesses, but they are always escorted by chinless, mumbling earls. Counts are a purely continental invention and most are poorer than a butcher anymore. I like that, since I am richer than most butchers I have met. At the time, I was suspicious as to whether this Romanian count was the real thing. To me, Europeans pick up titles like jacks. The ball bounces and a bunch of cousins' hands go snatching.

The flannel shirt I was wearing was what I called my Good Shirt. I found it on a coat rack at The Pelican, unattended and handsome, so I took it. It looked so lonely, just waiting for its owner to come back. I thought I could give it a better home, so I walked right out with it under my arm. Come to think of it, this is how I ended up with so many dogs.

My Good Shirt gave me the confidence to stroll anywhere I wanted on the ship. I believe confidence is the ticket to social mobility and that night I was feeling attractive. It only took me a second in the hallway to sniff out the Romanian count's room. The name written on the placard on the door was my other clue: *His Lordship Count Andrei Găvăneşti.* Bluish smoke wafted out from under the door and through the peephole, through the keyhole even. I doubted I would see him, and while my Good Shirt had given me some confidence, I was too shy to knock and introduce myself. Instead I turned around to leave, pocketing the name placard to use as a bookmark.

Two days ago, I was still getting used to being on the ship and could not easily fall asleep. When I would doze off, I would jolt up in bed, worried the London police were going to be waiting for me in New York. My sudden movement would cause the dogs to wake up, too. If they barked, Horace and I would rush to quiet them with kisses and ear scratches and soothing little words. In the morning, Horace and I would walk into the breakfast hall complaining about some damned dogs barking in the small hours of the morning to throw others off our own scent. Then I would steal a handful of sausages and tuck them into my pocket for their breakfast.

Because I could not sleep easily two nights ago, I wandered the ship to relax my mind and exhaust my body. I am a slender man, but I am not athletically inclined. I huff and puff walking around the deck. The only thing that seemed to soothe my lungs was the fresh sea air when I would take a break on a reclining chair and smoke a cigarette. I did this every hour or so when we first boarded the ship.

It was when I was having my second cigarette in one such chair that I had a small stroke of brilliance. The more I thought of that chimney of a man, Count Găvăneşti, the more I thought what a pity it was that the balcony was being ignored. Like my Good Shirt and my four dogs, I was sad that it was not being appreciated. That is when I decided that this balcony, being so ungratefully ignored, deserved someone like me.

So, for the last two days, I have been trespassing aboard the *Mathilde*. It is an easy enough thing to do. I just wait until the sun sets and up I go. This is a ship that drinks freely, so most people do not notice that I am carrying a pillow and a rope made from torn bed sheets. I walk with a smile on my face. If my Good Shirt is dirty, I will wear my second-best shirt, which is navy blue and missing a button on one sleeve. Otherwise it is in good shape. I have noticed throughout my years of trespassing that a smile and a clean shirt often work better than a key when it comes to access.

The rope made from a bedsheet is the reason Horace is my ex-best friend. Upon returning from the Count's hallway, with the stolen placard secreted away in my pocket, I began to form a plan for how I would use the count's balcony. I figured my best bet was to climb, unnoticed, onto the balcony from the main deck. It was my belief that the cigarette smoke would be too great for the count or his nurse to see me through the French door. If anything, they would mistake my silhouette for a large seagull, or perhaps a beautiful, leaping dolphin. I believe my hunch has been correct, and that I have thankfully remained unnoticed.

I could not ask any of the crew for a rope. And mine being an interior portside room, my linens were not refreshed regularly, so I decided to look for a substitute. Our room is small: two beds, one shared nightstand, a wash basin, and a cup for our toothbrushes. It is made even smaller by the dogs who cover both the floor and my bed. They do not sleep in Horace's bed. He has a tendency to kick them when he sleeps, so the dogs do not like Horace.

Horace's bed was unattended and his bedsheets were crumpled at its foot. Horace is a restless sleeper, even more so when he loses at craps. Every morning, I ask Horace to make his bed and every morning he grumbles. I have come to believe, and have told Horace this when we argued, that if he was nice to the dogs, if he had made his bed, I would not have been so tempted to use his bedsheets. Horace is sensitive about others touching his things.

Well, there they were and there I was. I took out my pair of manicure scissors and snipped the sheets into long strips. I was lucky to have remembered my grooming kit. We were in such a rush to escape for America, my packing was a blur. I then double- and tripled-knotted the strips of cloth into a long rope. I looped one end. I would use it to lasso the ornamental lantern next to the balcony and climb right up.

I am a very good knot-tier and was excited to show Horace my handiwork. He came through the door close to midnight, smelling of sweat and bourbon and cigar smoke. When I lifted my rope to show him, he asked, "What did you do to my bed?"

I told him about the Count, but that did not seem to interest him. He said I should not touch his things. He made mean remarks about the dogs, too, which I will not repeat. He said I will give him my bed sheets as repayment. I said I will not, my reason being that Milly, my pug, is eleven and shivers at night. He was being mean and unreasonable. He must have lost big at the tables. He didn't even notice how good my knots were.

Horace and I have not spoken since that night, which does not bother me. I have been camping out on the balcony chair, using the nearby lantern and starlight to write this journal. I usually doze when it is very late, but always wake up before sunrise. Having slept on many benches in London and avoided the policeman's baton here and there, I believe my body is well trained for this exercise.

We will arrive in New York in three more days, which gives me just as much time to finish this journal. I must account for the time I had spent in England and how I ended up in the deckchair of a crippled Romanian count with my ex-best friend Horace and four dogs.

I

A Very Influential Author

Like all great authors, I should introduce myself. My name is Arthur Croots. It is not an attractive last name and I would change it in a heartbeat, but I have a very nice signature and would not want to ruin that. Sometimes, when I do not have to write my last name, like at a hotel buffet or a darts competition, I will introduce myself as Arthur Boisseau. Boisseau was my mother's maiden name. She is dead now, which is sad. In the guestbook at her funeral, I had the best signature of anyone who had attended.

Horace did not attend my mother's funeral and, at the time, I did not have any dogs. I did not even know Horace then, and I was very lonely after my mom died.

You might think that with a last name like Boisseau, that she was French. Maybe she was, but she did not speak any French. In fact, she didn't even speak English very well, because she grew up in America. She looked pretty in the photos I've seen of her as a young woman. She was old when she had me, and she was not very pretty when she died. When I remember her, I force myself to remember her pretty and young and in black-and-white. It makes me sad to know she did not die beautiful. She died very grey-looking.

I am attracted to beautiful things; and, therefore, I like to collect them. The problem is that I am poor, so my collections are generally small. I own a very nice comb I found in the Earl of Lumley-Brummel's bathroom once. I also have one cufflink from the Duke of Lumbardo. I saw it fall off his shirt cuff one night as he danced. I do not speak Italian, so I put it in my pocket. I promised myself I would post it to him, with the help of the hotel bellhop, Stefano, as translator. Stefano did not know the address of the Duke of Lumbardo's house and I did not have any money for postage, so I had to keep the cufflink. I believed I would appreciate it more than him anyway. It really is a beautiful cufflink.

I hope it does not seem like I am bragging when I talk about my friends, the Earl of Lumley-Brummel and the Duke of Lumbardo. I am not bragging, I am simply telling you that I know them. Anyway, we are not really friends. The only words the Duke of Lumbardo ever said to me were, "*Che ore sono?*" I pointed down the hall to where the men's restrooms were. He seemed very confused. Perhaps even he did not speak Italian.

Being impoverished, I sometimes have to work. I prefer to take jobs that allow me to be close to people of influence. This means that I have worked as a waiter and a caterer. It has also means I have worked as a valet, a lifeguard, and an architect's apprentice. I nearly had a job once as a German ambassador's attaché. I thought if I answered every question with a *ja* or a *nein* that I could fib my way through the interview. Unfortunately, I mistook the janitor for the ambassador and he shredded my resume when I handed it to him. This upset me because the job paid well and I thought that, given the chance, I could have been quite good at it.

Come to think of it, had I got the German attaché job, I would not be heading to New York right now.

It is strange to think that I have been what some would call "down and out" in my life, but it is true. My mother did not have anything to leave and my had father died years before. If you met me, you would think I was being dramatic to say that I have been chased out of my last three flats at the point of landladies' broom handles. I am not the dramatic type, so believe me when I say it is true. It is not that I don't try to save money; but I simply believe I will go further if my money is shown outwardly. I hate the idea of it being hidden in a bank somewhere.

Finding myself holed up on a ship with Horace and sneaking onto a stranger's balcony, it's easy to think I might be less than shrewd about finances.

So, how did I become the owner of four dogs? It's quite simple, really: I just took them off the street. I would often see these poor, abused animals tied to lampposts and telephone poles while their owners went to cash a check or attend Mass. I was tired of seeing their restless, loving eyes target passersby. So eager were they for love from anyone who would give it.

I'm not ashamed to say that I feel a kinship with animals like this. So I began to carry my manicure scissors with me. I would cut their leads. I did it for about a year. Liberated, my new dog and I would run, run, run as fast as we could down to a street corner. I would buy us a celebratory sandwich and introduce myself. I am very good with dogs and children. Many would fall asleep in my arms on the way home where I would then sneak them up the stairs as quickly as possible. Dogs, that is. Not children.

The only complaint I have about owning so many dogs is that there is less money I get to spend on myself. Dog food is expensive, which is something I did not realize when I adopted these four. This meant many meals were rice, oatmeal, and broth for the lot of us. That is partially also why I liked working waitering jobs. After my shift, as the restaurant was closing, I would smoke a cigarette out behind the dumpsters and pick through them, putting food in two piles: one for me, one for my dogs.

You might be thinking that I am lying about owning four dogs in a small flat. If I wasn't living in the thick of it, I wouldn't believe me either. But it was not hard to adapt once I sat and thought for a minute. I do some of my best thinking in a hot shower. And I usually go to Horace's when I need a good think. The water pressure is better there and he lets me use his good soap—if I ask nicely. He really does not like his things touched!

I was lathering my hair when I had my stroke of genius. I could not go back and forth with four dogs twice a day for their potty breaks. That would be sixteen times a day, up and down the steps! I am not athletic by nature and I fear I have an allergy to excessive sweating.

I asked Horace if I could borrow some rope. This was when rope was easy to get and Horace was generous and he said he did, in fact, have some for me to use. Armed with my rope and my good idea, I strode briskly home to put my plan into action.

Milly, my pug, was the first to try my idea. I picked Milly because she is lazy and would not fidget in the harness. Plus, she is fat, so I wanted to see if the rope Horace gave me would hold her. She exceeded expectations. Like a wrinkly anchor, she dropped with aplomb and sniffed happily at the air, landing with the grace of a dog half her weight.

I was lucky enough to have a small balcony overlooking the garden behind the building. I was doubly lucky because Mr. Greaves' flat is front-facing and on the first floor. Therefore, he did not enter the garden much, if ever. The only time I had seen him do so was when a squirrel picked up a lit cigarette someone tossed and Mr. Greaves chased after it, worried about a fire.

I fashioned four harnesses, which the dogs wear at all times. One-by-one, I attached them to ropes, which I fed through pulleys I'd hung from the plant hooks overhead. I lowered them into the garden to do their business and get their exercise. When I felt they had had enough (or if I was running late for an appointment), I tugged them back up. I did this twice a day. I am sensitive to their need for fresh air, so I usually left my windows open, too. Only Henry, the Bichon Frise, did not like the window open, especially not in the Spring. I believe he was abused somewhere with a nice breeze. Positano, perhaps. Or Milwaukee.

I will make a note to look into dog psychoanalysts when we dock in Manhattan. But for now, he is doing very well at sea.

My pulley system worked perfectly for months. On Sundays, while Mr. Greaves was at service, I would go into the garden and kick about their messes from the week. I'm happy to say, we had better azaleas that year than any other. I heard my neighbor, Ms. Rublack, comment on the new growths in the Spring to her girlfriend, Mrs. Jean-Lyons. She took credit for the blooms, saying she had been using her old coffee grounds and watering them every day. Ms. Rublack took credit for everything, though. She also said she knew when George V was going to die because the morning of January 20 she had a stye.

"Don't you understand, Arthur? Don't you understand?" she asked when I heard her tell the story one morning on our shared front step. "I couldn't see a future without him!"

I was sympathetic to Ms. Rublack, but I did not like her. I was sympathetic to her because she was old and unmarried and because had a mustache. I did not like her because she was a braggart and had a mustache. I do not tend to be friends with ones so self-absorbed. But I could not very well contradict her to Mrs. Jean-Lyons, either. One, because I was eavesdropping from her kitchen, having snuck in to borrow her brass teaspoons I liked so much; and two, because the jig would have been up with my dogs. So I kept my mouth shut and climbed back through her window, teaspoon in hand and a few slices of cake for the dogs. If I recall, it was a plumb cake. It was very good. I will give Ms. Rublack that much: she was a fine baker.

I liked my apartment because it was cheap and the other tenants were all old and stupid, like Ms. Rublack. This meant they were hard of hearing and if the dogs got rowdy, I could blame it on the water pipes or my record player or the off chance I was having a cocktail party. Usually this was not an issue. My dogs are very quiet. I think this is because they are well-fed and therefore lazy. On Saturday mornings, when the rest of the neighborhood was sleeping, I would go through others' garbage bins to look for warm and comfortable things for them. I laid three perfectly good quilts in piles on the floor for the dogs after one such trip. I was surprised to see such waste when I would go looking in bins! I think the cigarette burns in one of the quilts gave it dignity and character, like a sea captain with a peg leg, or a schoolboy with a harelip.

What I liked most about this time was that I was never lonely. By nature, I am a lonely person. Not because I do not have friends, but because I do not especially like the friends I have. Many of the acquaintances I have work in banks and shops. One is a watchmaker. They are never around people of influence. We have very little in common because of this.

Dogs are different, I am pleased to say. They are very influential creatures by nature. I am often surprised how much I must cater to their individual needs. For instance, Milly will not eat off the floor, only from a teacup. Because of this, I have borrowed many teacups for her from the restaurants where I have been employed.

Sometimes, on the occasional free morning, I would take a couple of my dogs for long walks around the city. This proved to be influential, too. You would be surprised how many people will smile when you pass with a pack of dogs tied to each wrist. Because my dogs are very kind and I am very kind, I enjoyed many polite conversations and "Good mornings!" and the occasional child giggling and pointing. They usually giggled and pointed at Milly, because she is corpulent.

It was on one such walking trip that I met Mrs. Isabel Cormant. I suppose you could say she was my first customer, though I don't like to use that word since my dogs were only ever on loan.

Mrs. Cormant (I will not call her Isabel, as she was not my friend) was a tiny woman with a deep voice. I mistook her for an ugly, wrinkled child until she extended her hand and I saw how many rings she wore. I believe rings are a sign of influence, so I shook her hand and I introduced my dogs. On this walk, I had Milly, Rue, and Celia (Henry was sleeping and he hated to be woken up). All said hi back. Or I assume they did, as they cannot speak English but they did wag their tails vigorously at Mrs. Cormant's attention.

Mrs. Cormant was quite taken by my Celia. Celia is a cocker spaniel with sorrowful, cerulean eyes. I believe that is rare in cocker spaniels, which is why I took her home with me in the first place. Mrs. Cormant only gave Milly and Rue cursory compliments, which I felt was very rude. Rue is missing an eye, yes, but she is a gorgeous King Charles Spaniel otherwise.

We meandered through the typical pleasantries: the weather, the park, the weather again, our respective occupations. Mrs. Cormant was the Chair of some committee or another. It was volunteer work, as her husband was a barrister and they had no children. I believe this is why she was so interested in Celia. Celia has a very childlike disposition and I had placed a bow on her head that day, giving her a youthful appearance, even though she was nearly four.

I kept the conversation on Mrs. Cormant for as long as I could, asking follow-up questions and pausing for her to answer. At this time, I was not necessarily what one would have called a person of influence, so I avoided discussing myself too much. Finally, though, inevitably, she did ask about me.

"Are you a dog walker, Mr. Croots?"

I have to admit, the question was direct and I felt offended. Of course I was not a dog walker! Dog walkers are unemployable in other trades and untalented. I was neither of those things. But I am very good at hiding when I am offended and I did not show it to Mrs. Cormant. I smiled instead and answered in the negative, telling her instead that I was simply watching these three while my good friend, Lord Ranligh, was moving house.

This, of course, was not true. I did not know Lord Ranligh, but his name was already stuck in my head from earlier in the day. I had been flipping through *Debrett's* during breakfast that morning.

"Ranligh? Dougie Ranligh?" Mrs. Cormant inquired. She obviously knew who he was, but I nodded. "I thought he was in Lyons for the month."

I did not want to get caught in my lie, so I shrugged vaguely. "The dogs' passports were expired."

This seemed to satisfy her. Women like Mrs. Cormant, wives of barristers, tend to forget how to think. So much of their life is delegated to housekeepers and maids, they are happy to agree with anything handed to them, signing away divorce papers and birthday cards with identical disregard. I was lucky Mrs. Cormant was not the thinking type.

It was time to walk home and I told this to Mrs. Cormant, who had pulled a few breadcrumbs off her sandwich and was scattering them for Celia. She misunderstood this as an invitation to walk home with me, so she hitched her purse onto her shoulder and followed me out of the park gate.

It seemed Mrs. Cormant was lonely, but in a different kind of loneliness than what I was feeling then. Her loneliness was not because she did not have friends, but because she knew no one cared much for what she had to say. By this time, I had softened a bit to Mrs. Cormant and had forgiven her for mistaking me for a dog walker. To her, she thought we were friends and we spent two blocks with her asking if I thought she should paint her cupboards yellow (yes), how I had met Ranligh (it was so long ago I could not remember), and if I would be walking Celia again soon (I would have to check her diary, as she was a very popular spaniel). Again, I was annoyed that she gave so little attention to Milly and Rue. But they did not seem to mind as much as I did.

I did not want Mrs. Cormant to walk me to my building, as it is not a beautiful building and I would have been embarrassed. Plus, because I was hiding my dogs at this time, it would not have been easy for me to casually exit our conversation at the doorstep, since I would have had to smuggle each one in under my coat. Instead, I had the idea to escort Mrs. Cormant to her house. This was very smart on my part, because she would, of course, invite me in for a drink and I would also know where she lived in case we were to become friends or if I ever needed to borrow anything.

Slowly, I herded Mrs. Cormant and my three dogs towards her house. She did not stop talking about herself, which meant she had little time to ask about me. When she did stop to catch her breath, her only questions were directed to Celia.

"Are you a good girl?"

"Look how pretty she's walking!"

"Do you like the squirrels, sweet Celia?"

Celia tilted her head backward as to recognize that the questions had been directed at her. I did not ask Mrs. Cormant directly where she lived; but instead, at a street corner, I would point left or right and wait for her to tell us which direction we were heading.

Finally, after what felt like an hour but was really only fifteen minutes or so, we arrived at her doorstep. Mrs. Cormant seemed surprised to find us all in front of her green door. Awkwardly, she dug through her purse for her keys while the dogs sniffed pleasantly around the iron banister and garbage bins. I did not know if I was supposed to leave yet. It seemed a waste of time to have walked all this way to simply escort a stranger to her door. I was interested to see her house. If her rings were any indication, there would be many beautiful things inside.

Milly was panting heavily, being fat. I suppose Mrs. Cormant took notice of this and that is why she invited us in.

"Just drop the leads wherever!" she said as she opened the door, anticipating the dogs to rush in as dogs do. She breezily kept moving down the hall, past the formal living room to the left and the study to the right and three other closed doors along the way, leading us to the back of the house where her kitchen was. I immediately regretted telling her yellow would do nicely for a kitchen cupboard. Her kitchen was in shades of coral and lime green.

It was not that Mrs. Cormant had bad taste, it was that she simply had no taste at all. It was neither good nor bad. She was agnostic on the topic of fashion and, because of this, instead relied on what others told her looked good. This was probably the reason there were three separate fish mounted in her downstairs powder room and why the front door had a brass knocker in the shape of a cross-eyed cherub's face.

One could have easily mistaken Mrs. Cormant for a small child because of her house, too. A lot of it was mismatched patterns in very similar hues of distressingly clashing patterns. It was as if a small girl had decorated her doll's house with scraps from her mother's sewing room. I believe I have an eye for these things. I am a fashionable young man. Unfortunately, I knew my words would be lost on Mrs. Cormant.

She was comfortable surrounded by this ugliness. I worried for Rue. She may only have one eye, but it is discerning.

I like dining in old women's kitchens because old women will feed you to excess. They'll also turn their backs to you, rummaging through drawers for something they forgot to lay out, which makes it easy for me to pocket things. Mrs. Cormant had very little I wanted to pocket, though. Maybe her beautiful things were not in the kitchen. The only other room I had seen in her house was her first-floor powder room, and it held nothing beautiful, either. This was a pity. I did take three bananas.

Fortunately for both of us, we had run out of things to say to one another, so it was child's play to peel myself and the dogs away when I felt Milly had rested long enough on the cool kitchen floor. I could tell Mrs. Cormant was sad to see Celia go. I believe Celia was indifferent to Mrs. Cormant. But Celia is like this sometimes with other women. She is a jealous girl.

Upon leaving, Mrs. Cormant followed me to the front door and rested her hand on my elbow. "Thank you for coming over, Arthur. It was the most fun I had all week."

I am unaccustomed to sincerity. I am a sincere person myself, but it is jarring when I see it in others. Everyone I know is disingenuous. But this may be because I mostly know waiters from The Pelican. They are notoriously phony because the clientele are good tippers.

Because I am not used to sincerity, I was caught off-guard by Mrs. Cormant. I did not respond and the dogs were pulling me down her stairs. I turned around once while she was still at the door and yelled, "Pip! Pip!"

The entire way home I kicked myself for this, blushing and wondering why I had yelled such nonsense.

I do this sometimes when I am embarrassed. I focus on what I did wrong, trying to desensitize myself to my *faux pas*. It only works half of the time. Other times, I become so angry with myself I cannot sleep. Or I cry. One time, when I had tripped in front of a very important property manager, I got unflatteringly drunk at a pub and nearly cut my hand to pieces slamming down my pint.

Luckily, I did not have to wallow long. The dogs are an excellent distraction and I promised myself I would not get drunk or cry in front of them. That would embarrass me even more and Rue, who is finely attuned to my emotions, would get upset.

When I got to my flat after sneaking the dogs in front of Mr. Greaves' door, I sat down at my desk to write a letter to Mrs. Cormant. I like to write letters because I get to show off my elegant signature. Plus, I took a whole stack of paper before leaving my concierge job at The Rogers. It is faintly coral and it is very easy to write on. I wish I had taken more. I am covetous when it comes to stationery.

Dear Mrs. Cormant,

Thank you so much for treating Milly, Rue, Celia and me to a lovely afternoon. You have a beautiful home and such a unique style. I have never seen taxidermied doves before!

It was a nice surprise to make your acquaintance today and perhaps I will see you again soon.

I do hope I did not embarrass myself too much upon my leaving. I do not know what got into me. How much sugar was in that tea you made? Ha ha.

All the best,
Arthur Croots

P.S. Celia sends her love.

The last line was a lie. Celia did not say that, as she is a dog. And on top of that I do not believe she had much fun at Mrs. Cormant's house. The rest of it was only about thirty percent true. I am an extremely sincere person, but Mrs. Cormant is not very likable, which meant I felt I could not be honest with her so early in our friendship.

I shared one banana with Henry, my Bichon Frise, who likes them the most. The rest got a tin of beans and some leftover steak pie. Ms. Rublack had put it on her kitchen counter to cool while she went to the post office. The window was open and smelled delicious. She should be careful; how easy it would be for anybody to just walk right into her house!

Now that the letter was written and the dogs were fed, I had time to work on my beauty regimen. I cannot remember if I have described myself yet, so I will do so now.

I do not know if others would define me as handsome. I have never been told I am. But I think I am very good looking. This is mostly because my lips are hardly ever chapped, and because I have very nice brown hair that I part to the left.

I am of medium height, so sometimes I feel very short and other times I feel very tall. With Horace, I feel very short. He has a tendency to tower over me, especially when he is angry with me or when I cut up his bedsheets. I felt very tall that night, I remember, because Mrs. Cormant was so short. I usually wish I were taller, because I am around tall men all day. I believe this is why I have very straight posture; I am trying to squeeze every last fraction of an inch out of my vertebrae.

I also have slender hands, like a marionettist or a pickpocket. But I am not expressive with my hands. They fidget in my pockets when I am in a crowd. I never know how to hold a wine glass when one is handed to me at a party or a funeral. But I do not drink a lot of wine, nor am I invited to many parties or funerals, It has only happened twice in my life.

Because I have slender hands, I keep my nails trim. Very blunt, very masculine. There is a reason for this. The last time I had deposited money at the bank, I was called, "ma'am". The teller had not looked up from his ledger when I had handed over the paper notes. He had only seen my hairless, slender hands. I was mortified. He did not apologize and I hurried out of the bank. I now ask Horace to deposit my cheques when I am working. I am self-conscious about my hands.

My beauty regimen is uncomplicated, but it can be time-consuming. It requires patience. Spending so much time in front of the mirror also means I am acutely aware of my flaws. My gums are the same color as the paper I took from The Rogers. How can that particular shade of pink look so attractive as letterhead and so ugly in my mouth?

I first boil water in a kettle. While the water is heating up, I rub my face with ice-cold water using a rough cloth. I then cut a lemon in half. One half is for my beauty regimen, the other is for my tea. Once I have rubbed the lemon half on my scrubbed face, I use the steam from the tea kettle to open my pores. I splash a small amount of alcohol into my hands and rub this over my face, which I then dry off. Now I wash my face with a bar of soap and apply my unguents. I use three mixed together in the palm of my hand. Finally, I mist perfume onto my pajamas and I am done.

If I do not have perfume as the last step, I do not feel like the regimen is complete. So I am always on the look-out for a bottle or two when I am running low. I was nearly out of Chanel's *Bois des Îles* the day I had met Mrs. Cormant, so I slipped her small bottle of Bourjois into my waistband before leaving her powder room.

I could not fall asleep though. I do not know if it was the excitement of my day or because Rue was stealing all of the blankets. I was sleepless. I could still feel Mrs. Cormant's hand on my elbow. I genuinely believed I had made her day better with my visit.

Late at night, I am more compassionate than I am during the day. I think this is because, like the mind, the heart likes to dream as well. I found myself awake, twitching as the dogs do, trying to get comfortable and still Mrs. Cormant would find her way into my mind. The issue was, and I saw it plainly in the middle of the night, was that I knew Mrs. Cormant was lonely and I also knew how to fix it. She loved Celia very much, I could tell. But I also loved Celia very much, which is why I had taken her in the first place.

The other problem was that Mrs. Cormant believed that Celia

belonged to Lord Ranligh. I kicked myself for having lied in the first place, but I forgave myself. How was I to know Mrs. Cormant would know "Dougie" too?

This was how the mechanics of my new enterprise began to form. That night, at my most compassionate, I conceived a plan that would ultimately lead me to flee to America.

II

Arthur's Plan

By morning I had drafted my plan in full. I woke up early, a little jittery from lack of sleep. It has always been times like this when I regret having taken in so many dogs. No matter the night I've had, they require their time in the garden. Today, this would be an hour's long process, so I would't be able to put my plan into action until 8:00 a.m.

The first step was to call off work. Mr. Greaves is very cheap and does not own a common telephone. The other tenants are old and therefore anyone they would chat with on the phone would either be at church or is dead. Mr. Greaves, who does not like me, would not install a phone just for me when I had asked. Mr. Greaves thinks I am annoying.

I had no choice but to use the chemist's telephone next door. This was not usually an issue, but they did not open until 8:30 a.m. I had already dressed in a cozy jumper and equally cozy denim jeans and had combed my hair to the left. I had already brushed my teeth and had eaten a sensible breakfast of leftover pie crust from Ms. Rublack's pie, plus one more banana. After posting my letter to Mrs. Cormant, I sat on my bed with Celia on my lap, and thought the plan over one last time.

I awoke just after 1:00 p.m. I had fallen asleep and my dogs, not being able to tell time, hadn't bothered to wake me up. I was scheduled for my shift at 10:00 a.m. As I was three hours late, I decided there was no point in calling. The first step was de facto complete.

I was sacked the next day. But I did not care too much. I did not like being a waiter and, besides, I would be getting a cheque from Ms. Cormant shortly.

The next step was to get a French postage stamp. I knew Horace would have one but I also knew that Horace practiced his piano at 2:00 p.m. Horace is not good at piano. He is cruel to the keys. But he believes he is cultured and therefore he feels he must play the piano. I could have been a accomplished pianist, given my slender hands.

I walked three streets over from my building and tried to think of someone else I may ask who travels frequently and who is my friend. No one came to mind, as my friends are all very poor and most do not like me anyway. Instead I went to a bistro to dig through their trash.

I was lucky, as it was a Monday and trash is not collected until Tuesday on this street. I know most of the collection days for various waste companies; it is a hobby of mine to look through other people's bins. This particular bistro's bins were in an alley, which meant I would be hidden more easily. I was not embarrassed of digging through trash in search of a French postage stamp. I would be embarrassed if I were caught. While digging, my mind was already thinking of a lie in the chance anyone would find me, up to my elbows in snail shells. I decided I would say I lost my glasses and the *garçon* directed me to that very alley. Perhaps they would have felt sorry for me, in this hypothetical situation. Perhaps they would have given me a few dollars to buy new ones.

I affected a squint in order to appear as if I were looking for my glasses while digging through the garbage. I wish there was a mirror in the alley by the French bistro. I believe it was a very convincing squint. It involved an exaggerated crease in my eyebrows and a slight tilt of my head.

By the third bin, I was cursing the French. *Damn them!* I thought. *Don't these people write letters?* It was hard to believe in all of this trash that there was not one discarded envelope. Perhaps the French were not as talkative as I thought they were. I may have mistaken them for Italians.

I could not leave without a postage stamp. It was the second step of my plan and I did not want to waste any more time. Plus, I was covered in muck and did not have time to change into something clean. I was only wearing my third-best jumper, so I was not very upset by it being dirtied. I have two more jumpers which are much nicer, but not as comfortable.

Though it was not a particularly hot day, I was awfully sweaty. I wished I had a chilly glass of water, but I did not want to draw more attention to myself at the French bistro than I probably already had by asking for one. I was ready to give up or, at the very least, take off my suffocating jumper and rest along the shaded bricks of the alleyway. It was then, when I was at my most desperate, that I had a brilliant idea. I often have brilliant ideas when I am desperate.

It was so simple, I kicked myself for not having thought of it sooner, before I smelled of old mustard and stale wine corks. I simply marched out of the alley and reached into their mailbox and took a fistful of mail. I do not believe I was seen, as I am stealthy when I take things, but just to be safe I zig-zagged my way home. To be even safer, I have not gone back to the bistro since. I believe they would have remembered me, with my nice hair and medium build. Or at the very least, they perhaps would have recognized my third-best jumper. You can never be too careful. The French are very observant.

I did not look at the mail until I was safely in my room. Perhaps I should have, in case I failed to grab something with a French stamp on it. But as I said, I was, by then, exhausted, desperate, and more than a little sweaty. I could not waste the rest of my day in trash bins. My entrepreneurial spirit wouldn't have allow it!

Luckily, there was a birthday card in the mail that day, addressed to a child called Emmanuel. I believe the owners of the bistro live above their restaurant. I felt bad for poor Emmanuel, as he would think his *tante* Agnès did not love him. All the same, I pocketed the twenty pound banknote for myself. I would need it for the rest of my plan and I am sure Emmanuel had other birthday gifts.

I was very careful with the envelope now. I had done nearly an afternoon's work for such a little piece of paper. I did not put it on the table, in case a wind blew or I absentmindedly used it as a coaster. I changed into my dressing gown tucked the envelope safely into my pocket. The dogs were curious and it was time for their dinner, but I was too busy to notice. Usually, if I ignore them long enough, they harumph and fall back asleep. I promised them each a small steak, pending the success of my plan.

Next I would write a letter to Mrs. Cormant pretending to be Lord Ranligh. This was the easiest part of the whole scheme, I believe. It is because I am a talented writer and also because Mrs. Cormant is all but brainless, so I did not have to elaborate on any lie I was telling her.

Isabel,

I hope you have been well. My time here in Lyons has been wonderful. I am enjoying myself immensely and have got a nice suntan. Lu sends a kiss.

My very good friend, Arthur, called me last night and we gossiped about you. I'm surprised you have never met Arthur, as he has been my very good friend for many years. But he is also very shy, so that is why he has never been to any parties.

Arthur told me you fell in love with darling Celia. How could one not? You'll be happy to know that Celia has a twin sister, Amelia. Blue eyes and all. It just so happens I have heard that Amelia's owners, the Fenrics of Galway, cannot look after her any longer. Lady Fenric is an alcoholic, you know. But that is a secret and do not repeat it—even to me.

Anyway, all is well here. We let's make plans upon my return.

Dougie

It was a flawless forgery. Having been in the company of so many aristocrats in my life, I am expert at pretending to be one. I simply pretended I had money and a title and a suntan and the letter came spilling out of me. There were only two parts in which I had to pause. The first was when I had to research Lord Ranligh's wife in *Debrett's*. The second was when I had to make up an Irish peer. Most Irish titles sound made up anyway. I doubted Mrs. Cormant would be any the wiser.

I used my manicure scissors to cut the French stamp off of Emmanuel's envelope. I pasted it onto a fresh envelope (an ecru set I had for ages). I sealed the envelope and addressed it to Mrs. Isabel Cormant. I did not put a return address so she could not respond, but I did crumple the envelope a bit. I wanted her to believe it had traversed France as quickly as possible.

I then gave the dogs their garden time while I finished the rest of the day in my dressing gown. I was studying German then, for no other reason than I had found a primer on a bench and I had a very large fine at the library that I had no intention of paying. That night I learned how to say, "This pocket has a rabbit in it." and "No, that is not my hand." I was not sure if these phrases were meant for flirting or for a magician. Either way, I have forgotten both phrases now.

I am an impatient man. I believe this is because I rarely get what I want. So when there is an opportunity for me to be rewarded for my hard work, I do not delay. It is a psychosis I have, one may say. I put reason behind me in place of achieving my goal. This is why, without thinking of the actual delay a letter would have to take from Lyons to London, I snuck it into the Cormant's mailbox early the next morning.

For one week, I waited at home. I didn't even go to the park with any of the dogs. I did not want my acquaintanceship to be too sudden. I suspected lonely Mrs. Cormant found excuses to make her way to the park every day to see us again. I could not seem too eager. I wanted her to be very excited to see Celia and me the next time we crossed paths.

It was made much more stressful for me when I realized that, having been sacked, I no longer had any income. I became doubly stressed when Horace did not answer when I knocked on his door. This meant I would have to withdraw money from the bank myself. I was still very self-conscious of my hairless, slender hands, and did not want to be mistaken for a young woman again.

I slipped a note under Horace's door, instructing him to withdraw some money for me. I added that if there was no money to withdraw, to lend me forty pounds. I further added that if he did not have forty pounds to lend to me, then to disregard my note entirely and that we were no longer friends and he should take better care of his finances, for both of our sakes.

Luckily, Horace is a bosom friend and adroit with his finances and dropped off forty pounds at my flat. Horace does not like my flat, nor my dogs, so I met him outside and told him about Mrs. Cormant and my plans.

III

Convincing Horace

"You're not understanding, Horace! It will work!"

I had been walking for nearly four blocks trying to convince Horace that my plan with Mrs. Cormant was solid. Horace is a pessimist, so I do not often tell him my plans; he always tells me no. But I needed his help, so I had to convince him.

"Arthur, you're going to sell Celia but keep her?"

That was not the plan at all, and I was frustrated that Horace could not grasp the basics of my plan. How was I to trust him to help me if he couldn't even grasp the basics?

"No," I said. "I'm going to pretend Celia is her own sister, Amelia, and sell *her* to Mrs. Cormant." It was the third time we had gone over this.

"But why not just give Mrs. Cormant the real Celia?"

"Because Celia doesn't belong to me, she belongs to Lord Ranligh."

"But you said Ranligh is in Lyons and Celia *does* belong to you."

"Yes, but Mrs. Cormant doesn't know that. I want her to have Celia but I have to call her Amelia and I need your help with that."

"Won't you miss Celia if you give her to Mrs. Cormant?"

"Oh, yes, terribly. That's why it's really only a loan. I plan on stealing Celia back when I can't bear it anymore."

This was the part I think Horace was stuck on. Horace does not like the idea of stealing, as he was raised a Christian. I was also raised a Christian, but I am agnostic as to the question of stealing. I like it when it benefits me, but I do not like it when it does not.

I believe Christianity is a handicap in many ways, like a club foot, or a stutter. Horace's attitude toward my plan was proving me right. He was unfortunately myopic when it came to my ideas. He had very bad hands for the piano, and an even worse imagination for plans. This required me to repeat my reasons for even conceiving this plan.

"Horace, please listen to me," I pleaded. I hd grabbed his arm to both show the importance of what I was going to say, and also because he was dangerously close to running into the person in front of him. Horace is not particularly coordinated.

"It's simple, Horace. I need you to pretend to be an agent of the Fenrics so you can sell Celia to the Cormants. But Celia is Amelia in this case, don't forget. Then, when I feel Mrs. Cormant has had her fill of Celia's attentions, and when I am too lonely without her, I will simply take Celia back when Mrs. Cormant is not home. That way, if Mrs. Cormant ever sees me with Celia at the park again, she will think it is the real Celia and not Amelia, since they are identical twins. It's a perfect plan. And all you have to do is pretend for half an hour!"

Horace, I could see, was trying to find fault in my plan. Because I am a savvy planner, he could not find one. He knew I would not care to listen about the morality of taking Celia back. He did not bother to go down that road again.

"And will I get a cut?" Horace asked.

"Oh, yes! Of course. Let's say ten pounds."

"I just lent you forty!"

"Consider the remaining thirty as charity. Really, Horace, you are a terrible Christian!"

I was exhausted with all of our walking and my having to convince Horace of our plan. I asked if he would like to join me for a bite to eat. He declined, saying that he had to practice his piano. Because he agreed to help me with my plan, I did not want to anger him by saying he had been practicing for some time and was still not very good. Instead, I told him that was a brilliant idea and hoped he would invite me and the dogs over one night for a private concert.

We parted with a handshake and an understanding that I would see him tomorrow to finalize the details. I took a roundabout way home so that I could pass by Mrs. Cormant's house. It was easy enough to find, with her green door. Her curtains were drawn, so I watched her tiny figure in the window. Mr. Cormant was not home, and she looked lonely. He was probably still at the office, and she had probably spent all day alone. Celia would make the days more tolerable for Mrs. Cormant, I was sure. I hope she didn't mind too much when I took her back.

On my way home, I bought a stale loaf of bread from a bakery near my flat. I am very lucky to have this bakery so close to my flat, as they sell day-old loaves of bread at a discount. I can eat very well with very little money. The dogs would be happy. They are particularly fond of stale bread.

Walking up the stairs to my flat, I assessed my plan for flaws. There was nothing. I was confident, It would work. As I mentioned, I am a savvy planner.

The next day I met Horace at his flat, as promised. I know I have not described Horace very well, so perhaps the best way I can is to also describe his flat.

It is hideous and cramped and masculine. One would think that, living in one room with four dogs, my own flat would be cramped but that is not the case. This is because I do not own a lot of things. And the items I do own are tiny and beautiful - things that might be easily slipped into a pocket, for instance. Horace's place is the opposite. It is cramped with big furniture and big paintings and big books. There is never a place to sit and there is definitely no room to bring my dogs over. Not that Horace would let me. Horace does not like the dogs.

Horace himself is very similar to his flat. He, too, is ugly and masculine. Because he is ugly and masculine, his clothes never look like they fit him properly. They are either too loose in the shoulders or tight at the tummy. But they are nice enough clothes, I think. Horace likes corduroy.

Horace made space for me on a couch that had two identical leather-bound dictionaries. I don't know why he needed two. Perhaps they were gifts for a set of academic twins. Or perhaps one was for me, though Horace's gifts are usually not very generous. I did not ask and I did not offer to help him move the dictionaries. I stood patiently for him to gesture so I could sit down. I liked to pretend Horace was the *maître d'hôtel* of his shabby little abode. Horace was not in on the joke, nor would he have found it funny.

We hammered out the remainder of the plans to sell Celia/Amelia. Horace is not a dumb man, but he is cautious, so it took more time than I thought necessary and I was getting frustrated. I do not like to repeat myself and I repeated myself four times until Horace felt like he had understood the plan from every angle. We decided that waiting even a day longer would risk Mrs. Cormant speaking with Lord Ranligh, so we agreed to sell Celia that very afternoon.

To steel us both for the plan, I suggested we have a glass of something strong. All Horace had was cooking sherry (he makes a very good risotto). He wiped out two teacups with the bottom of his shirt and poured some out for us. He drank his in one gulp; I sipped mine a little more slowly. I have a very sensitive palate.

We agreed I would meet Horace in one hour a block from the park, where I had a hunch Mrs. Cormant would be that day. This would give me enough time to collect Celia, say our goodbyes, and for me to have a small cry if the need came over me. I am emotional by nature and was already anticipating how emotional I would be without dear Celia to greet me in my flat.

At the same time, Horace would spend that hour pressing his suit and shaving. His suit was corduroy and Horace has very rosy cheeks when he is freshly shaven. Both of these attributes seemed to lend themselves nicely to the image of a humble Irish agent. All he needed was a little dirt under his fingernails and a potato or two to complete the costume entirely.

When we met just outside the park, I thought Horace looked much less ugly and much more masculine in his corduroy suit and rosy cheeks. A small bit of tissue was stuck to his chin where he had nicked. I pointed it out and he brushed it off, only to have it fall down onto the shoulder of his jacket. I pointed that out, too, and he brushed it off again. Horace seemed aggravated the second time I commented on that little devil of tissue. I think he was getting nervous.

We kept our voices low and our backs turned towards the park, to avoid being noticed prematurely by Mrs. Cormant. I quizzed Horace once more on the details of our plan. I would be hiding out at a newspaper stand close-by—not handling the transaction myself.

"And you are?"

"I am Mr. Monteith, and I work for Lord Fenric."

"And why are you in London?"

"To look at some real estate for the Fenrics to invest in."

"Why do you have Amelia?"

"Oh, because the Fenrics cannot care for her and I thought she could use a good vacation."

"Is Amelia the Fenrics' dog?"

"For now, but they are happy to look for a home better suited for Amelia."

"Do you know Mrs. Cormant?"

"Never saw her before in my life, nor have the Fenrics. Only Ranligh knows her."

"And what will you say if Amelia recognizes Mrs. Cormant?"

"My goodness! She sure has taken a liking to you! You must be very good with dogs!"

"And if she asks if this is Celia, Lord Ranligh's cocker?"

"No, ma'am. Funnily enough, this is her sister, Amelia. She sure has taken a liking to you!"

"Now, Horace, this is very important. The minute—the absolute *second*—Mrs. Cormant seems interested in the dog, you must steer her into buying Ce—I mean Amelia. You have to push her towards loving Amelia. You have to play up that she lacks playmates and is lonely.

Pull at her heart a little. You remember how to talk to girls, don't you, Horace?"

I could see the additional quizzing did Horace good. He was calm and breathing slowly, confidently. He took a black, nylon rope from his pocket and looped it around Celia's neck. We had taken off her other lead and harness, as she was no longer Celia now.

I knew I would miss Celia terribly, but I would gladly welcome the money from this. I was conflicted. But I was also tired of eating stale bread and stolen bananas. Rent was also due, and I believe Mr. Greaves had been looking for an excuse to chase me out of the building.

Here is where we parted, with a "Good luck" to Horace and a big kiss to Celia. He was to meet me in front of a small bookstore that seemed to only ever sell books I was not interested in reading. I was not so nervous as I was pre-annoyed at Horace. I was emotionally exhausted already. I would miss Celia so much.

Being pre-annoyed is an emotion I have often. It is when I am thinking of all the ways something might go wrong. I will sit and think of how one can fail at this or that, how perhaps the grocer overcharges me or the barber cuts my hair poorly. Now I was thinking of Horace. How he could slip and say Celia, or mention me, or get the Fenrics and Ranligh's mixed up. Perhaps Mrs. Cormant would not be there or she would not have money with her. Perhaps Mrs. Cormant was smarter than she looked and would realize it was all a ruse.

I thought like this for nearly an hour, leaning back against the façade of the bookstore, my arms crossed and my head down, fuming. I had already concluded that Horace had failed in some way. I ran through all the possible ways in which he might have failed. I rehearsed a number of precise and cutting remarks to demonstrate my disappointment. Horace is good at making risotto but very bad at nearly everything else.

I was so absorbed in my own pre-annoyance, I hadn't realized Horace was jogging along the sidewalk to reach me. It wasn't until I saw a large man lumbering toward me in brown corduroy that I even bothered to look up. I thought at first he was a very bad pickpocket or perhaps a grizzly bear. But it was just Horace, no Celia. He had succeeded and all of a sudden I was no longer annoyed at him for all of the things I had imagined he had done wrong.

"Horace! You genius! You absolute brain!" I greeted Horace, slapping him on his shoulder.

He suggested we keep walking and I agreed. Along the way, Horace explained everything in perfect detail. The only parts I had him repeat were where he improvised. I needed this information in case I had to forge another letter as either Ranligh or Fenric.

Horace described himself as having been very gracious toward Mrs. Cormant. It seemed he thought her loneliness made her more credulous. This differed from my own hypothesis, which was that Mrs. Cormant's loneliness and her gullibility were both products of her husband's job. She was spoiled materially, but neglected emotionally. Either way, her current mental health was not really my concern. We had made fifty pounds in just an hour.

It turned out Horace was very good at improvising and only did so when it was necessary. He told Mrs. Cormant that both Celia and Amelia were from a Welsh breeder and that their breed was called a Siberian Spaniel (I thought this was an inspired touch by Horace). He said Lord Ranligh did not know the Fenrics well at all and, in fact, it would be best to never mention the Fenrics in person to Ranligh. Horace didn't say why, but said he was purposeful and grave in his delivery. All the better for Mrs. Cormant to remain vague at the vertex of reality and the lie.

There was one more thing that really evidenced Horace's genius. He had commented absently that he was heading back to Galway in the morning and was going to purchase his train ticket with some of the cash from the sale. Mrs. Cormant gave him an extra eight pounds for his travel. She really was an angel of generosity. Horace could really learn something from her.

I am a charitable person as well and let Horace keep the money. It was through his own improvisation that he earned it. Plus, that would nearly make up for the thirty pounds I still owed him.

We parked ourselves at a little cafe and celebrated with a slice of cake each and a soda. I would have liked a champagne, but Horace said the sherry we had earlier was enough for both of us. Horace is a bit paternal and, having never had a father myself, I find myself yielding to his rituals as my own. So neither of us had a champagne while we celebrated. It most definitely felt like a tedious birthday party. If it were not for the bank notes in my pocket, I wouldn't have remembered why we were sitting at the sticky cafe table to begin with.

We had, by this time, exhausted all talk of Mrs. Cormant. I was happy to let Horace direct the conversation. Plus, I admit I was pouting a bit over not having champagne, so did not want to talk much.

Horace was telling me about how he wanted to turn his kitchen into a woodshop. In the time I had known Horace, I have never seen him make anything but a fool of himself. I was not aware that he was also a woodworker. I'd of course noticed his calloused hands. I just assumed he did not have as good a beauty routine as mine.

I asked Horace where he was going to make food then and he said he would use a hot plate and survive mostly on fruits and cheeses. He didn't plan on having a proper kitchen at his flat ever again, from the sound of it. He said, rather annoyingly, that his woodworking would sustain him more than food ever could. It was annoying because I very much liked his risotto.

I told him I did not think this was the best idea and that he would get bored of woodworking the minute he craved roast chicken. He said he disagreed and that millions of people have a hot plate and do just fine - including me. I told him this was different, I had a hot plate because I was poor. He would get a hot plate not because he was poor, but because he was bored.

Horace had inherited money, so he could afford to spend time on selling dogs and playing the piano and woodworking. He also inherited his flat, so he did not have a Mr. Greaves of his own. Horace did not understand how easy his luck had made his life. He must have assumed that everyone's grandfather died when they turned twenty-two and left behind a two-thousand-pound-per-year allowance.

This annoyed me no end about Horace, that the things I was most embarrassed about in my own life were just the consequences of inconsequential hobbies of his.

He appeared set to build a woodshop in his kitchen no matter what I had to say about it. I knew I would never again enter his door with the flat smelling like something warm and delicious. Now it was going to smell like wood shavings and shriveled up stilton. And probably tins of beans. Horace understood adulthood in the same way I understood French - he stumbled through it, mostly incoherently but with little harm.

By this point, we had finished our cakes and Horace was dabbing his fingers on the plate to pick up the last crumbs. Horace was a tactile eater. This was part of the reason his clothes did not fit him well. The waiter came along with the bill, which included the two extra slices of cake I was taking home to the dogs. Since Horace had made a few extra pounds from Mrs. Cormant, I volunteered him to pay for us both. Horace really is a generous creature, he just needs to be reminded from time to time.

The waiter brought Horace his change and I thanked him again for helping to sell Celia. I believe he was proud of how well he did and seemed almost bashful at the compliments I gave him. He headed in one direction and I in the other, towards home, with my bakery box of cake and an empty harness in hand.

IV

The Eviction Notice

All the way home I was haunted by visions of Celia, nervous and hiding in Mrs. Cormant's big, ugly house. Her blue eyes searching for me, her nose sniffing for a whiff of *Bois des Îles* on the pillow cushions. It nearly broke my heart.

It was because I was so distracted by my own morose thinking that I didn't even notice Ms. Rublack until I was face-to-face with her. She looked especially arrogant and especially annoying to me.

"Good afternoon, Mr. Croots. Have you spoken with Mr. Greaves today?"

"Good afternoon, Ms. Rublack. No, I have not. Should I have?"

"Oh yes, I should think so! Seems he was quite angry when he left your flat this morning. Seems he's been trying to find you all morning."

"M-my flat? There's no reason he should have been in there. Why was he up there?"

"How am I to know? I just seen him slam the door shut and asked us if we seen you. I said not all morning but I'm not the nosey type, you know. I've been very busy with the azaleas lately anyway."

Not the nosey type my foot, I thought. But I was too nervous to respond to Ms. Rublack with anything but a weak, "thank you." I know she did not warn me in the spirit of camaraderie - it was a braggartly way of telling me she knew more than I did. Everything Ms. Rublack did bothered me.

My tummy was already upset, what with the emotional loss of my dear Celia and the cake I had for lunch. It doubled over as I walked upstairs to my door. Thankfully, I heard the *tip-tap-scratch* of dogs waiting eagerly inside. At least Mr. Greaves had not called the dog snatcher. If he had not done so yet, without me there, then he would not do so at all. This calmed me slightly.

I opened the door to my pack of three to greet me. Tails wagging and oblivious to our impending trouble. If Mr. Greaves knew of them, then we were to be evicted. It was as simple as that. I wished I had had some alcohol at lunch. I'm not afraid to say it: I was a nervous wreck.

After settling down the dogs and kissing each of their heads (I did not dare to put them in the garden just now), I noticed a folded up note tucked under my mug from the morning. It was in Mr. Greaves' wicked little scrawl. Because he is an ignoramus, words were misspelled throughout the note. I will not dictate those errors here, as I would like to protect others from his ignorance.

> You and your dogs need to be out of here in two days or I'll have the lot of you put away!!!!

I thought the four exclamation marks were excessive, but they did illustrate Mr. Greaves' anger, which I suppose was the point. In that moment, I found Mr. Greaves to be a caricature of himself, which diminished my distress but heightened my scorn for him and his silly rules.

I sat in my kitchen chair to think. I call it my kitchen chair, but it was also my only chair. It was chipped and uncomfortable, which usually did not bother me. In that moment, though, it did bother me. In my depression, I noticed how much squalor surrounded me. This was hard to reconcile, as I never saw myself as a particularly squalid person.

Rue came over and nudged my hand with her head. She may only have one eye, but she is very observant when it comes to emotions.

I sat in my kitchen chair and tried to think of how to approach Mr. Greaves. It was simple: I could not be put on the street. It would have inconvenienced me greatly. Not with my kitchen chair and my good perfume. Not with my third-best jumper, nor with my three remaining dogs. I had to think. At that moment, though, I found thinking arduous. I felt so successful after selling Celia earlier in the day, but I now felt like a downright failure.

I had nowhere else to go and nothing else to do, so I sat in my chair and watched the door, waiting for Mr. Greaves to knock. Just after dusk did Mr. Greaves finally knock. It was a quick one-two, an authoritative knock. He was in control of the situation. I hated him for having us both acknowledge that.

I patted my shirt to flatten a crease that had appeared from sitting too long and, in nervousness, ran my fingers over my beautiful, brown hair. I felt as smart as I ever would and opened the door with an exuberant smile. I was faking it for his sake, of course. And, to some extent, my own.

"Mr. Greaves, old boy! How are you? Thank you for the letter today. I'm happy you got to meet the family, so to speak. Ha ha."

"Save the charm for someone else, Croots. I'm just stopping in to see if you got rid of these mongrels yet."

This was a most unnecessary attack. Mr. Greaves, though uneducated, could see that all of the remaining dogs were of the best pedigree. That is, of course, why I took them home with me in the first place.

I thought it best to ignore his insult.

"It has only been a couple hours. I should think I need more time than that to say my goodbyes."

"Pound's open all night, Croots. Say your goodbyes and pack your things."

"Mr. Greaves, I pay my rent. I'm entitled to the remainder of my lease here."

"That's only if you don't break no rules. You broke 'em with these dogs. You know that and I know that. Don't need a lawyer to tell me that."

I was dangerously close to an eviction. I changed my approach.

"Okay, Mr. Greaves - Jon, is it? Jon. Okay, Jon. You're right and I'm wrong. I will get rid of the dogs and when my lease is up, I'll get rid of me, too. Two hours just isn't enough time, you understand. I've had these dogs in my care for months! I can't just say goodbye now."

"Months?!" Mr. Greaves said, his eyes popping at this detail. "Months?"

Oops. So I finessed my proposition. Mr. Greaves was being unreasonable and he was in authority. I hated it, but I was trapped.

"Look here, Mr. Greaves. It's been months. I currently have three dogs. No pound will take all of them and they are all quite bonded together now anyway. Please have a heart—and a little patience. And if you have neither then take this and shut up and give me a month to clear up out of here and you'll never have to see them again!"

I yanked the banknotes from Celia's purchase from my pocket and threw them at his chest. They scattered on the floor and I stood there, waiting for him to pick them up. Clark walked onto them, so Mr. Greaves had to wait for Clark to move to stoop down and collect the bills.

He counted them suspiciously. Twice. Licking his fingers before passing over each note. Fifty pounds—gone. But it bought me a month. I felt that was more responsible than a new suit in that moment, sorry as I was for having to put my spending plans on hold.

I knew by the look in his eye that we had reached an agreement.

"Fine, Arthur. Fine," he said, stroking his belly and smiling. "I'm a reasonable man. You get one month. Anything over that—even an hour, and I'm not gonna be so kind next time."

He left ungraciously without another word. He didn't even thank me for the money. It went to show, I thought, as I locked the door, that money really *can't* buy good manners. I was proof of this myself: I had very little money, but very good manners.

I spent the rest of the night on the floor, using the quilts I had found in the trash bins as a mattress. The dogs slept around me, conforming to the shape of my body. I rested my head on Henry. I used Milly's fat little body for warmth. I would sleep like this for the next month if I had to, saying my goodbyes and savoring their company.

I woke up the next morning only half-rested and only half-optimistic of how the month would go. No plan had come to me and it was too early to phone Horace. The dogs needed to be out, and keeping to our routine was a small comfort. At least that had not changed. Now that my owning so many dogs was an open secret in the building, I did not feel the need to use the pulley system that morning. My back thanked me.

Instead, I walked right out the front door and they all trailed out behind me. Their previous owners had trained them well. They did not go off running, but waited politely on the sidewalk for me to direct them. I walked to the fence of the back garden and picked each one up, one by one, being as careful as possible to drop them on the other side. Then, I see-sawed myself over by swinging one foot then the other. I am of medium height, so this was not easy for me. But I was satisfied at the sight, in Ms. Rublack's window, of her stunned expression.

This was the first time the dogs had their morning time together all at once and they must have realized it too. Diving and bouncing, crouching and tumbling, they panted and chased one another with abandon. For a second, I looked guiltily at their happiness. It was the first time I had thought that perhaps they really *would* be more comfortable somewhere else with owners of better means. But then I remembered I am a very good dog owner, that I just found myself in dire circumstances. This was a running theme in my life.

But it got me thinking. I was relaxing in the sun, and the dogs were happy, so thinking came much more easily to me then than it had the night before. I decided, then and there in the garden, that I would sell all of my dogs. All of them! Just as I had sold Celia.

And, just as I had with Celia, I would take them back, one by one, when I missed them too much.

It was clear this was the only way to save the dogs from the pound and me from being evicted in a month. It really was a sly plan. It would require a good amount of organization, but I had neither a job, nor friends, nor family, nor money to distract me from managing any of the details.

I left the dogs in the back garden to enjoy a morning gallop and sunbath while I sketched out on paper the general components of the plan that were floating about in my head.

V

Arthur Croots - London - He'll Call You

The first step would be to bathe all of the dogs to make them presentable. Having spent more time in my flat than anywhere else, they smelled slightly of dust and tobacco smoke and my various perfumes that mingled in their coats. While I found it a delicious combination, I could not guarantee others would. A bath of egg whites would make their coats glossy. I would put new bows in their hair. I also thought I may have been able to persuade Horace to lend me some of his aftershave. It had a very neutral, woodsy smell that I adored.

The next step was to make a list of potential clients. This would take time to research. I would need a library card (mine was revoked due to unpaid fines) and a motorcar. Again, Horace would have to help me here. He was the only friend I had who was both literate *and* knew how to drive. One would be surprised how rare a combination this is to find in a friend.

The criteria for potential clients went as follows: They had to be rich. They had to be childless (or their children had to have moved away recently). They had to have space for the dogs, either in the city or a country house—preferably a family seat. They had to be either very, very old or very, very young, when people are at their most gullible.

I doubted if *Debrett's* would be able to provide this information. *Burke's*, even, was not a guarantee. It would require looking through old newspaper announcements of marriages and deaths. It would require looking at old property highlights in *Country Life*. It may even require me to call in a few favors with friends of friends. More specifically, friends of friends of influence, those who could make the introductions for me.

I thought the best place to start with my research was looking for reviews of past dog shows in *The Tatler*. These attendees would be most interested in dogs, of course. And who else but the wealthy and withdrawn would want to watch dogs prance with their sallow-faced owners sweating in tweeds? I would then cross-reference their names using the resources mentioned above. I treated myself to a bit of stale bread and a bite of chocolate. How smart I was!

Finally, and perhaps the most fun, was that I would have to buy a very nice notebook to keep all of this information together. I have always loved shopping for notebooks, even though I rarely have anything to write in them. I get too anxious to use my nice ones. I feel that I cannot make a smear or a mistake or the whole integrity of the thing is ruined. I believe this was instilled in me early, this taking pride in things and this fear of mistakes. One can blame so much on one's upbringing.

Two blocks from Horace's place was an adorable stationery store where I was friendly with the owner. I often liked to visit his shop because he had nice wares, but he also had a glass eye. This always made for a fascinating time. His good eye was a dull blue-grey while his glass one was a striking green. It was strange how, because his glass eye had a brightness to it, it was that one which seemed the more expressive of the two.

He also had unkempt eyebrows and a pinky ring. He really was a fascinating man. It was a pity I could never remember what we talked about upon leaving the shop. I was so distracted by his eye and his pens I could never recall our conversations.

After locking the dogs in the flat, I made my way to the stationer. The name of the shop was H.H. Hargood & Sons. I assumed the current owner was "& Sons", as he could not possibly be the original Mr. Hargood. I couldn't imagine a man with a glass eye fathering children. At this my mind wandered to his bedtime habits. Did he wear pajamas? Did he have a comfortable bed? Did he put his glass eye in a vinegar solution by his bedside, as my granny did with her false teeth? Was he lonely?

I played this game often with people, most of whom I had no wish or intention of ever seeing at bedtime. I pretended Horace ate leftover chicken in his bathrobe from the icebox. I pretended Ms. Rublack wept with regret at being such an old crow to me. I pretended Mr. Greaves kept dirty magazines scattered around his bedroom. And I pretended Celia must have been exhausted, having stayed up all night waiting for me to rescue her. Poor thing.

I played this game to pass time on my walk to Hargood's. While I live in a city and do not own a car, I am not a fan of walking long distances. Because I am of medium height, I must take long strides to appear masculine or take very small and quick strides to blend into the pace of the crowds. This makes me feel feminine. Either way, I am not a leisurely walker. I am hyper-conscious of my gait, which causes me to stumble sometimes. I can be diffident. It is the other side of the coin when one is also extremely self-aware, as I am.

Alternating between long strides and quick paces, I reached Hargood's big oak door in no time. The bell tinkled when I entered and I was greeted by the shop cat. Its two eyes matched its owner's glass one, bright green and expressive. The curtains were drawn so that only small shards of sunlight glimmered on the pen nibs and diary locks. It felt ominous and sinister. I absolutely loved going into Hargood's.

Mr. Hargood's store always smelled vaguely of pipe smoke and tuna fish. This is not an altogether unpleasant smell and sometimes the paper I bought from him would smell faintly of tobacco and tuna fish when I brought it home. Today there was also a touch of citrus in the air. I found Mr. Hargood ripping the peel off a small clementine behind the register. What an odd man. He didn't seem to mind that the juice was spraying all over his receipt paper. Mr. Hargood was probably very sticky, if one was to touch him. I had no plans to find if my theory was correct or not.

"Arthur! Hold on what second and I'll be right with you."

I wanted to tell Mr. Hargood that I did not need assistance and that he could eat his clementine in peace. But he seemed so eager to help and I was so eager to see his glass eye, that I just nodded my head and wiggled my finger in the general direction of his cat. I am entirely indifferent to cats as a general rule. I liked Mr. Hargood's cat, though. He had one little spot above his nose which I was aching to tickle one day when we were on friendlier terms.

I shuffled a stack of notebooks and looked at a deck of playing cards which were printed with a tropical bird motif. I heard Mr. Hargood crumple a napkin and clear his throat. He pushed out his stool and approached me with a smile on his face. Again, it was peculiar how his real eye did not intimate a smile as his fake one did. Mr. Hargood was perplexing.

"How can I help you today, son?"

"I'm in need of a very nice notebook. I have a new business opportunity and I need to be well-prepared, as you know."

To Mr. Hargood, I was an entrepreneur of the highest degree. Every time I went to him, I had a new business venture. He also printed my calling cards for me. I was embarrassed to have them detail too much of my real life, so I left them to say, simply:

Arthur R. Croots - London - He'll Call You

Mr. Hargood got a kick out of this. He chuckled as he handed them to me. He thought I was being private because of my success. He did not know it was simply that I did not own a telephone. The calling cards cost me nearly four pounds. I used them exactly twice—once as a bookmark and once, folded up, to stop a table from wobbling. It was a surprise to me, too, to learn one did not typically need calling cards when one worked as a waiter or a lifeguard. But I felt important having them and it was important for me to have Mr. Hargood think I was a successful, if somewhat private, entrepreneur.

"We've a nice selection over here."

Mr. Hargood motioned for me to follow him to a small display of notebooks. Instead of opening a curtain or turning on a light, he grabbed a lantern from his desk to illuminate this little corner. I wondered if his cat ever knocked the lantern over. A paper shop is the one place you don't want a lit lantern and a mischievous cat, I'd think.

The notebooks, as to be expected, were of the utmost quality. I commented on the details of those I liked to Hargood, and together we narrowed it down to two: one a deep maroon with gold foil on its pages; the other in brown leather embossed to look like crocodile skin. I was torn. But I also remembered I still had money from Celia's sale, so I bought both. Mr. Hargood looked so pleased he beamed at my choice. There was clementine pulp in his teeth. I didn't point this out, though. He was already so ugly, I didn't want to make him feel worse about himself.

Buying from Mr. Hargood also meant he wrapped the notebooks in a fine blue tissue and tied the bundle with a navy ribbon. He handed me my receipt. He then picked up his cat with the spot above his nose, manipulating his paw to make him wave goodbye to me. I wished Mr. Hargood could be my landlord. Mr. Hargood would have let me keep twenty dogs, if I asked nicely.

Because I was in a good mood now and because I was so close to Horace's, I thought I would pay him a visit. It was the time that Horace would be practicing (abusing) his piano, but he may have still been in good spirits from the Cormant deal, and answer the door. I also needed to borrow his library card. And I needed to inform him about my housing situation. And I needed to tell him about my plan. So, really, it was imperative for Horace to answer the door and I was determined to knock until he did so.

And so I did. Loud, pounding knocks that hurt my fist. I could hear Horace taking short, exasperated pauses when the knocking was at his loudest, but still he went on. I was determined to keep pounding and I cursed the luck of the universe that Horace, all beef and no grace, had the luxury of playing the piano while I, with my slender hands and natural talent, was standing outside his door scheming to escape eviction. God has a sense of humor. It wasn't a very good joke, though.

"Horace! Please open up! Horace! Ope! En! Up!"

This did not work. So I tried another tactic.

"Ouch! Horace! Please come quick! I seem to have broken my small finger on our door! Ow! The pain! Please Horace! Bring ice!"

Horace was zealous when it came to his piano practice, but he was also an empath. He came running to the door. I could hear his big feet hurry as he took extra-long strides. I believe I even heard the piano bench tip over.

He opened the door and there I was, unharmed and smiling. Horace looked annoyed to find me in such good shape. It was like he was almost disappointed I was not injured! Horace really was a curious man.

"Hello, Arthur. Can I help you? I'm in the middle of..."

"Middle of practice," I said. "Yes, I know." My hand did actually hurt a little bit and I had worked up a thirst. Horace did not offer me a drink, so I drank a glass of water from the kitchen tap. "Horace, my landlord knows about the dogs. It's all up. I have a month to figure this business out or we're all on the street."

"I'm sorry, Arthur, but I don't know what help I can be. It may be for the best for everyone to give the dogs better homes anyway."

"Horace, I'm thinking the exact same thing. Old boy, we're on the same brainwave here. But just one thing—you *can* be of help."

I explained my plan. How I would sell my remaining three dogs to wealthy, companionless people and then reclaim them when I missed them. I explained how I would research my potential customers and I explained about making sure the dogs looked handsome and how I bought two notebooks for keeping it all organized. Unfortunately,

Horace didn't even compliment the notebooks. I was disappointed in him. Horace really has no eye for good design.

With Horace's characteristic bovine precision, he grasped the plan slowly and incredulously. He liked to ruminate on everything a little too long. It was maddening to wait for him to catch up.

"Now, Horace, here is where you'll come in. I'll need you to help me research, and I'll need your assistance on driving these dogs to their new owners. And also I'll need you to help me take the dogs back when I sneak them out of their new owners' houses. There may even be some work as Lord Fenric's agent, but I don't know for sure just yet."

Horace sighed.

"Okay. I'll help."

VI

The Newton-Wiggs Société

I do not know why Horace agreed to my plans. Perhaps he'd grown bored of the piano or, more likely perhaps, it was because I was so persuasive. Either way, I never asked. I figured if I were to press him on his decision he would revoke his offer. I needed his help no matter the reason. He had a very roomy car.

Horace was painting what looked like small army men on his dining room table and setting them on spread-out newspaper to dry. I pushed them aside to make room for myself and my notebook. I do not know why Horace surrounded himself with such inconsequential hobbies. If he was so good at painting, why didn't he try his hand at counterfeiting money or painting novelty keychains to sell? He never thought of the bigger picture.

We began planning over tea, which then led to a glass of sherry, which then led to Horace going out to grab two sandwiches for us. Thinking makes me ravenous. I gained nearly a stone during my semester at university.

I was glad for Horace's mind and for his sandwich. Both helped tremendously. It was Horace's idea to join the London chapter of the Newton-Wiggs Société, the preeminent organization for dog enthusiasts like myself. I was not a member of Newton-Wiggs. I did not have the money for dues. But it was Horace's idea, so he would pay for my membership. From this, I would receive a directory of names. Perhaps even a yearbook. All of this would then be cross-referenced at the library. An outstanding idea, indeed.

The hiccup in this plan, which we uncovered between bites of egg salad, was that we might be reselling dogs back to their previous owners. All my dogs were purebreds and were well-trained when I acquired them (that's why I took them in the first place). There was a chance that one of the previous owners would be a member of Newton-Wiggs. It was a risk.

This, we decided, would require a bit of ingenuity and perhaps a henna rinse. We would change the dogs' appearances. We decided dying would be the easiest method, but I had a friend who worked in theatre and perhaps could borrow a hairpiece or two. I wondered briefly if Mr. Hargood could recommend us to his glass eye purveyor for dear Rue. I decided against this. I am squeamish as it is.

I left Horace's with the agreement to meet the following morning at nine o'clock to head over to the chapter headquarters of Newton-Wiggs. I wanted to make sure I got home in time to give the dogs a little more time in the garden. I also wanted to measure Henry's head for a wig.

How nice it is to let your own dogs run free in a garden! No harnesses attached to pulleys, no whispering little shushes, no kicking messes into the azaleas. Too bad I only had a month left. We—all of us—could have easily gotten used to this freedom.

I sat and smoked a cigarette while the dogs lounged in the shade. It was close to nightfall and so my cigarette soothed me and warmed my fingertips. The dogs barked at squirrels and each other. I laughed with them. We all ate a pot of warm beans while the sun set. It was an excellent day.

The next morning I met Horace at exactly 9:00 a.m. in front of his building.

"You're late," Horace said with a grumpy look on his face. I could not figure out how I was late. I had the time written down in my very nice notebook. I'd even checked it in the morning.

"No, Horace, you're mistaken. You said nine. It is now 9:01."

I extended my hand so that Horace could see my watch, which said 9:01. Horace pulled out his own watch to show me it was 9:43 a.m. Damn! So that is why I had been late during my last shift at The Pelican. I reminded myself to check the time more accurately the next time I slipped a watch into my pocket from a department store case. It really was unfortunate that Horace had to wait because a shop girl did not wind the watch properly before I took it.

Horace seemed jumpier than usual that morning, and I believe this was due to having time to think over our plan again. I am gifted persuader, as I have mentioned, but I cannot persuade someone when I am not with them. Horace had all night to think, which in my experience, is never a good thing. I thought about asking if my three dogs and I could move into Horace's flat for the remainder of the month, so I could be there to persuade him more readily. I realized this would have defeated the purpose of my bribe to Mr. Greaves for the month's leniency. Business is an intricate and precarious thing.

I asked Horace if he brought his checkbook and he patted his pocket. We made our way to the Newton-Wiggs office for me to pay my dues to become a member. Horace and I had disagreed about which of us should be the member. My argument was that I should, as I was of medium height and therefore could more easily blend in with the crowd. Horace's argument was that he could grow a beard very quickly, so he could alter his appearance if need be. Keen arguments, both, as I cannot grow a beard, but also Horace is a giant.

We finally agreed that Horace would pay for both of our memberships and in return he would get forty percent of whatever profits we made, minus expenses for us in the due course of business, such as fuel, wig glue, and a new suit for me. He thought this was fair, and we shook on it. Two aspiring Newton-Wiggs Société members walked side-by-side that morning.

The office was shabby, but in the way Queen Elizabeth is sometimes shabby: it had an innate respectability, but was wrapped in ugly fabrics. I know what I will ask my dues to be put toward, I thought to myself, eyeing a red and orange tartan ottoman. We rang a little silver bell on the reception desk to get the secretary's attention.

A woman in a suit came to greet us. She wore her hair in a very low knot and wore no makeup. I was intrigued to make her acquaintance—she looked influential, I thought, but perhaps was just a lesbian.

"How can I help you gentlemen?" she asked, reaching the desk and patting her hair back a little on her crown.

I had already decided that I would do the talking. I was more charming than Horace and he was really just there to sign a cheque.

"Good morning, ma'am. My business partner and I are interested in applying for membership with Newton-Wiggs. We've our money here with us and hope to register today."

"Oh, I'm so sorry gentleman, but the NWS isn't accepting new members right now. We limit our annual membership to assure every member can contribute and be hands-on with our mission." She did look sorry when she said it, but it sounded rehearsed.

I did not falter. I am glad we had decided ahead of time that I would be the one speaking.

"Ms...Um..."

"Ms. Greenwood."

"Ms. Greenwood. You must understand. We have *money*. We are here to *pay*. Am I to understand that the Newton-Wiggs Société turns down money?"

"Not at all, Mr....Er...."

"Croots."

"Mr. Croots. Not at all, Mr. Croots. We simply don't need money right now. We got a rather large endowment from Lady Anthony Panáge this January. And our bylaws say we can only initiate twenty new members per annum. I am sorry for you both."

"But we have money! Lots of it! You can't tell me, Ms. Greenwood, that our dues of eighty pounds couldn't be used to reupholster this drab little room. Maybe there would even be enough to get your suit properly tailored!"

I was getting a bit heated. Horace cleared his throat to break the tension growing in the room.

"Mr. Croots and Mr....Um..."

"Mr. Wimbly."

"Mr. Croots and Mr. Wimbly, I appreciate your passion for our mission but we *cannot* accept you as members at this time. It's simply that we are at capacity! I wish we could have you both but, unfortunately, we cannot. Please apply in December to be considered for next year."

At this, she turned around and went back to a little room behind her desk. She had gotten the last word, so I yelled behind her, "We don't have months, Ms. Greenwood! We have four weeks! I need you to understand this, Ms. Greenwood! Ms. Greenwood!"

I continued tapping the little bell on the reception desk to get her attention until, finally, Horace escorted me out of the Newton-Wiggs Société's door. I did not like being told no. It is one of my most unbecoming traits.

VII

A Newly Appointed Chair

On the doorstep I cooled down quickly. It was Ms. Greenwood's indifference that upset me. Horace has a calming effect on me. He barely spoke, but I knew he was sympathetic at my annoyance.

"Let's go get something to eat, Arthur. I know it's a little late for breakfast, but it'll do us some good to get something in you."

He was right, of course. The toast and jam calmed me immensely. I consider the eating of toast to be a ritual. There is a pattern one falls into. The little lick of butter, the bite, the crunch, the sip of tea if the toast is too dry. Repeat. Repeat. Repeat until it's all gone. Rituals are sedative. You don't use your brain much when you have a ritual. My mother was a Catholic; there are lots of rituals during Mass. I often fell asleep during Mass.

Horace was drinking coffee this morning, which told me that he had not slept well. The waiter brought us the morning paper and Horace read it page-by-page. Horace gets very absorbed in newspapers. I think he was also embarrassed for me at having yelled at Ms. Greenwood. I was not embarrassed for myself, though. I had gotten the last word, and that was very satisfying. I ate my toast without guilt.

We sat like this for a good half an hour (or what I assumed to be a half an hour, having lost faith in my wristwatch). I munched on my toast and Horace read his newspaper. I was just wiping the toast crumbs from my lap when Horace put the paper down and looked at me, wide-eyed.

"Arthur! Who did Ms. Greenwood say the endowment was from?"

"Oh I can't remember - Spinage? Penrash?"

"Was it Panáge?"

"That sounds right. Why?"

"She's dead! Her and her husband, Sir Anthony Panáge! Dead! Their obituary is in the paper just today."

"Dead? Really, Horace? Are you sure? How coincidental!"

"More than coincidental, pal. That's two fewer people in the NWS!"

"Horace! Hand over the paper - let me read the obit."

In Loving Memory: Sir and Lady Anthony Panáge

Today we say goodbye to two patrons of London Society who will be very missed. Sir and Lady Anthony Panáges were found dead last night in what appears to be a roadside accident. No foul play has been considered. A bottle of Moët was found at the scene. A joint service will be held at Our Lady of the Labrador, where both were Chairs to the fundraising committee which oversaw a charity dog show for the blind. Sir Anthony received his CBE for his charitable work during the Great War where he supplied injured officers with dogs, which resulted in a therapeutic relationship between man and beast. Gertrude, Lady Anthony (née Tinker) met Sir Antony in Belgium during this time. She was a missionary who was very good at leatherworking, and often made leads for his therapy dogs. They celebrated their 19th anniversary together. They are survived by one son, Henry, and three Airedale Terriers. The estate will pass between these four heirs. Services will be held on this Saturday morning at 9:00 a.m. In lieu of flowers, the Panáge estate has requested donations be made to the Newton-Wiggs Société, of which both Sir and Lady Panáge were active members, helping to plan the annual dog parade each Spring in St. James Park

"Well, looks like Mr. Greenwood can't say no to us now eh?" I said, putting the paper down and meeting Horaces smile. I grabbed some coins from my pocket and tossed them on the table. We left to make our way back to the Newton-Wiggs office, feeling especially pompous that the Panáges were dead and I was full of buttered toast and going to be a new member of the Newton-Wiggs Sociéte.

"Ms. Greenwood!" I called as I swung the door to the office open. She was already seated at the reception desk, so I needn't have yelled. I was only slightly embarrassed.

"Mr. Croots and Mr. Wimby, hello again. You have some crumbs on your shirt."

Ms. Greenwood was a cool little thing. I brushed them off onto the carpet and proceeded to put the paper down in front of her. I pointed to the obituary, where the Panáges' portraits stared up to meet Ms. Greenwood's eye.

"What's this?" she asked, scanning the page.

"It's our membership into the NWS is what it is. Read it yourself, miss. That's two fewer members. And we make two."

"Now, Mr. Croots. I've told you just an hour ago that we are *not* taking new members. The Panáges were lifelong members and I need to type up a memorandum to inform the Board if they haven't been informed already. Mr. Wimby, Mr. Croot, have a wonderful day."

So went all of the jubilation I was feeling when I first walked in the door. It is a terrible feeling, to be deflated. It is worse than sunburns and worse than a hangnail. It is possibly not as bad as a hangover, but I suppose it depends on if there is fresh coffee or not.

I am not too prideful to say I was nonplussed. I'd assumed Ms. Greenwood would see the transaction simply. I began to wonder if Ms. Greenwood had a learning disability. Perhaps she could not count to two. Perhaps I should have drawn her a picture to illustrate.

While I was thinking of next steps, Horace had shuffled to Ms. Greenwood. Other than his name, he had not spoken to her. We had agreed that I would do all of the talking. Horace was going rogue—and on the very first day of our new business partnership!

"Ms. Greenwood, I'm sure this is a very sad moment for you. Mr.

Croots—Arthur—and I would like to extend our sympathy. Did you know the Panáges long?"

"For many years. They even invited me over for their Christmas dinner one year. I hear their Airedales had a turkey cooked just for them."

Horace put a hand to his cheek. "No! Just for the dogs!"

"I thought the same thing, Mr. Wimby."

"It's Horace."

"Mr. Horace. But they were like that, you know. Very good to their dogs and very good to everyone, really. It-it-it is a surprise, I must say!"

Here she began to cry and Horace pulled a handkerchief from his pocket. She took it and smiled.

"Arthur and I are very sorry for the loss this must bring for the NWS, financially and socially. We'd love to be of assistance. If we could be members today, we could take over some of the responsibilities of planning the upcoming dog parade at St. James Park. I know the Panáges were very important in planning. We'd hate for you and the Newton-Wiggs Société to suffer this loss any more deeply than is absolutely necessary."

"Mr. Wimby, that's very kind of you to offer. Yes, the Parade represents a substantial share of our fundraising efforts. Do either of you have experience in planning charity events?"

"Why, Arthur here is a professional! Tell her, Arthur!"

Finally, Horace had passed the baton.

"Oh, Ms. Greenwood," I said. "I'm so glad you asked! Horace is quite right. I am a professional planner. By day, anyway. I spend most evenings with my dogs. Or at Church, where I volunteer for the sick and the poor. Did you happen to read about the celebration tea for the Viscount Hencroft's daughter's engagement? That was all me. And the charity dance for St. Mercy of the Harpsichord? Me again! And did you get your ticket for the grand opening of La Pêche in Chelsea? My dear, do you go out at all? Do you even pick up a daily? I should be an ambassador for crêpe paper I'm photographed with it so often! Ha ha!"

"Well, Mr. Wimby and Mr. Croots, I must apologize for being so rude earlier. You must understand, the Newton-Wiggs Société can't just extend membership to anyone who wanders in off the street! But we will feel the loss of the Panáges, both at the Parade and in our coffers. If you'll fill out these membership forms, I'll take them to the Board for immediate approval this morning."

How quickly people change their minds when one tosses out words like "Viscount" and "grand opening" and "crêpe paper". By noon, we had received our membership cards and were fully initiated into the Newton-Wiggs Société, "the premier club for those canine-minded and those whose interests are canine-adjacent," according to the Club Charter we received, along with the current membership directory.

We felt very lucky the Panáges had died, and we laughed at our luck as we walked home. Horace was in an especially good mood and I complimented the tact he demonstrated with Ms. Greenwood. He congratulated me on being made the Chair of the Fundraising Committee in Gertrude Panáges' absence. On top of having to sell my dogs and leave my apartment in a month, I was now tasked with planning the largest fundraiser for London's richest dog lovers.

I wrote in my notebook on our way home a reminder to find out what the devil a dog parade was anyway.

VIII

In Loving Memory of Sir & Lady Panáges

I was very busy the following week, which was stressful. As a rule, I do not like to be busy. Instead, I like to have a day filled with tasks that I can dip into at my leisure, like a warm bath. This was not the case. I did not anticipate a dog parade to be so much work. Nor did I anticipate how many influential people I would meet following our membership into the Newton-Wiggs Société.

I went back and forth on whether I should chuck the whole thing and abandon all of my dogs at the NWS office one morning. I might choose loneliness if it meant I did not have to grow any more calluses on my fingers from all the note-taking. I have exquisite penmanship, but I cannot hold a pen comfortably due to my somewhat smallish hands. It seems every personal quality is a double-edged sword!

But one morning Rue came up to me and licked my hand, and I decided against abandoning the dogs. While they now had the entire back garden to run while I was working and planning and note-taking, I was spending less time with them. Here I was with just three weeks left, pushing lovely Rue away while I worked. I smeared ink on her little white head. I did feel a bit guilty, I have to admit.

I pushed forward with the planning. I am a diligent worker and something of a saint, if I am being honest. It is not bragging to say that the NWS needed me, and I was there to meet their challenge. I am a tidy, organized person. I bought four new notebooks from Mr. Hargood in anticipation of how tidy and organized I would be.

In that week of planning, I had only left my flat for strictly professional reasons, which included: meeting with the NWS planning committee, visiting Horace after my morning at the library, and for the Panáges' joint memorial service. I will describe all three here, as each event was critical to the overall plan on selling my dogs.

As new Newton-Wiggs members, Horace and I felt that it was necessary for us to pay our respects to the Panáges'. We thought of them fondly, the timing their passing being so serendipitous to our ambitions. We decided to attend the memorial service that Saturday to pay our respects. We also thought it would be a good way to meet affluent people. We felt affluent people would be more sympathetic to our plan when they were in mourning.

It was an ideal time for me to attend a funeral. I still had my waiter uniform from my previous job with George's Italian. It was a splendidly cut suit jacket and pants. Unfortunately, the pocket square was fake and sewn in permanently and it smelled vaguely of *pomodori*. Otherwise, an outfit appropriate to saying, "Goodbye" to my dear friends, the Sir and Lady Panáge.

I decided against the little vest that came with the outfit, though. I now regret this, as it *was* a charming vest.

Horace and I met in front of the church on Saturday morning. Horace was in his usual corduroy suit, which was handsome but not appropriate. At least his lapel was not stained with marinara, he said. I told him he was wrong—it was ragu. It did not come out with club soda like Ms. Rublack said it would. I do not know why I would go to her with housekeeping advice. Her windowsill was always filthy when I climbed through it to borrow something of hers.

Horace also wore his cap, which I do not believe I have described previously, so I will do so now. I believe it had previously been a cap common among younger lads than Horace and looked to have been ran over by a car once or twice. Perhaps Horace had picked it up from a crime scene of a boy who *had* been run over by a car once or twice. I had never asked him. It had the faint color of cigar smoke - brown and grey, but less masculine. Perhaps the underside of a rotting tomato leaf was more accurate. It had to be ancient and had to have been very cheap, and yet Horace always wore it at formal occasions. Horace had money, he just did not use it properly. And somehow I could not imagine Horace having turned up in anything else. It was an ugly cap, but it suited him perfectly.

My cap, on the other hand, was a simple black thing. It was the one I lost at sea on the *Mathilde*, as I had mentioned earlier. I had only ever owned the one, so it was a shame to lose it.

We sat in the very back pew and could spot only two people we knew: Ms. Greenwood, who blew her nose delicately when we entered, and a bishop who had made the papers recently. I believe this bishop was the nephew of an Earl. I would make sure to say my hellos. Ms. Greenwood did not seem to recognize us. Or she was ignoring us. Either way, I was pleased to see her, as I hoped she would introduce us to more influential people—-including more nephews of Earls. I was also pleased to see that she was wearing more feminine clothes, a rarity I find in London these days.

The service was stultifying and the little ladies who tend to help out at these sort of events did not have any coffee in any of the back tables, nor in the hallway, nor in the antechamber. I didn't really want any coffee, but I wanted an excuse to walk a bit to see who else was present for the Panáges. From my viewpoint it was a sea of tweed, littered with sniffling old women, and the bald pates of many men (and a few of the women!).

I was so distracted by the sadness that I hardly recall anything at all said during the memorial. I did learn that Lady Panáge was fluent in Danish, for some reason. I learned that Sir Panáge was not fluent in anything but English, but spoke English very well. He had written a book of poetry during the Great War. I learned that they had honeymooned somewhere in Africa, where neither Danish nor English came in handy. They had had a daughter who had died at birth. Their three Airedales sat in the front pew along with Henry Panáge, the son. The Airedales were very well-behaved. I wondered if they knew that the Panáges were even dead. I thought it best not to tell them. Airedales can be melancholy enough as it is.

It was only after the last remarks that I had any fun at the funeral. Some touched the caskets, some petted the dogs. Some rushed to the loo and some looked at the photo album propped up on an easel toward the front. Once the sanctity of the service was broken, it became quite a convivial, almost familiar, atmosphere. It was obvious most of those in attendance knew one other from their various intersecting social circles.

Most men would be cautious, even shy, to be at the edge of all of these intersecting social circles, but I was not. I am not like most men and I am not shy. That is, unless I am at the dentist or in front of a group of teenagers who appear mean, but those circumstances are rare and perfectly understandable. This was not one of those circumstances in which I was shy, though. In fact, Horace and I sat to one side of the mass and waited with our hands folded behind us. Sooner or later, someone would have to introduce themselves.

In a group like this, full of tweed and talcum powder, people like to shake hands as much as possible and compete over who was closest to the deceased. They say things like, "Oh, I knew So-and-so before the War!" And someone will reply, "Before the War! I knew So-and-so when we were children!" And someone will reply to *that* with, "As children? We shared a womb together!" On and on it goes.

It took only a few minutes for Ms. Greenwood to spot us and wave. She held up one finger to indicate, "Just a minute!" Because my watch was not working correctly, I could not time her precisely. She did sidle up to us very shortly after, though.

"What a nice surprise to see you both here," Ms. Greenwood said. I do not think she meant it.

"We thought that, considering how much we owed to the...the

deceased it was really the least we could do," I said, making sure I seemed like I genuinely cared about the Panáges.

"That's kind of you. I'm sure, had you all been members of NWS at the same time that they would have been fond of you both. They loved strays."

We talked a little more about the expectations for the dog parade and the Panáges' son, Henry. I mentioned how odd it was that there were no refreshments. Ms. Greenwood said it was not a diner. She was very tough on me. She was not tough on Horace, I noticed.

"Ms. Greenwood, I'm sorry to cut you off, but would you care to introduce us around? Horace and I have a very important business luncheon that we can't miss. But we would like to have a little assistance on paying our respects to those close with the Panáges."

I did not think this was an unreasonable request, but Ms. Greenwood seemed annoyed. I began to feel that that was her normal way of acting. Perhaps she thought Horace and I were people of influence and she was nervous around us. We were dressed very well, so one couldn't blame her for thinking these things.

In retrospect, I'm happy to say, this seems to have been our coming-out. With us in tow, Ms. Greenwood made the rounds. There was the Bishop of Nuthrop-on-Ham, who was indeed the Earl of Ham's nephew (twice-removed, but still)! There were the Rimshaws, who were young and American but spoke well enough. There were the Piersons, the Thompsons, and the Logues. There was Lady Derwint, Lady Yarlwood, and Lady Munlow-Temple-Pest. I believe they were sisters or perhaps all simply went to the same hairdresser. I was pleased to meet Lord Derwint, who had a barrel chest and toothpick legs. I was *not* pleased to meet the Viscount Spittlewind, who must have been taught it was rude to look people in their eyes. All were keen to meet *me*. I was becoming very influential among the Newton-Wiggs Société after only these few days, being the Chair of a committee, and being naturally charming. Horace remained respectfully quiet. I would ask him if he remembered everyone we met after we left. We agreed the information would be useful to our plan.

Before leaving the church, I signed the guestbook. My penmanship was superior to everyone else's. I noticed Ms. Greenwood's first name was Belinda. I did not care for that name much. I decided I would call her only Ms. Greenwood, never Belinda. Horace was silent when I commented on Ms. Greenwood's name.

At lunch we each had a small porkchop and some potatoes. We wrote down all of the names of those who we had met. Nothing exciting happened at the lunch other than Horace had a crème caramel *and* a slice of pistachio cake.

IX

The Inaugural Meeting

On Monday morning I received a telegram from the NWS reminding me that our first Fundraising Committee meeting would be held on Tuesday at 3:00 p.m. I thought this was Ms. Greenwood's work and felt it was excessive. I did not want my dues—-paid for by Horace's hard-earned inheritance—-to go to these little scraps of paper whizzing around London. It was a pointless reminder, anyway, because I had put the date in my new notebook and I am very good at remembering appointments, especially as I did not have a job then to muddle up my schedule. Ms. Greenwood did seem to be personally rather parsimonious, as her clothing was very old and she did not wear makeup. A telegram? Seems extravagant. Perhaps she was only careful with her own money. As the Chair of a committee, I would be sure to mention this to her.

I was enjoying the extra time I had with my dogs and they looked forward to the mornings in the back garden. I wonder if they remembered Celia. I wonder if they remembered the pulley system. I believe dogs to be very intelligent creatures, so I am sure they did remember. Perhaps Milly misses the pulley system, I thought. How exciting to be so fat and at the same time so weightless.

As my Committee meeting was the next day, I had all of Monday to begin researching those we had met at the Panáges' service. I could not decide who to take as top priority in my research and this was a subject hotly debated by Horace and myself over roast beef on Saturday night. I thought it would be best to start with those who held titles, as they would be monied and have family seats in the country. Horace said to start with the youngest, as their money was probably new and they may take a dog before wanting to have a child. He also reminded me that an earl's pockets were often emptier than mine—it was just that the bank couldn't repossess a name like they could a settee. He was right, of course. And the Bishop was out. Holy men are stingy.

We decided instead to split the list fifty-fifty. I did not bother to research Julius Rhodes nor Viscount Spittlewood, as both were on my Committee. According to the member directory, Monty Spittlewood was my secretary on this committee. I felt very influential at the thought of having him read minutes back to me, saying, "Yes, sir," at my recommendations. Perhaps his penmanship was better than mine, though. This made me feel insecure for a moment.

I had a tin of fish and two apples for lunch, while the dogs had bread rolls I had taken home from the restaurant with Horace. I studied a bit of German ("The cow is bringing coins to Mama," et cetera) and napped. When I awoke, just over four hours later, I was parched. I poured myself a glass of water from the tap and let the dogs run wild in the garden while the sun fell behind the skyscrapers. Only Rue stayed behind. She sat on my lap as I flipped through the paper.

There was a mention of the Earl of Ham. He was buying stock in a motion picture company. I took this as a sign that perhaps I would sell Rue to His Lordship. I always felt that Rue, being a King Charles, had a movie star quality to her. I believe it is her eyes. They are very similar to Bette Davis'.

I slept soundly that night. I was not nervous, even though I was to be meeting so many influential people on Tuesday at 3:00 p.m. If I stumbled through my notes, I would have the Vice-Chair take the lead of the meeting. If there was no Vice-Chair of the committee, then I would appoint someone and have them lead the meeting. I believe I am a natural leader. I believe the only way to flourish in a leadership capacity is to delegate. I'm very good at telling others what to do.

In the morning, I stretched my suit jacket over the hob to dry the last little bit of dampness out of my lapel. Fortunately, I had got most of the ragu out. I had my tea standing up at the kitchen window and smoked a cigarette for breakfast to calm my nerves. I was in my underwear and sunning myself like a cat. The dogs were down in the garden. Ms. Rublack did not seem pleased they were there, but she could do nothing about it. Mr. Engel in the flat across from mine waved cheerily at me. As I was in my underwear. I did not wave back. Mr. Engel must have been something of a pervert. I closed my kitchen curtain and finished my cigarette on my bed.

I had to ask Mr. Greaves to tell me the time when I left for my Committee meeting. While I had rewound the watch, I did not trust myself. A first impression was everything. I could not have both ragu on my jacket and be late for my meeting. I felt paranoid that the Viscount would record it in the meeting minutes. I did not want to be memorialized so soon in such an embarrassing way.

Mr. Greaves told me it was seven-after-two, which was what I had on my watch. I thanked him in the general, polite sense and he grumbled back to me under his breath in his little goblin language full of rudeness.

"Can I help you with something, Mr. Greaves?" I asked.

"Got any news on them dogs?"

"Why yes, that's why I asked the time. I'm going to a very important appointment as we speak regarding 'them dogs' as you call them."

"Good. Cause m'damn oven ain't working and your few pounds ain't covering the cost to fix it."

"I'm sorry to hear that, Mr. Greaves. Cold beans and a light salad can do in a pinch."

"I'm sayin', boy. You get me another fiver and you got yourself another week here with them dogs of yours."

Mr. Greaves was not a haggler and I was in a hurry. I gave him Horace's number and told him to tell Horace that this was considered an overhead cost for our business. Mr. Greaves eyed me as I walked out the door. Perhaps he saw the ragu stain, too. Perhaps I did not do as good a job as I had thought I had in getting the stain. Then I remembered Mr. Greaves was a suspicious old man and he was watching me go because he simply did not like me. Somehow, that wasn't a comforting thought, either.

On my walk to the Newton-Wiggs Société's office, henceforth known as The Office to conserve ink in my pen as I write this, I did not stop for a pastry, though I was hungry. I did not want to risk crumbs or rhubarb jam on the front of my shirt. I did not own many shirts then, so I could not afford to ruin the ones I had. I amused myself by thinking that, if I spilled any jam, I would just have to dye the entire shirt pink to match the rhubarb stain. What a thought!

I decided I would rather be hungry during the meeting than to be embarrassed during the meeting.

Today Ms. Greenwood was not at the desk to greet me. Instead a tall tower of a man, who introduced himself as George, waved at me as I entered. He wore a broad grin on his face and I could see that his teeth were not straight. This did not, in fact, bother me too terribly, as his smile seemed so genuine, even if it was a little goofy.

"Mr. Croots! How pleasant to finally meet you!"

I was awfully flattered. Usually when I enter a room, nobody knows my name. If they do, it is because I am late for my shift and the other waitstaff are angry with me. I shook George's hand and said my hellos back. I did not say he could call me Arthur and he did not ask to. I enjoy a bit of formality. A healthy buffer between us seemed appropriate, given my position as Chair of a Committee.

George asked if I would like any refreshments before the meeting began. I can never turn down free food, so I asked for a scone. I also asked for a knife and fork, to be safe. I was very worried that Viscount Spittlewood would be watching me closely while I ate, scribbling away, recording down my every social blunder.

The meeting room was round. Or, it felt like a very round room because there were dog beds laid along the wall. It was a windowless room and books were laid not on shelves like you'd expect, but in large piles on the floor. Every chair had a cushion in the same tartan fabric as the receiving area in the Office. I asked if this room was in the process of being renovated and Jane Raitland, a member who looked like a parishioner's daughter or perhaps a very sad nurse, said no and provided no further explanation. The subject dropped then and there. This was my first mistake as Chair.

Spittlewood read the minutes from the last meeting and kindly introduced me. He recited my credentials to the audience. All six of them. And I reacted modestly when he mentioned the Hon. Sarah Hencroft ("Oh! It was nothing!"). The Committee members seemed impressed. I looked the part of someone who was both influential and humble, sitting in front of the Committee with a Viscount to my right. I did notice my name on the nameplate was written in paint overtop Lady Panáge's own. I noted in one of my very nice notebooks to ask George to see to this matter immediately. I was very confident that George would not let me down.

The minutes made no sense to me and the topics of conversation seemed to be splitting hairs. Spittlewood would go down the list of something called an "agenda" and ask for everyone's input. When there was a debate, the expectant eyes would stare at me for a decision. I decided many things that day, including: dogs that were to be paraded would have matching red leads and collars; owners who paraded alongside the dogs were not allowed to wear pants (if women) or skirts (if men); this rule did not apply to our Scottish members (if men); no alcohol would be permitted at the parade, but members could bring a little tipple if it were for medicinal reasons (Toffie Montmaarten said it helped with her blood pressure); and that the parade would begin at 10:00 a.m. and conclude by 10:28 a.m. It seems we had only rented the marquee tent for two hours.

It was only after the meeting had adjourned—-I had never adjourned a meeting before and it was thrilling—-did anything substantial happen. I was able to meet all members of my little Committee and assess their value.

Fanny Maybrick was the first to introduce herself. But to me, being an avid fan of the social papers, she needed no introduction. She was not a peer, but she was tremendously wealthy. Her money was tied up in marriages, which was her full-time job in some ways. Her full name was Frances Maybrick-von Uttler-Smith-Jones-Carter-Unsworth. She did not have the presence of a widow or a divorcee. Instead, she had the presence of a Pekinese. I liked her immensely. She wore an outfit of green and terrible eyeshadow. I thought Rue would have liked to be her pet. Between marriages of course.

There was Jane Raitland, the dowdiest person in the room, who wore a pinafore that showed the dark spread of underarm perspiration before my very eyes. She mumbled a hello and gave cursory responses to my courtesy questions. Even her nods were mumbles, quick and nearly imperceptible, eyes down. She annoyed me greatly. But she appeared muscular under her pinafore and so would be good in setting up the tent, I was sure.

Julius Caesar Rhodes ate a pastry in two swallows and shook my hand after brushing the crumbs off on his pant leg. Usually this would annoy me, but he had a good handshake and most of the crumbs fell to the ground where I assumed George or a dog would see to them. Reynolds was the great-grandson of the Earl of Comphrey. He had the same good looks as the Earl. Both enjoyed racing, though I don't believe automobiles had been invented by the era of the 8th Earl. Who can keep track of other people's inventions?

I decided Julius would make an excellent member of the Committee board. He would be my Treasurer. Living so extravagantly, he would no doubt be terrible with money. I did not want someone to look too closely at the finances. I had to find a way to take a salary for all my volunteer work.

Hannah Grey-Downs was a firm handshake and a full bosom of a woman. I believe she thought she was to be the next Chair and she acted like it. Her husband was a newspaper baron somewhere in Portugal. Because Hannah could not speak Portuguese, she had stayed behind while he built his empire. She asked a lot of questions, which was flattering but annoying. I decided I would write to her that evening and make her my Vice-Chair. She would handle everything and I would take credit for it. Unless, of course, she failed. In that case, her handshake and bosom were my scapegoat. Either way, she would be useful.

Then there was Desmond Winnicott, Baron Ham-sur-Rye. He pronounced his surname as "Win-kit", as he was brought up in the aristocratic tradition of being quite *laissez-faire* about such things as consonants and vowels. He was the step-cousin of the Bishop of Ham and a baron in his own right. He had a Grecian profile and bushy eyebrows that knitted together at the faintest lull in the conversation. I do not know what his politics were that he should be given a barony. I wished I could have ousted Spittlewood and put Desmond in his place, as it would have been a fair excuse to be in his proximity. But I needed the Viscount as the Secretary. I didn't want to hurt his pride (him being a Viscount) and because he seemed to be the only one who knew where the extra pens were kept.

Desmond would be the Chair's Assistant, a title I made up then and there. He would do nothing except sit by my side during meetings. His first order of business was going to be to change my name placard. Delightful. I was a natural leader, I must say.

Toffie Montmaarten left the meeting immediately upon adjournment. She apologized and said the banks were closing and she had to cash a check. Considering her anxiety to get there before the banks were closed, I surmised two possibilities: either the cheque was very big and she had to cash it straight away; or her account was very small and she needed to deposit it to ballast her finances. I would be sure to inspect her jewelry more thoroughly next time I saw her to decide which of these two hypotheses were true.

I left the Office with a wave to George and a smile as goofy as his. I was euphoric. I had accomplished so much! There were connections to people of influence. There were free pastries. There was Desmond and his handsomely knitted eyebrows. I celebrated on the way home by buying a vanilla and lemon cake to share with the dogs. I was in such a good mood, I even contemplated buying a few chocolates for old

Greaves. But I decided against it. I remembered he was asking Horace for money. What if Horace had said no? Never waste of good chocolate on a bad landlord.

That evening, I cut a slice of cake for each of the dogs and we enjoyed them in the back garden. I saw Ms. Rublack behind her curtain. No bit of lace could conceal that monstrous shape. I waved. I was happy.

X

Horace's News

The next Committee meeting was to be on Friday. As the day of the Parade approached, I wanted to ensure that we were on a good path to succeed. I was happy to give the past vendors a phone call to ensure that this year's contract was no different than the previous. I was happy to call the ribbon maker to ensure the ribbons were still on schedule and that they were royal blue, like every other year. I was happy to call the park groundskeeper to verify that our spot was reserved. But I remembered I did not have a phone. I wrote to Mrs. Grey-Downs and delegated these tasks to her. I was sure she had a phone of her own.

I wrote to the other Committee members, too. I offered the positions to Julius and Desmond. I did not let Mrs. Grey-Downs know that she was to be my Vice-Chair just yet. I worried she'd turn lazy if I rewarded her too soon.

I whistled my way to the post box and all the way back. This was the first time that I had felt influential in a very long time. I did not feel influential when I had to ask Horace for rent money and I did not feel influential when a diner at The Pelican said I had stuck my thumb in their soup while I was serving him. I felt only slightly influential when I visited Mr. Hargood and I did not feel influential at all when I was snubbed by Ms. Greenwood. Life was a see-saw, and the weight of my own back luck had for so long held me down.

But this was different. I was a Chair! I even searched for the German equivalent in my little primer book. *Ein Stuhl*, it said. I was a *Stuhl*! Capitalized and everything. In two languages, no less.

The next day, I began my research notes. I started with those I had met at the Panáges' service and worked my way to the Committee members. I started with the funeral guests first because I was beginning to already forget their faces. They all looked so very similar. They wore dull smiles, and dull hairstyles. And they tugged dully at their dull hems as they stood in the dull nave among the pews.

Horace had lent me his library card. I would do my research at the library. I left the cardboard box that housed the cake from the night before on the floor for the dogs to lick. They were very thorough cleaners.

I have always appreciated the library. It is one of the few places I am content in being anonymous. I sometimes like to read books but more often than not, I like to sit and take in the inherent, if understated, drama of the library. There is the severe librarian whose hair is in a severe bun. There are the sullen aides who roll books down hallways like orderlies in a hospital. There are small schoolchildren who think they are whispering when they are not. There are comfortable chairs. In the Winter, there is even central heating. I go to the library often in wintertime.

I have not been to the library in a long while, though. This is because I am not allowed to check out any more books until I pay my fine. I do not believe in being punished for the pursuit of education; ergo I do not, on principle, believe in library fines. Instead, I borrow Horace's card. The librarian barely looks up from her nail file. And yet still, every time, I am nervous she will revoke Horace's card, too. How terrible it would be for him. But he is rich and I am not. He does not need to borrow books for free as often as I do.

The only time my penmanship is less than perfectly elegant is when I am rushed. When I am rushed, it is scribbly and I often annotate my notes with arrows and carets above and below the original script. In my excitement over our plan, I took less-than-perfect notes. I did not worry too much, since they were for my eyes only. If Horace saw how bad my note taking was, especially after my bragging to him about my great signature, I would be embarrassed. Horace has a way of making me very defensive about my mistakes.

Studying issues of *The Tatler* and *Country Life* and various society papers, I was able to work up a portrait of each my research subjects. I put a little X next to the ones I felt were lonely enough for a dog and a double-X next to the ones I felt were just status-obsessed enough to purchase one of my purebreds. Any with a country house would go to the top of the list, naturally. The reason being twofold: the dogs would have room to play, and I would be able to see the inside of a real-life country home. Too bad I would most likely only see the inside of the real-life country home during the nighttime, when I would be sneaking into their home and take my dog back.

I left the library feeling accomplished and famished. I bought a sandwich from a stand and told the boy to keep the change. I was in a very charitable mood. The sandwich was ham and cheese. It was warmed from the sun but not unappetizing. I tossed the wrapper on the sidewalk as I approached Horace's house. I didn't want him to think I had already eaten, as he may have some food for me, too.

I had caught Horace before his daily piano lesson and with his shirt sleeves rolled up. Horace has very thick forearms so the sleeves always look painfully tight on him. His two top buttons on his shirt were undone. He was unshaven, too. Horace is extremely casual at home alone. I doubt he even has a dressing gown, let alone a nightly beauty routine.

Horace was happy to see me, or that is at least what his smile said. Again, I had to move bulky items from his couch so that I could sit down. This time it was a very heavy brass sexton. I told Horace that if he was expecting me then he should make room for me. He said he was not expecting me. I told him we were now business partners and therefore he should always expect me. He said I still have to knock first.

Horace did not have anything for me to eat and it seemed that he had not planned to have lunch himself. This was not like Horace, whom I once saw eat an entire lobster for lunch on holiday. Perhaps he had had a big breakfast. I knew Horace liked to eat *omelettes* in the morning if he couldn't hold out until lunchtime.

Horace, who is naturally taciturn, was even less talkative than usual. I thought perhaps I should not have moved his sexton, as maybe that was what upset him. Perhaps it was sentimental. Maybe it was a gift from his grandfather, or a relic from the Norman Conquest. It didn't seem that old, but I know very little about nautical antiques.

Horace did not laugh at my jokes nor at my impression of the Committee members. I thought I did a ripping job of impersonating sad old Jane Raitland, but he didn't even chuckle. I told him about handsome Desmond and smiley George and strong-willed Mrs. Grey-Downs. Not even a blink! He only looked up briefly when I mentioned Mrs. Greenwood wasn't there and even that was more of a curious glance than an interested stare. There is a big difference. I am full of interested stares and often the recipient of curious glances.

I am accustomed to holding up my end of a conversation. I think this is because I am naturally influential. I have a phobia of dull conversations and therefore do not participate in them. This means I am often holding Horace's hand down the verbal path to something I like to talk about, like nice perfumes, or money, or lampshades. Unfortunately, Horace would have none of it. He didn't even care when I showed him one of my new notebooks from Mr. Hargood. That's when I knew it was serious.

"Horace! What *is* wrong with you? I didn't come over to watch you mope! I came here to discuss the next steps in our plan!"

"Oh, Arthur," he said. "I'm sorry. I didn't think you'd notice. I wasn't expecting company today so I'm a little dazed with some news I had with our estate manager, Mr. Driscoll." He meant his family's estate manager.

"Well, spit it out, man! You didn't even notice how good my impressions were."

"Well, Arthur. It's like this..."

"Like what, Horace?"

"Well, I've thought for some time..."

"Yes?"

"And I wasn't sure, but I had this feeling..."

"Horace! Spit it out, damn it!"

Finally he blurted it out: "I'm going broke!"

Talk about a news flash. I wish Horace had told me right when I had walked in the door. I would have saved my Jane Raitland impression for when he might have appreciated. Horace has always had terrible timing.

At first, I did not know what to say. As an empath, I am always ready to feel someone's pain when they suffer. But in this case, I naturally assumed it was Horace's fault, so I was more annoyed than anything. This meant there was a long pause, which Horace filled with a long explanation of how he got into this situation.

"I'm not sure how or if you know how my trust is set up with my grandfather's estate, Arthur. But it's tied to the success of his South American shipping company. A cousin of mine manages the business and I get my allowance. Well, the short version is, the money's dried up. This cousin had gone to seminary, so he had no idea how to manage a shipping business. Which means they're selling the business, and I'll be paid out for the rest of this year only. After that, I'm done. So I either have to start working or save up what I can this year and live off that."

Hmmmm, I thought to myself, *that doesn't sound right to me.* I thought his grandfather had a lumber mill in Germany. Perhaps this was how Horace was going broke—-he didn't know even the most basic thing about his finances. Now was not the time to correct him, though.

There was a long silence in which Horace looked guiltily at me. I was not sure if he wanted a hug, a drink, or for me to say something encouraging. I stayed silent. We both stared at our shoes.

I wanted him to speak first, but I gave in. "Well," I said. "I'm sure it can't be all that bad!" Even to myself, I did not sound very convincing.

I am usually a very good actor but I was a terrible one that afternoon. For so long Horace had been the only stable thing in my life.

More specifically, Horace's money had been the only stable thing in my life. It put our entire friendship into question. I wondered if I would like Horace nearly as much if we had to split a bill at a restaurant.

Horace, as I'd suspected, was not convinced of my optimism. Contrary to what I had said, it did seem bad. He went on to explain a bit about his finances and how taxes worked. He planned on selling the house and keeping the car. He thought the liquid cash up front was more important than keeping the money in his house and not being able to eat. Considering the only money to my name was what Horace had lent me and through the sell of Celia, none of this made much sense to me.

I told him it was a great idea anyway. I believe he needed to hear it.

The dots began to connect. Horace was selling those dictionaries and this sexton. He was gathering items from storage and shining them up for sale. It was also why he was trying his hand at so many hobbies—-in case he needed to fall back on one for a living. And, most importantly, and otherwise so out of character, it was why he agreed to be part of my dog selling scheme in the first place.

Horace looked doubly guilty when I addressed these points with him. I was not accusing him of anything dishonest, and yet I believe he considered his silence on the matter to be somehow duplicitous. While I am not a duplicitous person myself, I am extremely forgiving of duplicity in others.

That night, I helped Horace polish his brass sexton and we got roaringly, unrepentantly, stupidly drunk. He had some whiskey, which we mixed with tap water and little shards of ice chipped from the freezer. That night, I put away my notes from the library, and we spent the evening talking about running away to Cyprus and debating whether or not airlines took I.O.U.'s.

XI

The Esstäbchen Theatre

I woke the next morning to Horace prostrate on his bed, dressed only in his underwear. Mercifully, a sheet was tangled around his midsection, so I was spared that sight. I felt guilty, having left the dogs all night. They were probably hungry. The last thing they had eaten was the icing in the box I had brought home from the bakery. Poor dears. I promised I would rush home right after I had my breakfast.

I, too, was hungry. The last thing I had eaten was a measly sandwich. I was craving eggs, which I always find to be the best cure for a hangover. Horace only had two eggs. I had to make my breakfast quietly, so as to not wake him and have to share.

I decided the most silent way to make eggs would be to scramble them. I added a dash of mustard at the end, for which my hangover thanked me. I was very quiet with my fork and plate. I left my dirty dishes on the sofa cushion so they would not make noise in the sink. I wanted Horace to sleep as long as possible. I felt it would do him well.

I left him a small note for him to call on me later in the week. I also reminded him that he needed to do his share of the research on our potential customers. I put a postscript to remind him to buy eggs. I placed the note next to his keys so he would find it. He had two pounds in his wallet. I pocketed the money as I was going out the door.

I needed to buy the dogs a big breakfast to make up for not being home all night.

If you are thrifty, two pounds can go a long way. If you are thrifty and also very good at taking things, then two pounds can be a small fortune. On my way home, I stopped at three street carts. I bought two bouquets of flowers for a pound. I tucked two apples in my pocket there, too. At the next vendor I bought two egg sandwiches. At the last cart a loaf of sourdough bread found its way under my coat. Two pounds and a little stealth and I had nourishment for the rest of the day!

The dogs were overjoyed to see me. Absence is tough on all of us, so I felt especially bad to see sensitive little Frances shaking emotionally. I picked him up and we shared the two egg sandwiches between the four of us. I believe Rue, who has an eye for design, very much liked the way the flowers brightened the flat. All in all, they seemed to forgive me.

I decided the best thing I could do was to steam my face and undertake an abbreviated beauty routine. I believe even a little bit of moisture brought back into the skin can do wonders for one's face after a night of drinking.

I also took a three-hour nap. I believe sleep is the second best thing for one's skin, next to moisture. It was all very restorative.

After my nap, I had a small cup of coffee and an apple dipped in a bit of honey. The honey had crystallized slightly in its jar, but only slightly. It was a very good honey. I had taken it from The Pelican not two months ago. I looked at my notebook while I ate my little lunch. I have the dogs an extra hour in the garden. I decided that day was a good day to visit J.W. Dreisbach.

I have known J.W. Dreisbach for ages. I knew him when he was Johann Wilhelm Dreyfuss, and before that when he was Jonathan William Downing. He had studied cinema in Berlin and had adjusted his name according to how famous he got in the Weimar scene. From my understanding, he was not very famous there either. Perhaps that is why he did not choose a very good stage name.

Dreisbach was on my list because he owed me a favor and because he owned a theatre. I can hardly remember what the favor was that he owed me, but I vaguely recall catching a ferret with my good suit jacket. Now that the plan for selling the dogs was in motion, I would need to call in that favor for some wigs and other costume pieces to alter my dogs' appearances. I thought a little hairpiece on Rue would hide the fact that she had one eye. Perhaps something auburn. She was a fall. Everyone said so.

Dreisbach's Esstäbchen Theatre was shabby but neither he nor his theatre-goers ever seemed to notice. Perhaps they did not mind. Perhaps it was part of the charm, some export from Weimar that one didn't need an antibiotic to treat. I believe the theatre was a gutted Chinese restaurant with a stage installed. He'd given me box of paper fans when he remodeled. For months afterwards, I always had a paper fan on me. I would take them to parties as hostess gifts. I would whip one out any day that it was over 23 degrees. I even tried to fashion a few into a lampshade. But I tired of them quickly and brought the remainder to Horace's to use as kindling for his fireplace. To this day, you can still see bits of chinoise in the ashes.

Calling in a favour is always delicate, but I am naturally skilled at this social tightrope. It is all about friendship, reminding the other person you are a dear friend, and making them feel especially guilty for not upholding their end of the friendship. It has never come to tears when I have called in a favour, but I am not above pinching my thigh through my pants pocket to make my eyes brim a bit in anguish. Dreisbach is not the only one who is an actor. I hardly like the man, but I will feign best-friendship and hurt feelings if it means getting a few free wigs to glue onto my dogs.

Another thing I had to remember about Dreisbach was that he peppered conversations with French words. This was strange to me, as he lived in Germany and had taken on a German name. If he was going to be speaking French, I did not understand why he did not change his name to Devereaux or something else with a string of silent letters at the end. He really did annoy me. I thought of all of this as I tapped my knuckle on the utility door in the side alley next to the theatre.

Dreisbach answered, all five-foot-four of him, his face painted white, wearing only an undershirt, slacks, and round sunglasses. Dreisbach often painted his face, even when there was no performance. He was very ugly and shy, and the white makeup hid his ugliness. He was like a beetle who used markings to confuse predators about its shape and size. At cocktail parties, one could often tell which flute was Dreisbach's because he left a small semicircle of maquillage on the rim.

"*Quelle surprise!*" Dreisbach exclaimed as he found me at the doorway. "If it isn't Mr. Arthur Reginald Croots!"

"Hello, Dreisbach! I was in the neighborhood and had the idea to see how the old Esstäbchen was doing. And you, too, of course."

"Oh, Arthur, come in! Come in! *Vraiment*, we're not doing well at all. But I'll save my little tale until after you're settled in."

Dreisbach led the way to the small kitchen tucked between the dressing rooms and the storage closet. He kept his sunglasses on the entire time. The table was a bit shaky. It seemed the matchbook had shifted under one of the table legs. For fear of getting my hands dirty, I did not wedge it back into place.

Dreisbach put the kettle on and prepped our mugs with a bit of brandy. Even though it was a warm summer day, the kitchen was cold and drafty. I did not particularly want a drink, but I took it. Being a little tipsy would make Dreisbach all the more bearable. He handed me my mug. A bit of his white makeup had smeared onto the handle, which I found highly unappetizing.

"So, old man," I said. "Tell me what's going on with the theatre."

"Oh, Arthur! You always were so kind. Thank you for asking. It's a mess! A mess! An absolute *gâchis*! We've gone bankrupt! We're caput! The investors pulled out of the latest production, saying it was too profane for the public. I thought a modern retelling of *Lysistrata* with an all-male cast set in Prague was just what the people wanted. How was I to know that the investors wouldn't agree? Oh, Arthur! It's terrible. The actors aren't even coming in to rehearse anymore. They think I'm a dud. *Gâchis*!"

Tiny tears ran down his cheeks through his thick white makeup. He looked both pitiful and pitiable. It was nauseating, watching him pour his heart out. How was I going to find a way to ask him to borrow a wig or two now? I had to get the conversation back to me. And remind him of the favor he owed me.

"I'm sorry, old man. I'm sure the key is to just get new money or change the production to one more palatable for your current investors. Am I wrong?"

"That's just the problem, Arthur. There are no new investors. I've tapped out my resources. All my productions have been in the red. And I have no other play options. *All* of my plays feature an excess of male nudity. No one wants to back me anymore. For this last one, I had to beg my aunt's bridge club to invest. It isn't Berlin. That's for sure."

"Have you ever thought about..." I paused. "Not producing those kinds of plays?"

The answer hung in the silence. Apparently this had never, in fact, occurred to him. He topped off his mug with brandy and slurped it noisily without waiting for the tea to cool. He really was an unattractive man.

An idea must have floated into Dreisbach's head because he suddenly grinned a piggy little grin and looked up towards me.

"Arthur, you're a very talented man. Did I ever tell you that? Very...how do you say...*distinguée*. You wouldn't want to help a poor old friend out, would you?"

"I'm sorry," I said. "I would not. Plus, you know I'm poor. I might be *distinguée* but I'm also *fauché*. I have my own problems, old man. I can't be funding a play right now. Appreciate the thought, though."

"Come now, Arthur. A man like you! I seem to recall our last conversation involved the Duke of Lumbardo giving you some of his jewelry."

"Yes, but that's because he is my rich friend and I am his poor friend. You and I are just two poor friends."

"And what about your Horace?"

"My Horace? Horace is going *fauché* himself and he is not friends with the Duke of Lumbardo."

"My God, Arthur. Has the whole town dried up? Where's the fun in London if we can't spend a little money now and then?"

Dreisbach was a fool, but he spoke the truth. His economic philosophy and my own were very similar. But that is why we were both poor and why we sat at a tiny kitchen table drinking brandy with our tea in the middle of the afternoon. Both jobless. Both begging the other to fix things. The only difference was that Dreisbach was small and ugly. I was of medium height and not ugly. Small victories.

It was then that I realized my favor would have to wait. This annoyed me greatly, because I was not sure I could stomach another meeting with Dreisbach in time. Plus, if he were to go belly-up too soon, he may have to sell his wigs. It was a predicament, and one predicated entirely on my aversion to seeing Dreisbach more than once a year.

But I had a very good idea. The same way I think effectively in a quiet shower, I think effectively when I have a bit of brandy in me. I decided to rope Dreisbach into my dog selling scheme. We could use his resources and his wigs. I also thought he could use the cash, so he would be desperate and do as I ask without question. Dreisbach might also help solve the nagging issue of Horace and I having both joined the Newton-Wiggs Société, making ourselves recognizable to people in the canine community. We would need a third person anyway, to act as a count, or a breeder, or the humble agent of another backwoods Irish peer.

I asked for another top-off of brandy and said, "Dreisbach, what if there was a way to get you some money?"

After I related the plan, we agreed he would have to wear his makeup conservatively. It was too conspicuous. In my experience, an ugly little man is easier to forget than a white-painted gnome in sunglasses.

We further agreed he would receive twenty percent from each sale. This would mean a reduction to Horace's cut. I would write Horace a note and break the news gently. Who knows how being poor would affect Horace's good nature?

We tipped our mugs to one another to seal the deal, like proper businessmen. He asked me if I wanted to see the collection of wigs and prosthetics in the storage closet. We thought we may be able to sew a few of the longer wigs together as a sort of coat to put on Henry. He would go from a Bichon to a Barbet in no time.

We brainstormed the rest of the dogs' new identities until the flask of brandy was dry. It was a good time for me to leave anyway. Dreisbach was disgustingly sweaty, which made his makeup run.

He never took off his sunglasses the entire time I was there.

XII

Returning Celia

As I suspected, Horace was deeply affected by finding himself poor. It did not suit him. This was ironic to me, because I did not think being rich suited him much either. When he had his allowance, he had spent his money on dictionaries and piano lessons and oil paints. That, in my opinion, was a terrible way to be rich.

Now the piano was being appraised to be sold and the dictionaries, though handsome, were useless to him. In a few months, when his allowance ran out, he would be at the mercy of his savings. I believe this thought scared him very much, which was why he was angry with me for reducing his cut of each dog sale from forty percent to twenty.

I hate arguing with Horace because we see situations very differently. While I see the picture, Horace sees the brush strokes. He only saw the facts laid out before him, mainly that he had to share any profits with "that painted-faced weasel Dreisbach." I saw it differently: that Dreisbach's involvement would secure more sales, which would mean more money for us all.

Horace asked me why I did not reduce my own percentage. It was a fair question, so I gave him a fair answer: I did not want to. He asked this question in a few different ways, trying to be clever, trying to get me to concede, but I held my ground.

It was my plan. I had already made a substantial investment in notebooks. I had recruited Dreisbach and Horace. I had done all of the research at the library. I was exhausted by my participation in the plan while Horace skulked around his flat all day. Horace dropped the subject eventually. I do not think he fully understood the unfairness of his question, though.

I did not have time to argue anyway. I had only come to Horace's place to tell him about Dreisbach and to remind him that, between moping sessions, he would have to investigate his list of potential customers, too. I was in a hurry, as it was Friday and that meant I would be meeting with my Committee that afternoon. I couldn't be late just because I was offering Horace a drink and the odd word of encouragement.

I was beaming by the time I reached the NWS door. I was proud of the plan, I was proud of my position as Chair, and I was proud of keeping my percentage of the sales. But my smile dropped when I encountered Ms. Greenwood. I still did not like that her first name was *Belinda*.

"Good morning, Mr. Croots!" She said. "I thought I'd be seeing you today" She flipped through some paperwork and removed a staple with her fingernail.

"Good *afternoon*, Ms. Greenwood," I said. I emphasized the time of day as a way of correcting her. I was a Chair at the Newton-Wiggs Société and felt it was my duty to ensure that the receptionist knew what time of day it was.

"Yes, Mr. Croots. Good afternoon. Would you like me to take you to the meeting room now? I can get you some coffee or tea."

"I know the way, thank you very much. A tea would be great. And can you bring me one of those delicious hazelnut scones from next door?"

"We don't have those scones here at the office, Mr. Croots."

"Ah, well. The meeting doesn't start for another ten minutes. There's still time for you to grab one while I prepare."

I walked down the hall to the meeting room with its dog beds and piles of books, leaving Ms. Greenwood to her work. I did not feel confident that I would get the hazelnut scone, with good reason, as it turns out. Luckily, I had taken a boiled egg out of the pannikin in Horace's kitchen and ate it on the way over.

The Committee members entered the meeting room, one-by-one, and greeted me with smiles. I was genuinely happy to see everyone, especially since they obviously regarded me so highly. Desmond had brought his dog, an English Bulldog with a black spot around his eye. The dog looked like he had been in a bar fight. Desmond looked like he had just come back from Capri, so warm and citrus-smelling.

In the ten minutes before everyone had arrived, I had adjusted the seating. I wanted the Committee leaders to be facing the Committee members. This meant that on one side there was Julius, Desmond, Spittlewood and me. On the other side there was Jane Raitland, Fanny Maybrick, Hannah Grey-Downs, and Toffie Montmaarten, who wore a sizable emerald ring. I suppose you could include Desmond's bulldog Marcus on that side as well, though he slept through the meeting. I joked that we should include Marcus in the minutes. A few people chuckled.

Viscount Spittlewood and Hannah Grey-Downs spoke for most of the meeting. Spittlewood looked to the agenda and Hannah provided answers. I was pleased to know she had received my letter and had reached out to the vendors we'd used previously. She went one step further and had reserved all necessary supplies. She had used the charge account of the NWS. She was a very resourceful woman. The only thing missing from her list was a truck to transport the supplies on the day of the Parade. Toffie Montmaarten said her new beau had a moving company and we could borrow his truck. Mrs. Grey-Downs joked and asked that she not break up with this new beau for at least three more weeks, then. They shared a laugh. I was jealous of Hannah Grey-Downs' easy camaraderie with the Committee members. My earlier joke was now overshadowed by Mrs. Grey-Downs' better one. It infuriated me.

Spittlewood proposed tallying the final guest list and asked for volunteers. My ears perked up, as this would be a potential list for more customers for the dogs as well. Jane Raitland raised a shy little hand and so did Desmond. I could not think of a less likely pair. Spittlewood set a date for completing their task, asked Julius if there was any cash on hand to spend for final invitations, and the meeting was adjourned. I asked for a copy of the final guest list for myself from Jane and Desmond under the pretense that I should be in the know. Jane nodded without meeting my eyes. Desmond nodded and I think may have even winked a little.

Since the meeting ended earlier than expected and everyone had their marching orders, I decided to take a stroll to the Parade site. I bought a lemonade along the way. It was not an especially hot day and I was not especially thirsty, but I often feel uneasy if I am walking and there is not something in my hand. I worry I swing my arms too much when I walk. I believe holding something helps to balance this defect of mine out a bit.

When I entered the park, I wished I had not been holding a lemonade at all. I nearly dropped it right on the grass. I was surprised to see my Celia, blue eyes and all, running joyously off her lead, Mrs. Cormant trailing behind her, laughing. It was an uncanny sight. I did not like it.

Mrs. Cormant was dressed even more shabbily than I thought possible. She was in an old flannel shirt that must have been her gardener's chore shirt, plucked from the trash bin. She wore a long wool skirt the color of oatmeal and wet paste. She wore muddy trainers. A man, presumably Mr. Reynolds Cormant, Esq., strolled behind her in a tan suit. He was much more handsome than I expected. Perhaps Mrs. Cormant was a beauty in her day.

Were dowries exchanged?, I wondered.

I did not want to be seen, so I quickly found a bench that was shaded a bit behind two shrubs. I wanted savor the joy I'd brought to Celia and the Cormants without being seen. I also felt the terribble tug of jealousy. I could not decide if I was pleased to see the trio so happy or if I was upset by it. It did not help to see Mrs. Cormant in such ratty clothes. That alone compounded the intensity of any emotion I *did* feel while sitting on that bench, even if I could not name which emotion it was.

Not twenty yards from me the Cormants settled down to enjoy a break. Celia itched her back on the grass and wagged her tail happily at passersby. Celia had a new collar on her neck. It was a mauve satin. It brought out the blue in her eyes. If only Mrs. Cormant had an eye for her kitchen or her clothes as she did for her dog.

Mr. Cormant tapped his pipe onto the heel of his shoe while his wife sunned her face. To witness this moment of domestic bliss felt perverse, and yet I did not immediately turn away. Something had changed in the small frame of Mrs. Cormant. Her motions no longer betrayed a desperation. She was searching for neither approval nor affection. It seemed that Celia had filled the void in her. I am not a psychoanalyst, but I wonder if my dear Celia had even brought husband and wife closer together.

I have always said that dogs are very influential creatures.

Later that night at Horace's, I replayed the scene in my minds. I felt guilty. I had gone to Horace's to tell him that I was planning on taking Celia back that evening.

With Horace's new mood swings, I was not sure how he was going to take the news. It was inevitable that Celia would return to me. I am not so sure he thought it would be this soon, though. But we had just shy of four weeks to sell them all and put them on rotation back in my flat. There was no time for delay!

I explained it all to Horace, who agreed that very evening that we would return Celia back home to me. Having seen my dear Celia in the arms of another woman, it's no surprise my passion was so convincing. Horace, for his part, had been perfectly persuadable. I believe this was due to his being depressed. This worked to my advantage.

We debated the necessity of Dreisbach and agreed that we would try this one without him. For one thing, Dreisbach was annoying. For another, this was our first time taking a dog back. If we botched it, we agreed that the fewer people involved, the better. If the authorities were called in, I had an inkling that I would be a faster runner than Horace, but was not sure about Dreisbach. I did not share this reasoning with Horace. I do not think he would have appreciated this observation of mine.

The plan we agreed upon was as follows.

First, wait until it is completely dark. Horace and I agreed that elderly couples such as the Cormants probably go to bed around 8:30 p.m. To be on the safe side, we would wait until 10:00 p.m. We would just be doing reconnaissance work. It would be good to see how many people were out late, how many cars were in their driveways and garages, how many windows were dark. We would then go grab a bite at a diner and wait until midnight. At that time, the second part of the plan would be put into action.

I would be the one to actually sneak into the Cormants' place. This was a natural decision since I had already toured the house, and because Celia would know my scent. That is, if mean old Mrs. Cormant hadn't persuaded Celia to forget about me already. At the diner, I would change into a dowdy old dressing gown and cover my head with a scarf. Because of my medium height and my slender hands, it was our hope that anybody who noticed would mistake me for an old lady taking a nighttime stroll, dotty, perhaps, and maybe lost, but otherwise harmless.

In my experience, neighbors seldom call the police on unassuming old ladies.

Horace would then drive me in his car and drop me off near the Cormants' and then park on the next block with the passenger door open for easy getaway. I would climb in through the bathroom window. I did not want to risk the kitchen window with all the pots and pans that could be lying about. I would then find Celia. I would use the dressing gown belt as a makeshift leash and we would use the kitchen door to exit. This would be intentional. I wanted the Cormants to think they had left the door open and their "Amelia" run off. Naturally, they would blame themselves, not me.

Like all of my plans, it was faultless. And Horace, even though he was depressed, agreed.

I stopped by my flat and let the dogs out into the garden and fed them some brioche I had picked up. I collected the necessary plan accoutrements and promised Milly, Rue, and Henry that they would have their sister back soon. I also took a shot of vodka to calm myself. It was warm, having been on my vanity to be used for my nightly beauty routine. It burned and I belched. I excused myself to the dogs, who did not seem to mind. My dogs are very forgiving. Of me, anyway.

This was not the first time that I had successfully sneaked into someone's home, but it was the first time I felt nervous doing so. I believe this was due more to do with the fact that I would be reunited with my sweet Celia, and less to my fear of being caught. What would Mr. Cormant do if he saw a man in a dressing gown with a scarf on his head walking out with his dog? I doubt he'd shoot or even yell. Perhaps he'd think he was dreaming and forget the whole thing until the morning.

My mind is devilishly quick, and I was not able to slow it down on my walk to Horace's. I worried the bathroom window would be locked, but then remembered Horace mentioned he had a tiny screwdriver that would do the job if it were. I worried that I would slip on the perspiration from the toilet tank and hit my head and die. But this, too, was ridiculous because I had changed into my waitering shoes, which were very grippy. I even worried that the Cormants' lights would be off because they were Devil-worshippers and I would be interrupting some sort of orgy. I would be perfectly justified in removing Celia from an environment like that. Celia had a very Protestant air about her anyway, which I had always found attractive.

I stopped at a pub near Horace's and had a pint, which had a thick head of foam on it. It was mostly to cool the burning from the vodka but it was also to give me a moment's rest before my rendezvous with Horace. Horace, when he was nervous, was either very quiet or very talkative. I, on the other hand, was either very talkative nor very quiet. When he was talkative, I wanted to be silent. But if we were both silent, I would be more nervous. Horace and I are not totally compatible as criminals, I must admit. But I always tried to think the best of Horace, even then. At the time, he was my only friend.

I left the bartender a generous tip and was surprised to suddenly feel a little light on my feet. Horace was making risotto to honor the night. Some cream and mushrooms in my stomach would help me sober up. I envied Horace's mass. A shot of vodka and a pint doesn't even have him blinking.

I opened Horace's door without knocking and found him in the kitchen wearing an apron. The apron string cut slightly into his gut and had a tight, floral pattern around the hem. It was most likely a woman's apron. Perhaps his mother's, as I know he kept many of her things and used them frequently. He had a small knife in his hand and he waved in acknowledgement of my presence. The radio was on. The music was punctuated by the knife hitting the chopping block as Horace diced mushrooms and parsley. He really was a divine cook. But only when it came to risotto.

It was 8:23 when we began dinner and both of us took it slow. We had seconds and thirds and each had a bit of fruit for dessert. I don't believe either of us were that hungry. But if we kept eating, then neither of us could talk and inadvertently stumble upon some flaw in the plan. Horace unbuttoned his trousers halfway through his third helping of risotto.

At exactly ten we rolled past the Cormants' house. All the lights were off the sleepy street, so Horace's headlights seemed to glare brightly against the Cormants' green door. A curtain was only half-closed, making it easy to see into the house from the street. It was more handsome in the nighttime. If I were to ever see Mrs. Cormant again, I would tell her to only have friends over after dark. It was sound advice, but I couldn't manage to work it into the conversation.

We nodded to one another and parked to wait. At the diner, we each ordered coffee and I ordered a glass of water. I did not want so much liquid, being as nervous as I was, but I had to order something so we did not look suspicious. I also ordered a bacon sandwich, because it was the cheapest thing on the menu. I hardly touched it. I had the dressing gown bundled under my clothes so I felt slightly pregnant. Horace read an discarded, two-day-old newspaper. I felt reading old news to be unlucky so I ripped bits of napkin and pushed the pieces into small shapes. A giraffe, a snake, a letter H.

We must have appeared bored, as the waitress gave us the bill after just ten minutes. I ripped this up, too, and my little paper shapes became more substantial. I made a sheep, an elephant, and a motorcar. Horace didn't look up from the paper. He either cared deeply about the horse races or he was getting nervous and didn't want to show me how nervous he was.

"Horace," I finally whispered. I checked my watch and it was 10:24. Sitting any longer in the diner and I would have screamed. The dressing gown was making my stomach sweat and the coffee was making my palms sweat and the fluorescent ceiling light was making my forehead sweat. I was very sweaty.

He did not answer. His eyes weren't even rolling across the text on the page and he hadn't turned a single page. He fixated on a spot on the page just to ignore me. Horace, unlike myself, is a terrible actor.

I pushed the paper out of his hands. "Horace," I whispered again. "Horace, let's do it now."

"Now? But it's only..."

"I know. But I can't do this waiting around thing. Let's have a quick smoke and I'll change in your car and we'll do it now. An hour won't make a difference."

We paid for our meal and left quickly. The waitress, who I suspected had seen stranger things than two men whispering to one another at night, didn't even look up. She filed her nails as the cook rang the bell to announce orders were ready.

I was at the Cormants' powder room window in under ten minutes. The dressing gown was a ratty old thing and the scarf was no longer on my head. The cigarette had helped me immensely and I was calm and taking strong breaths. I have found cigarettes to be very good for my lungs and for taking strong breaths. I was no longer nervous or afraid. I was ready to be home in bed with Celia. I was also ready for another shot of vodka and my evening beauty routine. Perhaps I was a bit nervous, I admit that now.

I retrieved Horace's little screwdriver from my pocket and realized it was unnecessary as the Cormants left their window unlocked. This gave me a peace of mind, as I reasoned that anyone who left their windows unlocked could not be surprised if they woke up to find their dog missing. They were practically inviting strangers in.

After that, I did not feel guilty entering the Cormants' residence. I did not feel guilty when I pushed the screen out of the window. I did not feel guilty when I hooked my leg through the window. I didn't feel guilty when I maneuvered my body into the bathroom, nor did I feel guilty when a small porcelain dolphin figurine crunched under my shoe when I stepped on it on the shelf behind the toilet tank.

I had quite a shock for a second as I stood up in the powder room, as I found myself staring at a pair of beady, bulging eyes. No! Six of them! I stepped back. Perhaps the Cormants *were* hosting a demonic orgy. Luckily, a car drove by and the light from the headlights brought the powder room into focus. It was just the fish mounted on the wall that I had seen at my previous visit. Damn Isabel Cormant and her awful, terrible style.

I closed the window behind me and swept the broken porcelain into the trash. I have never been one to tolerate a mess, even when committing a crime. I walked into the hall where the coral and lime green kitchen looked suddenly subdued, almost pretty. Yes, I decided, if anyone ever wanted to admire the Cormant residence, they would have to do it at midnight, or with sunglasses on.

Something on the kitchen table caught my eye. Underneath a jumble of keys was a handsome, silver watch. I had always preferred silver to gold. Mr. Cormant must have taken it off when he, Mrs. Cormant, and Celia got home from the park that afternoon. I imagine him rubbing his wrist as he took it off and grabbed a glass of milk to cool off. I gently, very gently, moved the keys a bit so they would not jingle. I put the watch on my wrist and tightened the clasp. It was a bit big for me—-I have slim wrists to match my small hands. But it was a free and very handsome watch. Who was I to complain of such luck?

Perhaps the sound of keys, even the slightest little movement of them, alerted Celia that someone was either coming or going. I was very lucky as I heard her four legs come bounding down the steps and tip-tap into the hallway. She grumbled a low growl, which I was afraid would happen. I immediately got into a low crouch and threw her a bit of the bacon I had smuggled out of the diner in a napkin. She gobbled up the bacon and came up to sniff my hand. Some guard dog!

I threaded the dressing gown belt around her mauve satin collar and tied it with one of my sturdy knots. I gave her a kiss and let her lick the little bit of bacon grease off my fingertips. We slipped out the kitchen door as Celia wagged her tail and I smiled. I pocketed a small salt shaker shaped like a cardinal. We left elated.

XIII

Winston Meredith Tamassy

The next day I awoke to all four dogs curled around me. I tip-toed to the kettle so as to not wake any of them. It was an impossible task, not waking the dogs. Once they hear the first fork rattle, they jump up and expect to eat with me.

I ate a peach while the dogs sniffed Celia in the garden. She was overjoyed, if a bit perplexed, to be back among her friends.

The peach was not totally in season, hard as an apple. I ate it anyway. I was still very poor, as our business enterprise hadn't taken off yet.

I wiped my hands on Milly's coat and we all made it back upstairs in time for a second cup of tea. I had decided to celebrate getting Celia back by buying a small cake and taking it over to Horace's. I decided to dress nicely for the occasion and put on an elegant pair of slacks and a chocolate-colored, polo neck sweater, over which I wore a summer jacket. It was a nice outfit and it suited my mood. My new wristwatch, courtesy of Mr. Harold Cormant, Esquire, finished the ensemble.

I decided as I walked out the door to phone Dreisbach and invite him over for our celebration. I knew Horace would not mind because Horace's house was very big and Dreisbach was a small man. Dreisbach was annoying, though, so Horace may have minded that. Either way, I wanted Dreisbach over so that he could see, firsthand, how successful the plan had been. I could foresee him being very useful in selling the dogs. I did not want him to second-guess how good I was with plans.

As was my custom, I used the chemist's phone. The assistant was gracious and even silently placed a cup of coffee by my elbow while I was on with the operator. Someone picked up on the fourth ring. The voice was very deep and gravely.

"G'morning, who is this?"

"Dreisbach, is that you?"

"No Dreisbach here. *Vous avez fait un mauvais numéro, désolé.*"

I thought perhaps the operator had connected me to the wrong phone. But who in the hell else would be speaking French, on purpose, at 9:00 a.m.?

"Dreisbach? Johnny Dreyfuss, if that's you, it's Arthur!"

The voice changed immediately into Dreisbach's higher, nervous pitch. Dreisbach always sounded like he had just told a perverted joke at a party and was waiting for others to laugh. I did not like talking to Dreisbach on the phone.

"Arthur, *mon ami*! Good morning! So sorry about that. Had some debt sharks circling lately. Had to be careful. What can I do for you?"

"I wanted to see if you'd like to join me and Horace for a little morning party we're having. My, um, plan went into action last night. It was a success. We're celebrating."

"A party! A party! I'd be thrilled. I just got home a few hours ago from a party. Haven't slept since. Well, maybe dozed a little, but I could use a little *poils du chien* to pick me up."

I was not sure the idiom made it through translation with its elegance intact, but I caught his gist. I gave Horace's address to Dreisbach and thanked the chemist's assistant. I put a couple coins down. I hadn't touched the coffee. It was already lukewarm when she poured it. I only like very hot coffee.

In an hour's time, we were all enjoying the cake I had purchased. It was either apricot or orange marmalade. It was heavy on cinnamon, which confused my palate. I have a very sensitive palate and therefore was slightly disappointed in the cake. Horace seemed to like it. He had four slices.

Dreisbach had brought a half-empty bottle of Grand Marnier, which he presented to us apologetically. I enjoyed mine in a little demitasse of coffee. Dreisbach enjoyed his *poils du chien* neat. Horace enjoyed his as a little drizzle over his cake. I do believe it would have made the cake tastier.

Dreisbach looked awful. Even worse than when I had seen him at his theatre. His white face paint was smeared onto his temples and neck. It dusted his jacket collar like dandruff. There was a divot in his makeup where his sunglasses had rested on the bridge of his nose. Was he wearing lipstick, too? Perhaps he had a sangria that had stained his lips. I had seen it happen to a Spanish friend of mine more than once.

Dreisbach looked dreadful, and I wanted to keep the conversation away from him. And with Horace eyeing his fifth slice of cake, it was I who had to repeat to Dreisbach the events of Celia's rescue. Dreisbach particularly liked the part about the fish mounted in the bathroom. He said he would take that idea for an upcoming retelling of Perseus and Medusa. The mounted fish, he suggested, could play the vital role of the Gorgon. And it would save renting a fish would be cheaper than casting another actor.

Even today, I cannot be sure if Dreisbach was sly or stupid. I'm told this is the case with most geniuses, but I am also told this is the case with most psychopaths. I tend to think Dreisbach was clever, mostly because he knew some German and some French. I pondered this thought as Dreisbach sat on Horace's couch. I saw that he was wearing unmatched shoes. That settled it for me: only a psychopath could leave his home wearing a mismatched pair of shoes.

Now that we had celebrated and Dreisbach was caught up, it was time to plan. My time at my flat was running out and I felt that we had to pick up the pace. With the Newton-Wiggs Sociéte's Parade coming up, I wanted to have everything mapped out ahead of time. Being on the verge of bankruptcy, Horace and Dreisbach welcomed my suggestions eagerly.

Money can be very persuasive. I am not easily persuadable. I like money for the simple fact that I have to eat and also I like fine things. But Horace and Dreisbach seemed obsessed with not losing their home and theatre, respectively.

Horace, even with all his cake eating, looked thinner in the face already at the stress of losing his allowance. Dreisbach, on the other hand, looked much more plump in the face. But this may have been a trick of makeup. The streaks of white paint made him look like he was a candle that had only partially melted. Both looked at me, waiting to hear the next steps in our plan. Lucky for them, I had brought my maroon notebook. It was chock-full of brilliant ideas.

I suppose Viscount Spittlewood would have been proud of me—I had my own agenda! Too bad the subject of the meeting was illegal. I would have liked to have told good old Monty about my goings-on. One could easily tell that he was influential. He was, after all, a viscount. Not only that, but he had an exquisite fountain pen with which he scribbled his agenda notes. I was nearly as envious of the pen as I was of the peerage.

We agreed that the plan was a success and therefore could be recreated multiple times. What was needed now were Dreisbach and Horace's watchful eyes at the Parade so that we may see who would be the easiest (i.e. most gullible) potential clients. We also decided during this party-cum-meeting that we would dress up a couple of my dogs in costume as a sort of dangle, to see who among the crowd might be interested. We decided that Rue would have a fringe over her missing eye, and Henry would be dyed black with shoe polish. We felt Henry would enjoy the attention. Plus, Henry could not swim, so we did not run the risk of the polish washing out by accident if he was off his lead.

By now the Grand Marnier had kicked in and we were a bundle of giggles on the couch. We thought up preposterous disguises for the dogs. A peg-leg for Henry. A Fu Manchu mustache on Milly. Eyelashes glued onto Rue. How fun to have such self-confidence that we could laugh with ease, so sure were we of the plan's success!

We decided to give Dreisbach an alias. Dreisbach, being a limelight addict and an (alleged) actor, sat straight up at the prospect extra attention. I, of course, could not have an alias—-I was the Chair of a Committee. Horace was a member, but a wallflower. It would stay that way for now.

So for the third time in Dreisbach's life, he would answer to a new name: Winston Meredith Tamassy, art historian and expatriate from New South Wales with an interest in discovering new dog breeds across the Continent. Horace had suggested Meredith as a joke and I quite liked it, so it stuck. I had suggested New South Wales because I had assumed Dreisbach would drink a bit before the Parade to calm his nerves, as he did before any performance. And saying he was Australian might account for his slurred speech.

Mr. Tamassy was a cultured and erudite man, upon this we all agreed. We also agreed that Dreisbach would affect his new identity without the use of costume or make-up. But he begged to wear "just a little rouge," and we eventually capitulated. Mr. Tamassy was to wear a suit at all times. Perhaps Mr. Tamassy bowed and had a slight Edwardian lean to his manner. Perhaps Mr. Tamassy had a limp, which would play on people's sympathies, and leave them unsuspecting. Mr. Tamassy might have a pocket watch or a hilarious tie. He would be everything Dreisbach was not: charming in an understated way, comfortable in his ugliness, and in on the joke.

Still, I left Horace's a little uneasy. We all knew Dreisbach was a terrible actor and prone to impotent improvisations. I whispered to Horace to push Dreisbach into the closest fountain if he came in white makeup as a reimagined, flamboyant Mr. Tammasy. Horace winked. Horace always winked when he was tipsy instead of responding verbally. It was one of the few quirks of his I would classify as charming.

When I returned to my flat, I found the final list of attendees, mailed by the lovely Desmond. It was sent in a lovely, ivory envelope with a plump scribble that could only have been his. Very masculine. Given what Jane had worn to the meetings, though, I suppose it could have been hers. She was very masculine in her own pastoral, milkmaid sort of way. But I wanted to believe it was Desmond's, and so it was.

The list was divided between Walkers and Watchers. The Walkers' list, which consisted mostly of Newton-Wiggs, indicated each Walker's dogs. They had names like Sandy, Cork, and Samantha. The Walkers own names weren't much better, I will tell you. They were titled, and therefore their names were noble, and therefore their names were hideous. There were names like Montagu-Rinds, Pigdon, and Beltrash-upon-March.

The Watchers were less influential, but made a good list of potential customers for our plan. Their names were normal and not hideous, which led me to believe many were not tilted, but *nouveau-riche*. There were Jones and Pryces and Smiths. To my surprise, there was even a Raitland. Perhaps Jane's elderly father wanted to see what his daughter had done with her life in London. Surrounded by dogs and perspiring from under her arms. What a life.

In the garden, while the dogs played, I marked names with a little star to indicate for Dreisbach to introduce himself, along with Rue and Henry. I also added small notations alongside the names of attendees whom I believed would pair well with others. I was a voracious reader of the society papers during this time, so I knew a little many of the names already. There were about forty in all. We would most certainly sell a few dogs by the end of the week.

It was good to have my Celia back. I was tempted to celebrate with an old-fashioned walk with a few of their ropes tied around my wrists. But I could not risk it - by now I am sure that the Cormants were asking their neighbors if anyone had seen a blue-eyed Cocker who went by the name Amelia. Mrs. Cormant, in her thoroughness, may even by now retraced her steps to the park where I had first met her. She would, undoubtedly, have asked other park-goers if they could recall a handsome, medium-height man with nice hair. Perhaps she was ringing her pal, Dougie, in a panic, to see if Amelia had run away back to Galway. She certainly didn't have Horace's number.

These were the risks. But they were small, so I was nervous, but not anxious. If anything, I was more preoccupied with the thought I had when reading over the attendee list one last time: Why hadn't Desmond written a little note with the list? It seemed very formal of him, to do exactly what I had asked without any deviation. Perhaps Desmond was intimidated by my title of Chair. This, I reckoned, made the most sense. I made a reminder to myself in my notebook to be kinder to Desmond. I was, after all, influential now.

That evening I rested with a small lamp and a tin of biscuits, which I happily shared with my dogs. I decided to continue with my German practice, because the lamp I was using was very dim and the text in the German primer was very large, so I did not have to squint much. I would have to remember to ask Horace for another lightbulb. Perhaps I would be lucky and find him in the middle of a selling spree, so I could harvest the lightbulbs out of his antique lamps before they were all sold off. Surely, the new owners could afford their own, I thought.

Now that I was an influential person, I felt slightly responsible for setting a good example to those who looked up to me, like my dear friend Desmond. I have always felt that knowledge of a second language was the most influential quality one could have. After having a title, of course, or being the Chair of a Committee devoted to annual dog parades. I devoted nearly two hours to my German studies.

I studied a chapter on how to order food at a restaurant. Or, as they say in German, *ein Restaurant*. I learned how to say mustard and mayonnaise. I learned to ask for a bill, and to inquire whether one takes traveler's checks. I learned how to reserve a table for eleven and tell the waiter I was allergic to shellfish. I am not allergic to shellfish myself, but I enjoy pretending to be someone else when I am abroad. Perhaps the Berlin version of Arthur would be allergic to shellfish. In that case, this information would be vital.

By the second hour, I was tired, and my mind began to wander. Plus, the biscuits were all gone. I could not focus on the page, even when I read a paragraph twice. This was due to my curiosity as to Desmond's potential allergy to shellfish, or if Desmond liked still or fizzy water, or if Desmond's traveler's checks said Baron Ham-sur-Rye. It was a nice thought to have and one that did not last long, unfortunately. My beauty routine awaited. I did not have any more time for my curiosities or to contemplate the German language's reckless use of the genitive case.

XIV

Arthur Hears the Truth

I went straight to the chemist's as soon as they opened the next morning and used their telephone. The girl assistant was not there that morning and her replacement was a rather fat old man. He was friendly enough but he did not smile, nor did he serve me my practically promised free cup of coffee. I left a handful of coins on the table and called up Dreisbach. He answered on the ninth ring.

"Who the hell is calling at this hour?"

"Dreisbach, it's Arthur!"

"Arthur, I'm so sorry! I thought you were this automobile salesman. He has been calling at the strangest hours, begging me to return the car he let me borrow for the weekend. It's only three days late. I told him I'd bring it back next Monday, but he just..."

"Dreisbach, I don't care at all. Horace has a car. I don't need to hear about yours, too. Listen, I wanted to see how your Mr. Tamassy was coming along."

"Oh, yes, very well! I wrote him a bit of a backstory. I think Mr. Tamassy has a dark past, don't you? I think he must have had an abusive father, or perhaps a sadistic aunt who burnt him with cigarettes. Something...under the skin about him. Something to explain why he surrounded himself with dog people, you know?"

"No, I don't."

"Oh, well, think about it. This Mr. Tamassy is trying to fill some emotional void he didn't get as a child, so he travels the world trading dogs and breeding dogs and wearing tweed and sunning in parks. Doesn't that seem like something someone with a dark past would do?"

"I'm not so sure, Dreisbach. A lot of people like parks, you know."

"Yes, but park *and* dogs? At his age? Seems perverse. Also, I was thinking that Mr. Tamassy should be a distinguished man, the debonair sort. Don't you agree, my boy? A real *gentilhomme*."

"Yes! Horace and I think..."

"Oh, I'm so glad that you agree. I will buy the eyepatch right away."

"Eyepatch?"

"Don't you think it just screams *distinguée*? Think of all of the most distinguished men you know. What do they all have in common? They all lost something in a war or a fishing accident. Mr. Tamassy's eyepatch will attract exactly the right sort of attention."

"Yes, but we don't *want* a lot of attention, Dreisbach. We want you to hide in the Parade crowd and leave. Remember the plan?"

"Oh and another thing, before I forget. I'm not a fan of his name, Tamassy. I was thinking something more... exotic. Continental, you know? What if we went with *Gnädiger* Herr Jakob van Lieben, an Austrian baron."

"I thought you were going to be from Australia?"

"You're so burdened by details, Arthur. No one will know the difference, especially when I have my beard glued on. Oh, thank you for the chat, *mon ami*! It did me good to plan this out with you. Your ideas are always so helpful! I'll see you next week at the Parade! I will be totally *indisponible* until then. Avoiding the car man and all. Must go. Bye now!"

Dreisbach hung up, and the last thing I heard was him blowing kisses into the receiver. I began, and not for the last time, to regret the decision to invite him into our plan. I would not have been surprised if he showed up at the Parade in stilts and a Father Christmas beard. Dreisbach made me nervous.

I have found that the only way to combat my nervousness is to do the following: I must first be wearing very comfortable shoes. Because I was wearing a pair of brown loafers at the chemist, this required me to return to my flat to change into my second sest pair of trainers. I must then have a cigarette in my hand and a matchbook. I will then go for a very long walk in my comfortable shoes and smoke my cigarette. Sometimes I will think, but other times I will try my hardest not to think. I will sometimes buy a comforting drink like cider. And sometimes I will buy a comforting food like a madeleine. Or six madeleines. In one of my nervous fits, for no known reason, I bought a melon. I sat on a bench and stared at the melon. I didn't know what to do with it once I had it. I can be absent-minded when I am nervous.

It was this absentmindedness which led me to wander right in front of the Newton-Wiggs Société's front step. I was not wearing my nice loafers, but I decided to go in anyway. I heard a faint laughter as I opened the door. I wanted to laugh, too, so I would not be so nervous.

I walked into the ghastly entrance room of the office and still the tinkling of laughter called to me. Little did I know, it was a siren song that would leave me dashed upon the rocks.

I followed the sounds of people to the back room, behind Ms. Greenwood's desk, past the file folders and cabinets, past the ink blotter and old newspapers left in the rubbish bin. I had never been in this space before, so I was immediately critical of it. Poor George, I thought, having to work in Ms. Greenwood's mess. I wondered if he minded the sandwich crumbs on the rug as much as I did.

I was now close enough to begin making out words and voices. There was, of course, Ms. Greenwood's. There were two other voices, both men, that I could not identify. I assumed they were high-ups within the NWS. I detected a little guffaw that I assumed came from sweet, toothy George. Last came a little rattle of a giggle from a woman. I could not identify this, either.

"He dresses so *terribly!*"

"And he practically bathes in women's perfumes. Isn't that right, George? Didn't you say you had to hold your breath?"

"I did, Lindy! I don't know how he even tasted his tea with all that scent on him."

"Oh, the *scone!*" This was Jane Raitland, I could then be sure. "Why on earth would he eat it with a fork?"

"Maybe his hands are too delicate to pick one up, ha ha!" said one of the unknown men.

Whoever they were talking about sure did seem to be a joke, a real dud. Most definitely not the influential type. I was surprised to hear them all laughing away so merrily. They should, indeed, be more concerned with excommunicating such types from the esteemed Newton-Wiggs Société. I stood just outside the door so I could hear a bit more. I thought, as Chair of a Committee, I had some authority in canceling this misfit's membership. They weren't taking any action, other than laughing to themselves!

Ms. Greenwood's voice came in again.

"I wouldn't mind him if he was more like his friend, Horace. But he's so delicate, so silly, so oblivious. And his clothes! I nearly gasped when I saw how ill-fitted his suit was at the funeral last week. He looked more like a concierge at a cheap hotel. I just gave him whatever he wanted so he'd leave me alone. I figured I wouldn't have to breathe in his perfume if he just said yes and we'd have Hannah do the labor. It worked!"

That was enough for me to realize they were talking about me.

When I am embarrassed, I usually like to have a good cry. This is something I do not like about myself, but it is something I have very little control over. The sight of my boyish cheeks and my slender hands often lead people to assume I am still a teenager.

I took a second to gulp down the knot in my throat before I made a couple loud coughs to announce myself. I tucked my hands firmly into my pockets. I did not like that they had mentioned how small they were. That was the most embarrassing part.

As Ms. Greenwood opened the door, her eyes widened in recognition. I did not say anything to her, but instead set my eyes to the small crowd behind her. There was, as I had suspected, George and Jane. The two men I could finally identify. One was the President of the NWS,

Felix Alabaster Reynolds (I recognized him from his portrait in the toilet) and the other was Desmond. He had his hand on Jane's knee. The knot in my throat rose again.

"What a party we have here!" I said. I am very good at lying and I hope my voice did not give away my emotions.

No one spoke and all looked like they had seen the Devil. Perhaps Jane Raitland, who was fingering the tiny crucifix that hung from her neck, actually did think their jokes had conjured me. I paid no attention to them.

"I wanted to say, Ms. Greenwood, *Lindy*, I wanted to say that the Parade arrangements are all done. I was just in the area, so thought I'd stop by instead of phoning or writing. I see you are all very busy, so I will leave you to your fun."

All Ms. Greenwood could manage was a stammer, "Th... thank you," she said.

Even Desmond, whose eyebrows are usually so expressive, remained frozen. I thought for sure he would have got up, put a hand on my shoulder, and say *something*. He did not. I was disappointed.

When I left, my nervousness did not subside. In fact, I felt shaky. I had never felt more insulted. I had never felt more vilified. I had never felt more offended, affronted, or slandered. This even included the time I was accused of cheating in a church bingo game in front of the entire school or when the Archduchess of Battenwig sneezed in my pint at a bar in Chelsea two years ago. This was, of course, after her date Count Achtenberg had heavily seasoned his shrimp cocktail with pepper, as he was wont to do.

I was not sure how I was ever going to forgive Desmond and that dowdy succubus Jane.

But I had also never felt more lucky, either, once I cooled down a bit on my walk home. What luck to have eavesdropped on them! How fortunate it was to muster up the courage to inform them I had heard everything. They were bound to feel guilty, and I would use their guilt to my advantage. Perhaps I could even sell a dog or two if they were feeling especially guilty. It really was a very lucky thing for me to have been so insulted. The more I thought about it, the better I felt.

But now there was the issue of buying a new wardrobe. I did not have the money for a single sock, let alone a whole suit. Dreisbach was too short and ugly to loan me anything and Horace was too large and dull. My only option was to buy new.

This was very frustrating for me for two reasons. The first was because I was poor and had no way to pay for a new suit. This would not have been a pressing issue if the parade wan't so soon. I could have sold a few more of my dogs. But I wanted to have a new suit for the next time that I saw Desmond and Jane and Ms. Greenwood. I do not know if George would be at the Parade. If so, I wanted to have a new suit for him to see, too.

The second reason it was frustrating was because I thought my clothes were nice. I was unaware that they were shabby. This upset me, as I take great pride in how I dress. I looked into my wardrobe to see what else I owned. How many of my best shirts, which were so beautiful to me, were actually hideous in the eyes of others. I began to lose self-confidence. If you have ever experienced it, then you will agree that it is a most disagreeable feeling.

I let the dogs into the garden while I considered my options. Ms. Rueblack had made bread rolls so I reached through her window and took one while they were cooling. She had made six, so I figured she would not notice one missing. I ate in silence while I thought.

The money from Celia's sale was all about dried up. Between cakes and bouquets of flowers, I had only a handful of notes left. I wondered if other people's budgets ever included flowers and cakes and perfumes. I doubted it. That was why other people had more money than me. It was difficult thinking. I simply could not see how having money in a bank somewhere was any more fun than vases of flowers.

I suppose there was another good thing about having eavesdropped at the NWS. I would now save plenty of money I would otherwise have spent on perfume.

But that was all in the future, the idea of saving money. I needed cash quickly. I was desperate enough to eye up Ms. Rueblack's kitchen a second time. Unfortunately, her purse was not in its usual spot on the kitchen counter. I was full of bad luck that day.

I often say that the unluckiest days produce the best ideas. (Just ask Horace. I've said it to him twice this week.) When I returned to my flat, it occurred to me how much I hated it there. How I hated Ms. Rueblack and how I hated Mr. Greaves and how I hated the drip-drip-dripping of the kitchen faucet. I hated the crown moulding and I hated the azaleas. I hated having to use the chemist's telephone and that Horace did not like coming over.

I was in a bit of a depression when I made the decision to move out. I think one makes the best decisions when they are depressed because they have no happiness to gamble with. It was a dump and, despite everything that Ms. Greenwood said, I was still a very influential person. I needed to stay in a place that reflected my newfound influence. It also had to be free, as what money I had for rent really needed to go toward the purchase of a new suit.

It was then I decided to move into the Esstäbchen Theatre with the dogs. Of course, that also meant living with Dreisbach. But I was willing to sacrifice my patience if it meant proving those who laughed at me wrong. I would have a very nice suit and I would not be paying rent. I would even buy cakes and bouquets of flowers whenever I pleased with the money I would be saving. It was a brilliant plan.

I never formally told Dreisbach I was moving in, nor did I ever formally tell Mr. Greaves that I was moving out. I simply did not give Mr. Greaves an envelope of money at the end of the month and I began taking dogs over to the Theatre under the pretense of them meeting Dreisbach. I would then say that I had to run an errand and ask if he could watch one of the dogs. I would simply leave them there. I did this four times and four times Dreisbach never mentioned it. He was drunk a lot of the time, being upset at not finding a backer for his all-male *Lysistrata*. Such luck!

The Esstäbchen is cavernous, which provided the dogs with hours of exploration. When they annoyed me, I would hide bits of ham around the theatre and then retire to the props closet I used as my bedroom. I had chosen this room because it was where Dreisbach kept a stack of various rugs he used for set design. It became my makeshift bed. I was not able to take the bed with me when I moved out of my old flat. Mr. Greaves had nailed the frame into the floor. That just goes to show how little he trusted his tenants.

I bought the suit. It was a deep navy, more subdued than I typically liked. But it fit well and had never been worn as a server's uniform, so that was already a positive. Because I could no longer trust my own taste in fashion, I had asked the salesman four times if he liked it. One would have thought I was buying a Daimler, the way I went on and on with worry. I was finally convinced that the navy suit was the right choice for me. It did complement my hair. I decided to wear it out of the store. I also bought a beige sweater. I had seen Desmond wear a similar sweater in a society write-up. I thought he may compliment me if he saw me in it. Perhaps we would get to talking about how I have a wonderful style. Perhaps, then, he would forget about Jane Raitland altogether.

With the last few pounds I'd saved on rent, I invited Horace to dine with me at the Pelican. It is not that the Pelican is my favorite restaurant, it is just one of the only places I have been to in a while. Because I do not have a lot of money, I do not dine out often. I knew the menu at the Pelican very well, too, having worked there. I also hoped that some of the waiters would remember me. Perhaps Horace and I would get some free bread or perhaps a hunk of cheese. It was worth a try. It was also my excuse to wear the new navy suit. I just wore the jacket with a pair of slacks. It was a most versatile purchase, with so many available permutations between jacket and pants for different occasions.

Horace, when I called him from the Esstäbchen, asked me three times who would be paying. I found this to be vulgar, as I had been the one to invite him. Bankruptcy had obviously changed him for the worse.

Upon hanging up, I found myself wishing that his depression had taken a form more akin to Dreisbach's. At least with Dreisbach he mostly slept and when he was awake he didn't ask too many questions and simply trusted me. But, then again, if I were wishing for things, I should probbably just wish that Horace was wealthy and generous again.

The Pelican is an exquisite restaurant. I am not saying it is exquisite because the waiters did end up remembering me and gave me a free dessert. It is exquisite because it is glamorous and also it has a very cheap lunch hour. While I waited for Horace, I imagined myself as a business professional taking my lunch with another business professional. Perhaps I was a typist for a veterinarian. I would have been very busy in the morning and so looked forward to the lunch hour with my colleague. We would muse over other colleagues' love lives and complain about taxes or the price of private schools. We would laugh and laugh and I would put my hand on the bill first, offering to pay for the both of us.

In my daydreams, I am very prosperous and own a closet full of beautifully tailored navy suits. I also have many friends from work and I am happy to pay for their meals because we eat lunch together often and so my friend will buy for me the next time. In my daydreams, I do not have four dogs but a more manageable one or two. And in my daydreams I do not live in a converted Chinese restaurant, nor do I sleep on a pile of rugs.

It was this thinking that caused me to be slightly irritable when Horace lumbered into the restaurant. I knew it was unfair to Horace, and yet I could not help being short with him at first. Daydreams are like warm milk; they can comfort you and make you sleepy, but they spoil too quickly.

Horace and I sat down at a booth upholstered in a fine, emerald leather. The table was marbled in a seafoam with hints of golden vein. I commented on its beauty twice. Horace said it reminded him of Positano. I told him I had never been to Positano. He said he knew that. I asked him why he would make a reference I wouldn't understand, if he knew that I had never been. He ignored the question and returned his gaze to the menu.

It was not the lunch menu, rather it was the more expensive

dinner menu. So I began to remark on how delicious the cheaper items sounded.

"Doesn't the side of radishes sound appetizing?"

"I could absolutely fill up on creamed spinach!"

"I believe a plain baked potato and a glass of ice water sounds good. Shall I order two?"

This experiment in persuasive psychology failed, however. Horace ordered a steak and a side of chips. He also got a glass of red wine. Horace absolutely must spend more wisely, or he won't make it, I thought. Didn't he know how many bouquets of flowers he could have gotten for all the money he wasted on food? Not to mention perfumes!

I believe a part of it was Horace getting back at me. Horace is a simple giant and I feel I am able to read him easily. For years I have been the one knocking at his door for cash and rent money. Now it was his turn. My side of creamed spinach tasted particularly bitter as I watched him savor his steak.

"So, Arthur, why did you invite me out? All going well with the plan?"

"Oh yes, quite. No particular reason, old man. Really. I just had a few extra quid and thought I'd share."

"A few extra? You? How'd that happen? Did you sell another dog without me?"

"Nothing like that Horace. Besides, I'd need your car as a getaway. I simply stopped paying rent at my flat. Did you notice my new jacket, Horace? Isn't it nice?"

"Stopped paying rent? Arthur, you're going to get yourself and your dogs kicked out. And you can't all move in with me."

After years of friendship, I never did learn with Horace. He always liked to talk about my finances and never noticed my nice clothes.

"I know that, Horace. I know. I don't plan on moving in with you. I plan on *you* moving in with *me.*"

Here I proposed to Horace my plan for turning the Esstäbchen into the headquarters for our business operations. If Horace could sell his house, then that would be extra cash on hand for him. The theatre had plenty of space for his junk and and I believed I could split my pile of rugs in half and still be comfortable. Plus, we would be all in the same space. This would make it easy for the plan to succeed.

Horace actually grimaced—-he actually grimaced!—-when I suggested moving into the Esstäbchen. I knew it was because of Dreisbach. To be honest, if it wasn't saving me so much money, I would have grimaced too. While I agreed with Horace, I don't think he was thinking very clearly. He was still thinking as if he was a rich person, for whom options are limitless and owning a home is a genuine possibility. We, none of us, were in that position now. I lived with Dreisbach and ate creamed spinach; Horace owned a home and was eating steak. But who was paying for dinner that night?

Horace asked many questions, all of which I had an answer for. I embellished, of course, but I believed I was doing Horace a favor and therefore needn't tell him the truth. I told him he would have his own room and that we would share a bathroom. This was only half-true, as he would share a bathroom with both Dreisbach and me and his room would be a section of the backstage, partitioned off by Chinese curtains. He asked if he would have to see Dreisbach much and I said not at all. Certainly he would see Dreisbach often, but Dreisbach would be passed out, drunk, and would not bother Horace much. He asked about utilities (covered by Dreisbach) and cleaning (we would get a charwoman) and food (each man would fend for himself). Frustratingly, he asked if he would have to care for the dogs at all. I told him that if we did our jobs right, there would hardly be any dogs for anybody to take care of. That seemed to quiet him down.

We had dessert, which, as I mentioned, was free, thanks to my good friend Balthazar. On the way out the door, I spotted a rather fetching flannel shirt hanging on a coat rack. It was a chilly night, so I took it with me. This was how I came up on my Good Shirt.

XV

Parade Day

By the day of the Parade the following week, Horace was halfway moved in and Dreisbach was nearly fully recovered from his bender. It seems he was very worried about the debtors who had been calling. I solved that problem the night I had moved in: I unplugged the phone from the wall. Not a single call since.

I got used to the pile of rugs as my bed and so had the dogs, who, even though we now had an entire theatre to ourselves, still liked to sleep close to me. It was endearing, but I worried about poor, sensitive Henry catching a cold in the drafty storage room. Luckily, Dreisbach had put on an adaptation of *Taming of the Shrew* in which the characters were all cavemen. He had kept a ratty fur thing I can only assume was a woolly mammoth pelt. This was to be our bedding until I could afford proper linens. Frances seemed happy, if a little sniffly from the dust.

I loved performing my beauty routine at the Esstäbchen because I did so in the long corridor where the actors did their makeup. This meant bright lighting and very polished mirrors. I sat at one of the vanities the morning of the Parade, fussing over my various flaws and coiffing my hair with some grease Dreisbach had on hand. I put on my beautiful beige sweater and my full navy suit. I felt dashing, which, perversely, I resented. I only bought the outfit because of the embarrassment Ms.

Greenwood and her company had caused me. It was also the reason I was now even living in a run-down theatre. In some ways, she had ruined my life, but she had made me feel so very handsome. It was too much influence for one person to have over another's life.

Regardless, my handsomeness bred confidence in me. It was 8:00 am by the time I had washed the pomade off of my hands. I woke Dreisbach in his room. He slept curled up tightly in a ball. Even his fists were clenched. I believe this was due to a repressed violent temper. The more I was around him, the more Dreisbach made me nervous.

Dreisbach had not drank the night before, as I had asked him not to. He woke grumbling a pillow-muffled word in French that I did not hear and that I did not ask him to repeat. I kept the ceiling light on so he wouldn't fall back asleep. I kept his door open so the dogs could jump on his bed and wake him up. They were good at that.

I laid out all the supplies necessary for his part in the ruse: the shoe polish to paint Henry, the glue and wig to attach to Rue, the pressed suit for his role as Tamassy. I hid his white powder under the sink to be safe. I kept his rouge out though, as promised.

Upon leaving the theatre, I waved goodbye to the dogs and banged the door very loudly to wake Dreisbach up again. He had two hours to do everything. The plan hinged on Dreisbach. I felt nervous because of that.

I was doubly nervous because I would be seeing so many of the NWS members who had embarrassed me. I had skipped the last Committee meeting because I had not had my new suit pressed yet and so did not want to show up in the old rags they had seen before. I could have worn my Good Shirt from the Pelican, but I did not want to waste wearing it for the first time on that turncoat Desmond. Instead, I sent a telegram saying I was extremely ill. I hope everyone felt very worried for me.

I was unnerved in the way I became unnerved by drinking and smoking too many cigarettes. It is an electric kind of nervousness, one that does not make me hungry. I did not want a comforting madeleine nor did I want a comforting cider. Instead, I wanted to rest my fore-head on a cool brick wall and to have some poetry read to me while I fell asleep. I had never had poetry read to me while I fell asleep, but it seemed like the right medicine for this of nerves I was suffering.

The Esstäbchen is just a brief walk to St. James Park, so I was there before anyone else. We had only rented the marquee for two hours (budget) and the rental men had not arrived yet, either. I was not alone, though. There were other park-goers. Women in flimsy hats and men with flimsy newspapers tucked under their arms. I always wondered why people bothered to read the newspaper. They do make one's hands dirty. I laughed to think, what if we had rubbed a hundred newspapers onto Henry to color his coat. Ha!

Because I was early, I took a bench far away from the set-up area for the marquee. I wanted to be a voyeur. Perhaps at the last minute before the Parade was to begin, I would come out to greet the guests. I was, after all, still Chair of the Committee. Ms. Greenwood and her acid tongue could not take that from me!

I am an excellent voyeur, slightly built and keenly observant. I like to watch how others interact. I believe this is due to my having so few friends of my own; it is a novelty to see how others do it. I see small nods, a very masculine greeting. I see kisses on both cheeks, a typically French form of greeting that looks ungainly on the thick-calved women who inhabit parks on Saturdays. I see wide smiles and hugs, very feminine. I see children admonished to stop feeding pigeons and I see nannies shooing the pigeons away again and again.

I used to be an adroit voyeur when I was a lifeguard and also when I was a waiter. This is because there are many different types of people to observe who like to swim and who like to eat. On my way home after a shift I would practice interacting with people. I would pretend to have many close friends whom I would see around town. I would kiss the air when I was around women and I would lay a firm, masculine hand on the shoulders of men. I would get so caught up in my fantasy that I would sometimes walk right past my own building. This was before I had my dogs, of course. I am not as lonely with my dogs.

According to my new silver watch from Mr. Cormant, it was 9:07 am when the marquee people arrived, and by 9:18 am there was Toffie

Montmaarten with her truck driving boyfriend. He was a compact little man in an undershirt and suspenders. They clearly enjoyed one another's company. I waited ten minutes before approaching them because they were moving things and I did not want to help.

Hannah Grey-Downs joined the group and immediately began directing the scene. She was authoritative to the point of bossiness and I was grateful for her energy. My nerves had not calmed themselves while I was on the bench. I usually find bossy women unattractive, but I was charmed by Hannah Grey-Downs taking the role of Vice-Chair so seriously. Desmond and Ms. Greenwood were making themselves downright useful, the sight of which unnerved me so that I was all but incapacitated.

Luckily, I did not have long to sit with my nerves as many people began to show up all at once. The Walkers were motioned to a part of the tent while the Watchers milled about the pastries and drinks cart that was set up for them. Many lifted a cup of tea to their mouths and steam danced around both the men's and the women's mustaches alike. It was an ancient crew, on the whole.

For all the terrible things I could say about Jane Raitland and Desmond (and there were many), I had to admit that their guest list was thorough. There was Lady Montagu-Rinds with her little Abigail and Cork. There were the Pigdons with their wolfhound, Sandy. The Hon. Tibbery Beltrash-upon-March with his tiny Corgi called Samantha. There was Heywood Linten (with Josephine the Pug) and Heywood Unset (with Cunha the Shih Tzu). There were the Muirs (with Wilfred), Farley Gingham (with Nanny), and Lady Ipswin (with Manny). Every name they had written down for me was accounted for. I spent little time worrying about the Watchers. They were not connected to titles, so they were not that important to me.

I made my rounds and introduced myself. I like to introduce myself because I believe I am skilled at it. I say my full name for them to remember and sometimes I will repeat it before I go, especially if they are elderly and therefore more likely to forget. I made sure to tell everyone that I was the Chair of the Committee that planned this event.

When asked what business I was in, I said I had ties to importing and exporting, but also had close business with the theatre. People were impressed.

When I introduce myself to new people, I will also compliment them on something like a brooch or a sturdy shoelace. People like when one notices these things. I knelt to greet the dogs, too, which is a very important step many other influential people neglect. I have found that if a dog dislikes a person, their owners will too. Dogs are very influential.

In my periphery, I saw Jane Raitland and the man I assumed to be her father. He was exactly the man who would have a child like poor, dowdy Jane. He used a cane that was too short for him and bent severely. His shoes were covered with mud and his face was the color of dust. I don't believe he was sick. I believe, like Jane, he simply did not care about what he looked like. He was probably an accountant. He had the air, even from afar, of someone whose pride was attached to his stinginess and ability at correcting others. Maybe he was a Justice of the Peace, presiding cases of noise ordinance and sheep rustling.

Desmond followed closely behind with his bulldog Marcus in tow. He sported a finely tailored grey suit, the severe cut of which somehow managed to enhance his broad and expressive eyebrows. He nodded, as gentlemen do, to those he passed. He was comfortable with the attention. It drove me to jealousy, so I turned to introduce myself to a Watcher named Archibald Dafydd. His wife, Helen, was eating a clementine she had pulled from her handbag.

When we had all settled and had our fill of tea and introductions, Hannah Grey-Downs cleared her throat authoritatively and commanded everyone's attention. The Parade was not very populated (I counted about 52 guests and 22 dogs) so she did not have to shout to be heard. When everyone turned their attention to the Committee, Hannah showed them a phony smile that I believe was intended to demonstrate confidence and hospitality. She had crumbs on her bosom from a biscuit she had been eating.

"Welcome, everyone! Thank you so much to all who could come

today. As you know, the Newton-Wiggs Société is proud to sponsor today's Charity Dog Parade. This is the largest event of the Spring season and we appreciate the endowments you have made to fund the continuing work our little club does for the canine enthusiasts of London!

"It is my deepest honor to begin the procession. Our NWS members have volunteered their morning to show off some of the finest purebreds in the Commonwealth. Without further ado, I say we start the fun. Shall we?"

Hannah Grey-Downs was a take-charge woman and such aggressive chairmanship would typically have annoyed me immensely. It would have annoyed me because giving a speech was to be part of my role, as Chair of the Committee. It was my duty to be influential and to set the tone of the Parade. But, I was not annoyed at her dominating that particular moment. In fact, I welcomed it. I did not have a speech prepared (no one had told me I should have) and I was in a very stuttering type of mood seeing Desmond in his flannel suit. Ms. Greenwood smirked as I surveyed the audience. I believe she was tickled with Mrs. Grey-Downs usurping these duties. She probably thought it bothered me. Ms. Greenwood was, as usual, wrong.

I searched the crowd for Dreisbach and did not see him. I had asked a man standing next to me, a Mr. Wargle, if he happened to have met a Mr. Tamassy. He said no. I was pre-annoyed but tried to tamp down this feeling quickly. Horace, too, could not be found. Perhaps they had both overslept or had got the address or day wrong. It made me *extremely* pre-annoyed.

The Parade was a quick affair and ended in exactly 28 minutes, as Mrs. Grey-Downs had anticipated and as Viscount Spittlewood had prophesied in his meeting minutes. Those who had brought their dogs walked in front of the group of Watchers with their dogs in tow on leads. They would turn once, twice, three times then return to the line of Walkers. The audience clapped politely. There was the odd chuckle when one of the dogs got excited or acted silly. One woman oohed at the site of Thomasina Burkley's Borzoi. "It looks like somethin' outta a fairy tale!" she whispered loudly in her American accent to her husband, Garrett Burkley, 6th Baronet. He had married her for money, we all could tell. Probably for a quick injection of cash for his family seat in Wales. I wonder if he or his eardrums regretted it yet. You may not know this, but Welsh houses echo terribly.

As the last of the Walkers strolled down the marquee, the audience broke up. Many went for another cup of tea, as it was beginning to rain and therefore was quite chilly. As the crowd dispersed, I was pleased to see Dreisbach in the very back of the crowd. I had simply not seen him earlier, him being so short.

My pre-annoyance was for nothing. There Mr. Tamassy stood before me, dressed smartly and indeed with a slight limp in his gait. He winked at me in acknowledgment. He, I thanked the Lord, was not wearing an eyepatch. Behind him trotted two regal but nearly unrecognizable dogs. A pitch-black Henry and a Rue sporting a stylish fringe bang to cover her eyes. Both wagged their tails vigorously. I did not approach the trio. They all had a job to do and I did not want to distract from their work.

I made my rounds again. This time with something to actually talk about that wasn't banal introductions or small-talk about one's brooch or shoelaces. Many people liked Desmond and Marcus. Many people commented on the quality of the food, for which I gave all the credit to Toffie and Hannah. A few complimented my beige sweater (which I knew flattered me). Fanny Maybrick hardly looked up from her teacup when I waved at her. She must have been going through another divorce. She looked forlorn. This was great news for me. I believe the best medicine for a divorce is a dog. Rue, who is a very good companion, would be the ideal balm for Fanny's broken heart.

Out of the corner of my eye I watched Dreisbach do his work. We had only rented the marquee for two hours and therefore, he would have to hurry it up a little before the rental men began to tear it down and the Parade festivities would be over. He bowed at women and shook everyone's hand equally. He protected Henry from being petted to conserve the shoe polish on his coat. Rue was oblivious. I wondered if the fringe was too thick. Perhaps she was a bit blinded.

Still I did not see Horace, which did concern me a little. But only a little, as I was very busy myself. Between grabbing a few biscuits to take home to the dogs and nodding my head to every passerby, I scarcely had time to breathe.

As I shoved a handful of shortbreads into my jacket pocket, I was tapped on the shoulder. I nearly jumped out of my Nice Brown Shoes. I spun about and found myself staring straight at Ms. Greenwood. I winced. She smiled.

"It's really good to see you today, Mr. Croots."

"Thanks, Ms. Greenwood. Can I help you with anything?"

"I just wanted to say...how wonderful it is to see you."

"How wonderful it is to see me in a suit that isn't crummy, you mean?"

"No, Mr. Croots. I don't mean that. I'm sorry for whatever you may have heard. And misinterpreted."

"Oh, no apology needed. I don't believe I'm mistaken about what your mean little get-together was laughing at. But even if I were, I suppose I too would be very, very sorry and very, very embarrassed at the pain I caused another person. Especially one of such influence as me."

"Yes, that's right, Mr. Croots. We do feel awful."

"How awful do you feel, Ms. Greenwood?"

"I-I beg your pardon?"

"How awful do you feel? I'm curious how awful you must be feeling right at this very moment."

"I guess pretty awful, Mr. Croots. I don't think I understand."

"How awful does Desmond feel. Do you know? Do you think he feels singularly awful?"

"I'm sure he does. I haven't actually asked him."

"Can you? Can you ask him if he feels awful? I want to know."

"Mr. Croots, this was just for me to say that I am sorry for any hurt feelings. I don't think it's my place to ask Lord Ham-sur-Rye if he's feeling bad about something said nearly a week ago."

"Oh, you don't think it is? Then you must not feel that awful then. I know when I am feeling awful for hurting someone's feelings, I would do whatever was necessary to atone for it. I suppose that's the difference between you and me, Ms. Greenwood. I care about people more than I care about my own pride."

I am not sure if we looked especially heated or if Toffie had had too much to drink. Either way, she darted over with her beau and threw her arms around Mrs. Greenwood's neck.

"Lindy! Isn't it lovely? Didn't we do good? Didn't Aleksi do good?"

Both Ms. Greenwood and I were a little stunned at the abrupt shift in mood, so neither of us answered right away. But this did not seem to bother Toffie who, it seemed to me, was accustomed to filling silence with her own words. Aleski was, in fact, Russian and could not speak a lot of English. This did not seem to bother Toffie, either.

"Thank you both for your hard work today," I said, after a calming breath that calmed me only slightly.

"Oh, Arthur, we enjoyed helping. Besides, it's been great free advertisement for Aleksi. Isn't that right, dear?"

Aleksi, with his short, muscular stature and severe Slavic expression, nodded curtly.

"Plus," Toffie continued, "we met the most fascinating man. From Australia! His name was Thomassy or something. He's says he's a celebrated dog breeder. Very popular in Croatia, he says. He brought two brand-new breeds to the Parade for us to see. A *minuit frise* and something called a Ruffled Spaniel. Both darling. Both very continental."

"I've never heard of either of them. Are you sure you heard the names right, Toffie?"

"Of course I am, Lindy! My goodness, I think I'd know what he said. I was right there."

"It's nothing to worry about, Toffie. I just haven't heard of these breeds before. That's all."

"Yes, Belinda, but that's because they're *new* and *exotic*. You know, Britain is a very small island. There's a whole continent full of breeders out there. Many people probably thought pugs were overgrown moles until someone put a leash on one and house-trained it. Come with me if you don't believe me!"

We followed Toffie to the corner of the marquee where Dreisbach was entertaining a few NWS guests by introducing them to Rue and Henry. He appeared to be telling them some made-up story about a hot air balloon trip in Buenos Aires. His accent was very bad, but people enjoyed themselves anyway.

Toffie, who was accustomed to getting her way, cut to the front of the crowd and put out a hand.

"I'm sorry to interrupt, Mr. Thomas."

"Tamassy, mate."

"Mr. Tamassy. But my friends here don't believe me when I tell them you have two new breeds with you. Can you please take a moment and introduce the *frise* and the Spaniel to my dubious compatriots?" At the last phrase, Toffie smiled sweetly to the crowd to apologize for her interruption. This was obviously not the first time she had command the attention of a crowd. I would not necessarily call this influential behavior, though. I believe she was just pretty enough, just fragile looking enough, that people did not like to yell at her to shut up and move aside.

"Of course, mate! Here they are. Got my little pair right here. Black one's name's Alfred, and the little sheila is Bunny."

He gestured to the two disguised dogs. Henry wagged his tail so vigorously I swear I could see polish falling off in droplets.

Everyone leaned in to get a closer look. Toffie began to walk closer to the pair but Dreisbach put his hand up to stop her.

"My dear Ms...erm..."

"Montmaarten, from the sugar family."

"Ms. Montmaarten from the sugar family. How many people do you think want to see and play and touch these two new breeds here in the United Kingdom? Hundreds, one must assume, at a minimum. We must protect their health. We can't allow just anyone to pet them. They're one-of-a-kind, each of them."

"Well, Mr. Tamassy, that's a bit of a surprise. You're telling me you brought these dogs all the way from Australia just so we could *look* at them?"

"That is correct."

"And now that you're here, at our event, we can't even *touch* the dogs?"

"Also correct. But let me apologize, Ms. Montmaarten. I didn't know this was your event."

"Well, it's the Newton-Wiggs Sociéte's event and I'm a member of the planning committee."

"But not the Chair?"

"No, that's Mr. Croots. He's right over here."

I began to take back all of the negative things I had said about Dreisbach. He led Toffie masterfully toward a sale. She wanted what she couldn't have. The onlookers whom she had interrupted were now just as curious. And I, being an influential person at this moment, just had to let Dreisbach do the work. I would follow his lead. Perhaps he wasn't an idiot after all. It was very hard to tell with Dreisbach who, in all the years I had known him, had always seemed like an idiot to me.

"How do you do, Mr. Tamassy?"

"Hullo, mate. Lemme apologize for taking time away from your event, my good man. Just got a little too excited 'bout these new breeds, you see?"

"I understand. I'm sure many members today will be more than anxious to get their hands on a--what was it again?"

"A *minuit frise*, mate!"

"A yes. And the spaniel, too! What a specimen."

"Yes, both were bred for mild temperament and shy demeanor. We took a lovely King Charles and bred just the most beautiful parts of a bearded collie. Which are, of course, the bangs. And you'd never believe how easy it is to get a pitch-black Bichon once you begin breeding them with labradors and rottweilers and setters. Why, he's a whole bundle of purebreds!"

Somehow this was a selling point for the onlookers and many began to mutter in approval.

"Mr. Tamassy. May I ask, why bring such wonderful specimens of their breeds if you are not willing to have our guests enjoy their presence?"

"Why, mate, I never said they can't touch! I just said they can't touch if they aren't willing to give these beautiful creatures a new home, is all. Anyone with a wallet can pet them all they like. These two are here to be sold in the UK. I don't have the proper paperwork to take them back to Australia with me, so I thought the Newlon-Wink Société would be the ideal milieu in which to find suitale homes for these two."

I could almost feel Toffie shiver with excitement. She wanted them both and she wanted them fast. A woman like Toffie surrounded herself with the slightly exotic: emerald rings, ermine-lined dressing gowns, Russian boyfriends who owned moving trucks. Rue and Henry, in their disguises, would only add to the fabulous lifestyle she had curated for herself.

"Wonderful, Mr. Tamassy. That's great to hear. Well, perhaps not great for you, as I'm sure you'll miss them frightfully. But I think it's aces you'll be giving them away to the devoted members of the NWS. Now, let's see. I think the fairest way to handle this is to start by inquiring if anyone would even *want* one of these handsome, brand new, exotic breeds. All who want a *minuit frise*, raise your right hand. All who want a Ruffled Spaniel, raise your left."

Mr. Tamassy, with his ringleader bravado, summoned quite a crowd. When I turned to look at the audience surrounding us, it was nearly all of the Watchers and a few of the Walkers. Even Desmond was in attendance, though I suppose it was more out of curiosity than actual interest. Neither his left nor his right hand was raised.

But many hands were raised, and I even saw a few elbows being thrown as people jockeyed to be seem. Toffie had both hands raised. Fanny Maybrick had her left hand raised. I was pleased to see that. She had looked rather melancholy during the Parade.

"Well, this is a nice show of support for Mr. Tamassy! Ms. Greenwood, please grab a piece of paper and make two columns: one for those who want this beautiful *frise* and one for those who want this gorgeous example of a Ruffled Spaniel. I will examine the list very thoroughly and reach out to those I judge best suited. I believe this is fair. Don't you Mr. Tamassy?"

"Oh, yes! Very, er, fair dinkum alright! Take their names down, Sheila. I'll leave ya to that. But just so's we have it out there, the prices will be about 150 pounds per dog. That includes travel costs and food and such. You understand, I'm sure."

A few raised hands wavered at the sum , but pride won the day and not a single hand came down. In fact, Toffie grabbed Aleksi's hand and pulled it up alongside hers. Trying to double her vote, I presumed. Little did she know how fruitless that was. I was having everyone go through this little ruse so that I could collect the names of all the fools who would take any dog we threw at them if we labeled it a purebred. I had already decided that Rue would go to Fanny and that Henry would go to Toffie.

Tamassy said his goodbyes and the crowd broke up. We had to, anyway, as the marquee rental men were standing closeby, and angrily. We had kept the tent for an additional 40 minutes.

That was a problem for Mrs. Grey-Downs. Not for me.

XVI

And Get Some Sleep, You Look Like Hell

Even as the crowd dispersed, I still made no attempt to show my recognition of Dreisbach. We were playing to strangers and both of us were very good actors. I walked away casually, trying to see behind shrubs and picnickers if perhaps I had missed Desmond. We had not chatted once during the Parade. He must have felt horrible laughing at me.

I looked for Horace. His absence worried me. Horace, oafish as he was, was usually punctual. I knew that he was living between his house and the Esstäbchen. Perhaps he had lost his diary in the shuffle of boxes and had forgotten the Parade was today. Most unlike Horace. Worrisome.

Like a handsome deck of playing cards and crisp white taper candles, I believe punctuality to be a sign of influence and class. I wondered if, now that Horace had sold his handsome deck of playing cards and could no longer afford crisp white taper candles, he would lose the small vestiges of class he had managed to muster. Perhaps the ornamentation of his life no longer influenced his behavior. His bankruptcy, it seems, threw the corduroy-clad baby out with the insolvent bathwater.

This was a pity for me because up until a week before I did not have a very reliable wristwatch. This meant I often depended upon Horace for the hour and for important dates. If he was now useless in this regard and also poor, why were we still friends? If he sold his car, he and I would need to have a very serious talk.

I did not search too far for Horace, as I could see his back hunched over a pint close to the park. The pub was dim but I could make out his corduroy suit. It seems he had dressed up for the Parade and then simply chosen not to attend.

A chime on the door tinkled as I entered the pub, but still Horace did not look up. He made no motion at all until tapped his shoulder. I will admit, it was rough, as taps go, but I was annoyed.

When Horace turned to me, I was at a total loss for words. He looked awful. Horace was never handsome, exactly; he is no Desmond! But he looked particularly awful at that moment. His eyes red, from drink or from tears, or from both. His hair was matted on his forehead in sweaty clumps. He had stubble all the way down his chin, and where the stubble ended the crumbs began. He had crumbs all the way down to his chest hair where they mingled with peanut shells he had been chewing. This was no longer a man of influence, I thought. This was a fat and greasy ghost before me, an apparition of my once best friend.

But still he said nothing. We just stared until the barman asked if I wanted a drink. That day, in my beige sweater and new navy suit, I did not want a drink. I did not think that a man with my nice clothes would want to have a tepid beer in some pub. I ordered a soda water with lime. This seemed like something someone in a navy suit would order. Also, it was very cheap and I planned to put my order on Horace's tab.

"So, Horace, I didn't see you at the Parade today. You were supposed to be watching Dreisbach."

"Oh, I was watching him. I saw him come and go. He looked fine to me."

"Fine to you isn't fine to me, Horace. You know how Dreisbach is. I needed you on him. Luckily Dreisbach did swimmingly, thank you for asking."

"Well, then what's the problem, Arthur?"

"The problem is that I needed you and you weren't there. That's the problem."

The barman put my soda water down in front of me on a small square napkin. He raised his eyebrows and I scowled back. Had he never heard two men fight about trust and fidelity and friendship before?

"But it all worked out, Arthur. You don't need me. He did fine, he wasn't wearing makeup or an eyepatch. I decided to get a drink and I would see you later to hear the details."

This dismissiveness hurt me. The soda water fizzed merrily on the counter. It was oblivious to the tension between Horace and I.

"Horace..."

"Arthur, it's nothing. I just have a headache. I haven't been sleeping well. This is the first time I've had time to just *think*. And you talking isn't helping my thinking."

"Well, old man, let's think together then! What are we thinking about?"

"I'm thinking about how a month ago I had my life before me and now I'm looking to sell every book I own to keep myself afloat. I'm thinking about how much money I've wasted over the years on picking up other people's dinner bills and dry cleaning and birthday presents. I'm thinking about how, at thirty-six, I have to move into a dingy theatre with a failed actor and a man whose only talent is lying! And our only hope is that I keep my car so we can steal dogs!"

"Horace, lower your voice. You're being hysterical."

Horace wasn't making sense. I have many other talents besides lying. (As I've already mentioned, I am very good at tying knots.) Plus, we weren't "stealing dogs", as he so crudely put it. We were renting the dogs out and returning them. The marquee men weren't stealing the tent from us when they tore it down after the Parade. They were simply reclaiming what was theirs. Horace knew so little about the way the world worked it was astonishing.

"Well, Horace, I'm sorry you are in this situation. Perhaps next time you won't put so much faith into someone who went to seminary school. I could have told you that! They put that little basket in everyone's face and live off other people's pocket change. I hope to see you when you're a little kinder, Horace. I'm off to have some calling cards printed up with Hargood, so I'll be in your neighborhood today if you want to apologize. And for your bad behavior, I'll be putting this soda on your tab. Bye for now. And get some sleep, you look like hell."

Getting the last word in the argument usually leaves me quite self-satisfied. But my satisfaction does seem to hinge upon the recipient of my wit being left flustered. And Horace was not flustered, which left me deflated me as I exited the pub.

Horace hadn't looked up from the counter during my speech, nor had he looked up when I left the pub. (I looked back in through the window just to be sure). He didn't even notice my new beige sweater. This was not the first time I wished that Horace was Desmond and Desmond was Horace. Desmond would have noticed my new beige sweater. I would have liked that.

This was not the ideal circumstance in which to get our plan moving forward. Due to Dreisbach's great performance, we now had a definitive list of potential customers. We had an unlimited supply of costumery, and were no longer bound by Mr. Greaves' strict deadline for evicting me and my poor dogs. In short, we were free for the first time to begin making money!

All in all, this was the most successful I had felt in a while. Horace was sulking but he would snap out of it. If not, then Dreisbach and I would simply split Horace's share. I'm sure with the cash from the sale of Henry and Rue that we could find a nice little coupe. I became convinced we wouldn't need Horace for anything. I did not know how to drive, but that was a small matter.

XVII

Tarzan's Grip

Horace did not come home to the theatre that day or the next. He did not answer the phone or the door or the four letters I slipped into his mailbox. He was either dead, in jail, or ignoring me. In any case, he was of no help. Cuustomers were waiting. He was being unprofessional.

I am a shrewd entrepreneur. I have to be, given the economy in general and my penury in particular. I had to strike some deals soon. I could feel my influential status waning as the days passed after the Parade. For instance, I thought for sure more people would have sent me a congratulatory note (preferably on a coroneted letterhead). But, alas, no one did. I believe this was Miss Greenwood's doing. I'm sure she did her rounds, speaking ill of my small hands and my *penchant* for good perfumes. It was easy to see that Ms. Greenwood was a gossip. Her eyebrows gave it away. They were thin and deceitful-looking. An honest woman's eyebrows are never that thin.

Over breakfast, Dreisbach and I discussed next steps. He was confident we could go on without Horace, but I needed convincing. Dreisbach said he knew an American taxi driver who knew very little English and who could possibly help us. The difference, I reminded Dreisbach again and again, was that we'd have to pay a taxi driver. Horace's car was free.

Dreisbach, as you may already imagine, was a disgusting eater. He claimed that smacking his lips made the food taste better. I found this strange, given that he was eating porridge, which doesn't have much taste to begin with. I did not like eating breakfast with Dreisbach. I preferred it when he was hungover and ate in his bedroom. But these were desperate times and all I could hope for was that the bowl of porridge would be finished soon and we could discuss next steps in a relatively on-disgusting atmosphere (though Dreisbach did like to grunt and clear his throat after every meal).

I turned over an envelope that was stamped NOTICE and began to make notes. While Dreisbach huffed and puffed and digested his porridge, and since Horace was nowhere to be found, it looked like it fell to me to make money. Mentally, I changed our splits. I would now take ninety percent.

Again, I am a very shrewd entrepreneur.

Dreisbach helped himself to more tea while I crumbled the first envelope and moved on to a second. This one was stamped SECOND NOTICE. How very kind of them to keep track, I thought. I assume it was one person's job to have a running list of everyone's first, second, and final notices. I'm sure they were paid well for this work. It wasn't easy remembering everyone in London's bills, nor was it easy inking a stamp day in and day out. I would imagine one would have to wear shabby frocks to avoid inking all over their Good Shirts, too. Perhaps if this dog business didn't work out I could be a Notice Stamper.

I made a small reminder in the corner to check the classifieds for openings. Then I cursed myself, forgetting that only Horace bought newspapers. When was he coming back?!

My thoughts were interrupted by Dreisbach coughing. He had mistaken a dog biscuit for a dessert and was spitting it out onto the table. I do not know how he had made such a mistake. The dog biscuit was shaped like a miniature bone. He threw the rest on the ground and drank his tea in one gulp to wash away the biscuit. I believe I had bought chicken-flavored biscuits. If Dreisbach was anyone else, I would have felt sorry for him. But he was Dreisbach, and his ugliness elicited no pity. All of my respect for his acting as Mr. Tamassy was long-gone. Isn't it amazing how fast such things evaporate when a person has terrible table manners?

We agreed that Horace's presence was not needed for at least the next two sales. Toffie and Fanny could be handled by Mr. Tamassy and me. While not ideal, I had to hope that Dreisbach could keep it together for at least a couple more days. I could already see that his composure was crumbling; he was overdue for a bender. I would have to keep a close eye on Dreisbach's diet. He would need to keep his ingestion of drinking and dog biscuits to a minimum. We needed Mr. Tamassy to be as clever and charming as he was at the Parade.

With three hundred pounds in our very near future, Dreisbach and I had a renewed sense of vigor regarding our plans. Even with Horace's absence, we were in high spirits. Dreisbach, now energized, showered and took out the garbage. Me, now energized, lay in my makeshift bed and read a catalogue. I must have been too energized, though, because I awoke some time later with the catalogue functioning as a perfect shade to cover my eyes.

I was pleasantly surprised to see two things on the kitchen table. The first being that none of the mail Dreisbach collected had any red stamps on the envelopes. These, my deductive skills predicted, would soon be stamped with FINAL NOTICE. This was a very good thing, indeed, considering I was not sure when Horace was returning to sign the checks.

The second good thing was that Dreisbach had already finished his letters to Toffie and Fanny, which was a surprise. Dreisbach, for all of his problems, is always surprising me. The letters were nearly identical. Luckily, Dreisbach's handwriting is very bad and so his spelling errors could be easily overlooked by an untrained eye.

Toffie's read:

Dear Ms. Montmaarten,

I am so pleased to have met your acquaintance the other day at the Newin-Tinks Parade.

Thank you for the interest in my beloved minute frees. After much deliberation, I have decided that he would do well in your home. I trust your Slavic husband would like a companion as well.

Due to a delay in my schedule I will be staying in the Merry Olde for a few more days. I am available Thursday morning. Shall we meet at the Park again? Full circle!

Please have your payment ready in small bills. With conversion rates and taxes, the total is 200.

Fanny's read:

Dear Ms. Maybrick,

I am so pleased to have met your acquaintance the other day at the Nitwit-Trunks Parade.

Thank you for the interest in my beloved spaniel. After much deliberation, I have decided that she would do well in your home. You seem extremely lonely and as we always say in Austria, "A lonely sheila needs a friend!"

Due to a delay in my schedule I will be staying in the Merry Olde for a few more days. I am available Thursday afternoon. Shall we meet at the Park again? Say 2:00? Full circle!

Please have your payment ready in small bills. For 180 I will throw in a lead.

Dreisbach could not tell a dog biscuit from a scone, but he could net us an additional 80 quid just by the magic of a few misspelled words and stroke of a pencil. Perhaps there was a bit of Christian teaching in me, as I decided after reading the letters that morning I would give Dreisbach a thirty percent cut *and* I would pay for the stamps to mail the letters myself. I was a fine Christian friend indeed.

And where was Horace, I thought as I walked back to the theatre after posting the letters? Bah! Who cared? If we never did another sale again, the money from Toffie and Fanny would be plenty for a few months. Perhaps Dreisbach and I could even get ourselves a chauffeur. Someone reliable, trustworthy, and who perhaps owned more than one shabby corduroy suit.

When I returned home, I threw a couple of slices of ham on the floor for the dogs and then suited Henry and Rue up for a goodbye walk. I needed to get more wig glue for Rue's fringe and more pigment for Henry's coat. His shoe polish was, unfortunately, rubbing off every time he laid down. We would either have to find a more reliable alternative to shoe polish or we would have to make small braces for his legs so he could not lay down at Fannie's. The solution was entirely dependent on cost, as I had not eaten lunch yet and only had a couple pounds left.

I dropped the dogs off back at the Esstäbchen after we had circled the block. I was worried Henry would rub up against my nice trousers.

With a stroke of brilliance brought on by a delicious apple tart I had grabbed on my walk, I went straight to the upholstery store that was very close to my old apartment. I had only been in there once before, when I had experimented in making modern art out of old milk crates and had needed some upholstery supplies. I remember they were a very kind elderly couple and had even asked when my exhibit was to be held. I had lied and said Morocco. This seemed to impress them greatly.

As the bell tinkled when I opened the door, I remembered they had asked for a postcard. I would remind them that the Moroccan mail is slow.

This was not necessary, though, as they did not remember me when I entered. In fact, the shopowner's wife didn't even look up from her hand of Solitaire. Now, I know I was losing my influence, but I didn't realize it could sting so, even before these ragtag seniors. Perhaps they were senile.

"Hullo, sir. Can I help ya?" the shopowner husband asked me. He was crouched down inspecting a drawer. He wore sleeve garters like a banker. They lent him an air of authority that was lost the moment I noticed he was missing three teeth.

"Yes, hello. I'm in need of two things. For my *art exhibit* coming up. It's in *Istanbul.* You may remember, I am an artist. An esteemed artist."

"I'm sorry, sir. I'm not sure we can place ya. Have you been in here before?"

"Nevermind that. I've been touring the Levantine for a few months now for inspiration for my upcoming show in Istanbul."

"Very nice, sir. We're a furniture place, though. Do you need help with anything?"

Obviously the man's senility had rendered him immune to my influence. Perhaps once you get to a certain age, you lose your your wonderment at class and influence along with your teeth. Not a bright future to look forward to, given my strong and attractive teeth.

"Yes, I am in need of fabric dye and your strongest glue. I mean, your *strongest*. I need it to hold in transit. As I mentioned, my show is in Istanbul."

"Ain't that in County Roscommon? That ain't that far." These were the first words the wife had spoken. She looked back down at her cards, her head dancing a little to a song heard only by her.

"No, ma'am. It's in Turkey."

"Sorry, son. We don't sell turkeys," she said. "You can try next door, though."

I was not sure where she meant. Their shop was sandwiched between an optometrist and a Girl Guide outpost.

To my surprise, the shopowner didn't even seem to notice. He walked back to a cabinet and returned with two items. One read: TARZAN'S GRIP. The other read: LIQUID IRON.

I asked which one was safe for dogs. The shopowner put on his glasses to inspect the label for any sign. I was grateful he did not ask if I would be using it on dogs. Unfortunately, the labels gave no indication of toxicity to canines. I asked which one was cheaper and went with Tarzan's Grip, which I felt was a little more natural-sounding than Liquid Iron.

He then led me to a little back room that held a cabinet of curiosities. From underneath he pulled a hamper that held sachets and bottles of fabric dyes. Bright cornflowers and deep yellows the color of curries. Some were startlingly beautiful and I hoped suddenly that one day we could dye a dog green, even if it was just for the hell of it.

He rifled through his stock and looked up apologetically.

"I'm sorry, sir, we're all out of black dye. We won't get a shipment in for another week."

"Well, that just won't do! Istanbul is expecting my work by this weekend."

"You can always use my phone to explain, sir. I don't believe it's terribly expensive to call County Roscommon from here."

I grabbed the deepest purple and hoped it would do. I took the coins from my pocket and laid them on the table and walked out quickly and exasperatedly. Out the door I heard the wife say, "He must not want turkey that bad, the butcher shop's in the other direction."

XVIII

A Wig for a Spaniel

The only thing I had ever dyed was Easter Eggs, and I will tell you that dyeing a Bichon Frise is not the same. For one, an egg is usually dyed in small cups and they end up being very pretty things. For another, the whole process takes about half an hour, after which one can enjoy a roast or whatever else for Easter supper.

To dye a dog is an undertaking. It takes two grown men and a large tub. The tub came from one of Dreisbach's all-male productions of *Othello*. Perhaps the spirit of Desdemona got into me as I scrubbed and scrubbed the tub after the dyeing was done. I was manic and yet for days I still saw spots of purple every time I closed my eyes.

Henry, for his part, was troublesome. It was especially disheartening because we had explained to him that two-hundred pounds was a lot of money. We also explained to him that Toffie was very rich and he would not have to share slices of ham with other dogs. In fact, he may not even have to eat ham (unless, of course, he wanted to). It was useless, though. Bichon Frises are not known for their cleverness. And Henry, though a swell companion, isn't even a clever Bichon Frise.

Horace's brute size would have easily pinned Henry to the tub, but Horace still was nowhere to be found. Instead, it was Dreisbach and me. I have very small hands, so I was no use. All I could do was hold onto

Henry's collar and dodge the torrents as he splashed. Dreisbach, who is very short, was eye-level with Henry while he poured the dye mix over his coat. We both wished we had pairs of sleeve braces for ourselves. Perhaps the furniture owner and his wife also had an entire dog-dyeing business in their shop. Perhaps this was why his sleeves were protected and he was out of black dye.

No one can ever be trusted completely, I am finding out.

When Henry was done, he was aubergine. I cannot deny it was a beautiful shade of aubergine, but it was not black. We thought that if he had stayed in longer he would have gotten darker. Instead, it seemed as though it just intensified the purple. He looked very regal. His teeth were slightly purple, too, which was alarming. I supposed I would just avert my eyes from the lower half of his face. Was this how the Austrians felt when they saw a Hapsburg?

When it was all done, eight towels were now colored in shades of lilac, plum, and mauve, each subsequent towel a shade lighter than the last. Dreisbach's shirt and trousers were totally ruined. My left hand was mottled and looked like a bruise. Henry, oblivious to his new shade, sat on the cool floor, panting in delight at the extra attention.

"Sorry about your clothes, old man. We can buy more when the cheque clears, as they say."

"*Pas de soucis*, my dear chum. Just a bit of paint. Really adds to the look I'm going for anyway."

"And what look is that?" I said between breaths.

"Why, I thought it was obvious, with me giving up drinking on Sundays. I've become very inspired by the Papacy. I saw a very impressive get-up on a priest the other week. He was buying some matches and was wearing these beautiful purple robes. *Je ne sais pas*. Anyway, what do you think he was buying matches for? Don't you think the Church would give them away for free? Well, either way. I like the way he dressed, so I think I'm going to convert. If I have a confirmation, I think I'll take the name Jude. Isn't that nice? Jude Paul Driscoll. Has a nice ring to it, *c'est vrai*?

How nice it would be to reinvent yourself whenever you want, the way Dreisbach does. Myself, I was cuffed to my name, and all because of my splendid signature. Alas! How many more lives could I have lived if not for my outstanding penmanship?

Dreisbach went on and on and I was no longer listening. Both Henry and I settled down to rest. I was careful to not rest my hand on my head while I napped. I didn't want to wake up with a heather-colored stain on my face.

It was a small nap because we had work to do. Rue was next, but she would be easy. It was a simple matter of spreading a line of glue over her eyes and holding her still for thirty seconds. It was so easy, I did it myself. Dreisbach would have found a shortcut. He would have only pressed it on for twenty seconds or not used enough of Tarzan's Fist. I said he could take a shower and that I would handle it from there.

I am am unusually honest man and remarkably humble. I am not too masculine to admit when I have made a mistake. I made a mistake with Rue. I was holding her on her back against my lap with the glue applicator in my hand. She has always been very easy to handle and so I had let my guard down. Well, if you have never handled a King Charles Spaniel then you would know that they are not very good at breathing. I had forgotten and by the time I had craned her head to apply the glue she was snorting and sneezing like mad. The glue went in a diagonal line from eye to ear. I panicked and slapped on the first wig I managed to lay my hands on. It was blonde and curly, utterly unlike the one Toffie had seen Rue in. Not only that, but it was crooked.

Rue smiled, coughed, and smiled again. I cried for Dreisbach. He came running in, dripping wet with his towel mercilessly held over his frontside by one hand.

"Jesus Christ, Arthur! What the hell did you do?"

This was not very Catholic of Dreisbach, but I guess all good endeavours take practice. For instance, I should have practiced gluing a wig on a dog. For Dreisbach, he should practice not using the Lord's name in vain.

"Is it...noticeable?"

"Well, that depends. Are either Toffie or her Russian fellow particularly nearsighted?"

"Not that I know of," I said, remembering that Aleksi drove trucks and Toffie could dress herself fairly well.

"Hmmm. Well, we can try to cut it ourselves, but I'm a little shaky lately, Arthur. I haven't had a drink in a few days."

"And all I got are my manicure scissors anyway."

"I do have a friend, a *coiffeuse* who helps with my shows sometimes. She would do it, but she may want to be paid if she comes over."

"Paid? To fix a dog's hair?"

"Well, paid for the wig. It was hers, you see."

"Fine. Call her. But it's coming out of your cut."

"*Naturellement.*"

Tully St. Germayn stood at the door of the Theatre. Tully did not blink. She stared. A lot. She was not, otherwise, unattractive, but the no blinking and lots of staring thing made her so. She made me self-conscious about my own movements. She made me wonder if I was blinking *too* much. I hid my hands in my pockets as much as I could. If her eyes wandered to my slight, feminine hands, I would have been more aware of them than ever before.

Luckily, Tully must have trained as a naval officer before she became a hairdresser, because she immediately walked in with a straight spine and shook our hands sharply and produced a pair of shears from her jacket pocket. She grabbed Rue by the scruff of her neck (ignoring Rue's surprised yelp, I may add) and began chopping.

A minute later she was done, looping her shears around her finger like a Western cowboy with his pistol, and replaced it in her pocket-cum-holster. She still did not blink, nor say a word.

"Tully, you did wonderful work! The only problem is...err...you trimmed the wrong hair. It was the wig that needed trimmed, not her ears."

"Huh? Oh...Oh! I'm sorry, Dreisbach. I just got my eyes dilated. I thought I did a pretty good job."

"Well, see here, Tully," I said. "Now we have to glue a second wig to her ears to make up for your mistake!"

"Not one of my wigs, you're not!"

"Yes, one of your wigs! Two, if we need them!"

Finally! I got a blink out of the old drill sergeant! She tightened her fists and walked towards me. Both Dreisbach and Henry stood in her way.

"Now, *mes amis*, let's consider this. Tully, you really should have told us you had an eye appointment and Arthur, you really shouldn't have glued that wig on the dog. So really, you're both wrong. So, Tully, here's an envelope. Write your name and address and we'll send you your money by Friday morning. And keep your shears here. We'll fix this right up and I'll drop those off too."

As Dreisbach was talking, he pushed her toward the door. As he opened it, she walked into the frame. And as she stumbled out he shut it.

Dreisbach apologized with a shrug. "Tully's always been a little off," he said. "But she's very good when she can see."

"Are we really going to pay her back for three wigs and her terrible service?"

"No, *mon ami*! Didn't you see? She wrote her address on the forwarding slip for the Post Office. Now the debt collectors will bother her for a bit—-and leave us alone!"

I was beginning to think Dreisbach would make an excellent Catholic. After all, he was perfectly capable of robbing Peter to pay Paul.

Rue, tired from the excitement, snoozed on my lap while Dreisbach glued two halves of a red wig to her ears and cleaned up the fringe a bit to not look so sideways. She sneezed when the bottle of Tarzan's Fist wafted too close to her nose but looked very fetching when the process was complete.

The small crisis that Dreisbach caused, he also solved. I conjured an image of St. Peter scratching his head as Dreisbach arrived at the Gates of Heaven. His list of Good Deeds would be exactly as long as his list of Bad Deeds. Peter would have to call in for back-up. He may even have to consult the Lord for his advice, so equally helpful and harmful had Dreisbach been to his mortal compatriots. Ultimately, he would be put in Limbo, I suppose, along with crying babies and clueless pagans. Which was a perfect place for Dreisbach, who looked in his white face makeup like a mix between Dionysus and a Gerber baby.

Lucky for us, we had an entire day for Henry's coat to dry and for us to fix up any trimmings we had on Rue. Henry was sequestered to one of the back dressing rooms. He did not seem to mind too much. Dreisbach was worried he would turn the red carpet purple. I was worried for dear, nervous Henry. He really does not like surprises.

Dreisbach had also dipped one of his dressing gowns into the tub before we had drained it into the alleyway. It was drying in the cellar. It did look quite papal.

And as for me, my hand was still bruised-looking and splotchy. I was only slightly upset, as I now had an excuse to wear a pair of opera gloves I had found in a vanity drawer while I was looking for a match. While I am terribly embarrassed by my small hands, it is no secret that women's gloves are generally of a higher quality than men's. And when they are tucked under the sleeves of a sportcoat, who can tell the difference?

Luckily, I did not have gloves on that morning because Horace showed up at the Theatre. He was unshaven and looked even more like a Neanderthal than usual. He held his hat in his hands in front of his belly like a school boy asking for forgiveness. I simply continued to eat my boiled egg.

"Hullo, Horace. You haven't been around lately!"

"Dreisbach," Horace answered as his response. I suppose in those few days he was gone he had not developed a softness for Dreisbach as I had. And I doubted he'd like Dreisbach any more once he found out Dreisbach was getting his share of the next two sales.

"Arthur, I got your letter."

"Which one? I sent four."

"I got all your letters."

"Did you leave your glasses here? I figured perhaps you couldn't read the letters. Why didn't you respond?"

"I needed some time. A lot's going on, Arthur, and I'm not like you. Or him for that matter."

Here, Horace nodded his head at Dreisbach, who was in a flimsy towel tucked at his waste and was eating a handful of peanuts over the garbage can.

"Yes, we know, Horace. You're not influential. That's the difference."

"Well, I wouldn't put it like that. I'd say I do a pretty good job of..."

"A pretty good job of calling me a liar and a thief."

"That's why I'm here. I wanted to tell you I was wrong. You were just helping. I didn't understand that at first and I needed some time to think."

"Well, while you were thinking, we were very busy, weren't we, Dreisbach, old man? We have two sales tomorrow. Almost five hundred quid! Both are within walking distance, so we won't need your car. Is there anything else I can do for you?"

"Arthur, come on. I needed a little space. I needed some time. I can't just be pushed into breaking and entering and expect to forget about it."

"Breaking and entering? You mean the Cormants? Oh, come now! You tell that to Celia. I doubt she'd call it a crime to come back to her family."

"Well, Arthur, I don't think Celia would care about the watch you're wearing from Mr. Cormant. But anyway, I needed to think, Arthur. I move at a slower pace than you."

Oh, thinking! Everyone who has ever thought has never been influential. The Duke of Lombardo, when I served him his ice water, didn't think. He just knew he was thirsty. He didn't think about the calories in it. He didn't think about tipping me (he did not tip me). He simply existed in the moment and laid the drinking glass back on my tray. People who think are not influential. A simple fact of life that Horace has never seemed to grasp.

I went back to my egg, which was all but finished. I scraped the inside of the shell with my spoon. I did not want to move and I had nothing to say. I did not want to raise my left hand too much, for fear of waving Mr. Cormant's watch around. It was a Very Nice Watch. Was it a crime to like Nice Watches now, too? I think Horace didn't see the same picture as I did. Once we had rotated enough dogs through the Newton-Wiggs, then we could start to buy our own watches. I would buy my own Very Nice Watch and return this one to Mr. Cormant. I would probably hide it in a potted plant or something for him to find next Spring. I believe a fellow like Mr. Cormant would think this was a funny story to tell at parties later in life. So, really, I was doing him a favor. Horace, though he did not wear glasses, was very short-sighted indeed.

Horace waited motionlessly for me to answer. I am not sure if you have ever been watched while you were pretending to eat from an empty boiled egg shell, but it is disconcerting. I coughed just to make noise. I chewed the little white bits on the spoon more than was necessary. I reached for a drink and for the salt shaker after each little bite. Finally, I put my fork down and put my hands on the table.

Horace gasped. His eyes focused on my left hand, the one dyed purple.

"What—what happened, Arthur?"

I am a good person and a good friend, but Horace was wrong to ignore my letters. Dreisbach had taken his peanuts to share with the dogs so I was free to make up a story for Horace, and so I did.

XIX

The Nicest Room in the Theatre

Horace thought I had been seriously injured since I had last seen him at the pub after the Parade. He looked very worried on my behalf, which only slightly assuaged my annoyance. I say only slightly, as I lied to Horace all the same to make him feel guilty.

"So kind of you to notice, Horace—-after berating me and ignoring me—-just how much pain I've been in."

I winced and held my purpled, mottled hand for dramatic effect.

Horace has a face like a potato sack, by which I mean there are large pores and deep creases no matter how it rests. His eyebrows furrowed inwards. He was curious to know more.

"Arthur," he asked. "What happened? Did you get into an accident?"

"Something like that," I said. "Dreisbach and I weren't sure how we would transport the dogs to and fro, as the demand for Mr. Tamassy's purebreds picked up after the Parade. The only option was to learn how to drive myself."

"You didn't!"

"I did, old man. I absolutely did. And I have to say, I miss the days of palanquins or even ox-tows. Let me say, the only clutch I am familiar with was Mrs. Rublack's purse when she left it on her kitchen counter. I had no idea there were so many parts to an automobile."

"Doesn't Dreisbach know how to drive?"

"Oh, he does. He does. But seeing as how he had not given the car back to the salesperson yet, and it's going on two weeks, he thought it best to not be seen in the driver's seat, on the off chance we encountered the salesperson strolling along on the same road. Salespeople really aren't good at letting others borrow their things. It's an affliction they bear."

Horace nodded. He, too, must have had certain somebodies calling him to return the odd Daimler or spinning globe. As I have said all along, Horace only now, at thirty-six, was beginning to understand the world. Finding himself suddenly poor opened his eyes a bit, I think.

"So, I don't want to go into the gruesome details of just how it happened, Horace." (I did not know enough about driving to lie confidently.) "But suffice it to say that we hit a tree and my whole body is banged up and it's quite your fault."

It is not that I wanted to put the blame on Horace, but that blaming him did alleviate some of remaining anger I had toward him. Horace and I, in our years of friendship, did not fight often. So when we did, I held onto it quite badly. Plus, I rationalized, perhaps Horace knew of a better place to buy black fabric dye. I would not have had to settle for an aubergine dog had he been at the Esstäbchen. So, in a way, somehow or other, my purple hands were his fault.

When I was younger, we did not own much of anything, including a radio. I would often hear music on my teachers' wirelesses in the silent periods between classes and exams and I would catch a small verse here and there. I would replay these verses in my head over and over again to hold onto while I was resting in bed. Eventually, through such repetition, the words would lose their meaning.

Apologies sometimes have the same effect on me, and Horace's were no different. He apologized so often that day that, eventually, I didn't want to hear another word from his mouth. I became utterly annoyed at Horace's apologies, in fact, because I tend to believe apologizing to be highly *un*-influential. It was not the way men handled business and I told Horace just that. Instead, I asked him for cash, which I believe is a more effective business practice. Horace only had a one-pound note on him. I pocketed it, wincing theatrically to remind him of my bruised hands.

We were now even, which was a blessing. I would eventually need Horace's car, so I was grateful for his guilty conscience.

The next step was to hide Henry's botched dye job while also keeping it from Horace. Even Horace, who is generally an oaf, would have been able to put two and two together when he saw my purple hands and Henry's purple coat.

I needed to get Horace out of the house and sell Henry to Toffie quickly. For this, I had to find a moment to speak with Dreisbach without Horace. Who knew that, in less than a month, I would be conspiring against Horace with Dreisbach as my confidante? I suppose we were all a little desperate then.

I excused myself with a vague and slightly ominous excuse: Dreisbach needed me to assist him with some bandages from the car accident. And no, Horace could not come to help as they were in a very private location. I believe the thought of Dreisbach's private locations repulsed Horace enough to stay in the kitchen while I searched the rest of the Theatre for that toad, Dreisbach.

He was asleep in his room, surrounded by peanut shells. Fat, snoring Milly was by his side. She had taken a liking to Dreisbach over the past week, if for no other reason than that she could be his Hoover when he dropped a peanut shell here or an apple core there.

I had no time for Dreisbach and so I shook him a little too roughly. Milly moved complacently aside and I sat on the bed with Dreisbach, who was bleary-eyed with half of his make-up now smudged onto his pillow and forearm. I explained the situation quickly and quietly and all the while Dreisbach was only half paying attention, having spent the time fishing for his sunglasses, which had been lost in a pile of blankets.

"...so, we need to get Toffie here *today* and Horace out of the house until at least tonight."

I was not sure if Dreisbach heard anything I said but he looked up and nodded. He had a glass of water on the floor next to his bed and drank the entire thing in a single gulp. He scratched his stomach and said in just one word:

"Paper."

I grabbed a pad from a milk crate stack he used as a sort of bookshelf and he pulled a hidden pencil from a flower pot that had long since bid farewell to the Aloe Vera plant within. A plant like that can last months or maybe even years in a desert, but that on didn't survive in the Esstäbchen for a fraction of that time. I took this as a terrible omen, which fueled my desire to get the dogs sold.

"Gimme a minute," came Dreisbach's next command. He was clearly in a contemplative mood. Perhaps his luncheon of peanuts had had a sobering effect on his otherwise flamboyant attitude. Whatever the case, I did as I was told. (It is important to make this distinction clear: I did as Dreisbach told not because I respected him, but because we were in a hurry.)

I stepped back to give Dreisbach space and surveyed his room. It was not a nice room, but it was the nicest room in the Theatre. I will describe it here.

I believe that when this place was a Chinese restaurant, this room housed the beverages, as a corner of the room was occupied by a large icebox. On top of that icebox sat a lot of framed photos, as one might arrange on a grand piano. Some were of Dreisbach, portraits taken in his younger (and thinner) days. Others were photographs of starlets. The majority, though, were of young men. Many at the beach, a few at what appeared to be a gymnasium set up in the photographer's studio. One even held a riding crop, although there was no horse to be seen. One thing all the men had in common were that they were hairless and wore no pants. I was unsure if this was a new fashion in actor's casting photos or another perversion of Dreisbach's. Either way, I turned my head, slightly embarrassed.

One wondered: were these photos acting as a sort of subconscious incubus? Did they poison Dreisbach's mind as he slept, leading him to direct such venereal productions as the all-male casting of *Taming of the Shrew*? The all-male casting of *Carmen?* The all-male casting of *The Greeks Had a Word for It?* This last one did quite well, until people realized just what the Greek word was.

The room also housed three braided wicker baskets, each one urn-shaped and topped with a braided wicker lid. They were of the sort one sees in illustrations of snake charmers in India. It appeared that wherever one set one's eyes in Dreisbach's room, one found danger. I turned away, not the least bit curious what those baskets may have contained.

On the wall hung a dartboard, empty of darts but full of pencils, many of which were scarred by angry-looking bite marks. Below that was a pile of newspapers. Next to that was an overflowing ashtray. Next to that was a hat box full of wine bottle corks. Next to that, a telephone, unplugged (to avoid debt collectors) but still a very pretty shade of robin's egg.

My stomach was nauseous. Not least because I found Dreisbach's room to be gross and disorderly, but also because it was the Nicest Room in the whole Theatre, and it was being wasted as a sort of venereal den, a museum of Dreisbach's many pecadillos and transgressions, an exhibit of his various vices.

I found it to be entirely corrupt.

Interrupting me as I wallowed in the injustice of it all, Dreisbach handed me back the paper I had given to him. On it was a note, in a rounded and feminine handwriting. It read:

> Mr. Wimbly,
>
> I am not sure if you remember, but I am Vanessa Smith. I am an assistant at the auction house where a few of your items were sent. I wanted to inform you that one of your dictionaries was worth quite a lot.
>
> At the request of the purchaser, I would like to provide you with an additional cheque, the difference being adjusted for the slight windfall we received from the auction.
>
> I will be at your house on Wednesday of the week to hand

deliver the check. Due to the amount, I must have you sign a ledger for us.

Thank you in advance.

As with all letters we sent during our dog selling enterprise, it required a little bit of creativity and hope that the recipients trusted in the social contract in believing that which is written, unless marked FICTION on its spine, is hardly ever a lie. Luckily, Dreisbach was a creative man and Horace was altogether too naïve.

I returned to the kitchen and handed Horace the letter. I told him that it had arrived just that morning. It seemed too important to wait so I opened it and no, I did not have the envelope it came in. He read the letter once and was out the door in a minute.

I could have kissed Dreisbach for being such a help in getting that oaf Horace out the door, but I am glad I did not. He had a bit of peanut shell stuck in his teeth.

Next, we had to ensure that Toffie would take Henry before Horace returned. I did not want Horace to find the purple-dyed dog and discover that I had been lying about my accident. I found the lie to be useful, as now Horace would feel too guilty to refuse to chauffeur me around. It really was quite a good lie.

This required quick thinking but also an active phone line.

Our quick thinking centered around how best to get Toffie to take Henry without realizing that he was purple and not black. I thought that we may have to pour a well of ink on him, but ink is expensive and I had many letters to write in those days. Instead, we used our setting to our advantage: we would blind Toffie with the Essstäbchen's stage lights and force her to wear sunglasses while we handed Henry over.

Next, the active phone line.

Because we all of us were avoiding debt collectors, no phone in the Theatre worked. Dreisbach's neighbor, a Miss Bonnet, had a phone line and it was a very active one indeed. I knew this because she was forever cackling into it at all hours of the early morning.

Miss Bonnet was not home, thankfully. And I was even more

thankful to find that her back door was unlocked. To be on the safe side, I brought Celia with me to Miss Bonnet's as a guard dog, as she was very protective and also because I had not walked her recently. We shared a few leftover pieces of chicken that were left on Miss Bonnet's countertop and I rang Toffie. Her number was listed in the NWS directory. Given her exchange code, I was not surprised it was listed. Toffie was the kind of person who practically walked around with a magnifying glass, looking for any little crevice into which she could insert her wealth.

She picked up on the first ring.

"Ms. Mountmaarten? Toffie? This is Arthur. Good afternoon."

"G'afternoon, sir. But I don't believe I know any Arthurs. Are you looking for Aleksi?

"Toffie, it's Arthur Croots from the Newton-Wiggs. I'm the Chair of our Committee."

"Oh, yes! I'm sorry. I was filing my nails and only half paying attention. For some reason I thought your name was William or Roger or something."

I was not sure if this was a compliment and it has eaten at my pride ever since.

"Well, it's Arthur. Or at least that's what my mother called me, ha ha. Anyway, I wanted to let you know that Mr. Tamassy was very impressed with your credentials and your obvious kind heart and would love for you to have his *minuit frise*. But you must hurry. It was my understanding that you were to meet later this week in the Park. Well, he has had a call from his mother and he must return home expediently. I'm sure you understand. Are you free now? Can you take Hen--the dog now?"

"Oh, I suppose, but I really was quite busy with my nails. I hope Mr. Tamassy won't mind if only half are filed."

"Well, to be frank, Ms. Montmaarten, he'll only be looking at your hands to see if you have the cash in them. He's very distraught about his mother and this money will help with his grieving I am sure."

"Oh, how terrible. Yes, I understand. I'll be right over. Where is Mr. Tamassy staying? The Ritz?"

I nearly laughed aloud at the idea of Dreisbach at The Ritz. I had an idea that the concierges at such places have a discrete signal for the security man to kindly escort the Dreisbachs of the world out onto the street where they belonged.

"Oh no, he isn't staying anywhere in particular. I cannot quite say if he has even slept since the Parade. You know how Australians are, Toffie. They live in the Outback and all that. He's currently at a small theatre called the Esstäbchen. He's in talks with the owner about putting on a play about his life."

I had just enough time to give Toffie the Theatre's address before I had to hang up abruptly and feed Celia another piece of chicken to keep her from growling as Miss Bonnet's keys jangled onto the table in the other room.

XX

Blinding the Sugar Heiress

It was an hour and a half later when Toffie's cab pulled up to the Essstäbchen. I believe the delay was due to her finishing her nails. She seemed also to be trying something new with her makeup. Her eyes were dark with purple eyeshadow. She did not immediately smile when she looked up from the cab window.

I welcomed her tardiness, as it gave me more time to get Dreisbach into character and be made presentable, meaning no peanut shells in his teeth, for example. The extra time also made me a bit nervous, as Horace could have returned at any moment, frustrated by having missed Vanessa Smith, whoever and wherever she may have been.

I shook Toffie's hand as she entered the Theatre. We both looked down. I was wearing a Very Nice Pair of opera gloves. And her nails were, indeed, filed.

"Tamassy doesn't want me touching the animals. Germs, you know." It was the best excuse I could muster.

We made a sharp left into the main seating area of the theatre I gave a quick knock to signal our arrival, at which point the dogs began barking madly. Dreisbach took his cue and opened the door quickly, but not before turning all the stage lights on and pointing them directly at Toffie's face.

She held a hand to her face and stumbled. It was a devious of us, but we really did want the cash and had to act quickly.

"Can someone please turn off the lights?"

Dreisbach, as Mr. Winston Meredith Tamassy, took her newly manicured hand and kissed it.

"My apologies, Sheila, but no can do. We're about to film here and the lighting has to be perfect. I know it's bright. I know. But we're recreating the sunny Outback and all that."

"Of course," she said. "I understand show business all too well."

"I knew it! Ask Arthur. Arthur, didn't I say that Ms. Montmaarten was a movie type of gal? Didn't I just say that? Here, darling, take these sunglasses."

Toffie put the sunglasses on and smiled. I was surprised at how sensitive she was to the lights. Perhaps she was hungover or perhaps she was part albino on her mother's side, the way one can be "part French" or "a quarter Cherokee."

The dark sunglasses we had given Toffie were shaded even darker with a wood varnish from Dreisbach's set design closet. When I tried them on, I saw only shadows and indistinct objects. Henry no longer appeared purple through the glasses, which was good. But he did blend into the floor a little bit, which was bad.

"I'm sorry to hear about your mother, by the way, Mr. Tamassy."

"Oh, my mother? Yes, she's dead. Now do you have the two-hundred for the *minuit frise* on hand?"

"Oh yes, I usually carry a lot of cash on me. Can I see the beautiful puppy first?"

"Of course!"

Dreisbach whistled using his two index fingers like a Texas rancher and four dogs came bumbling onto the theatre stage, with fat little Milly taking up the rear and panting happily.

I, too, had sunglasses on and I could see that Henry's coat had mellowed slightly. I picked him up off the stage and handed him over to Toffie.

"Oh, he's beautiful! Such a lovely coat. And how friendly! I love him already."

I am convinced dogs possess a supernatural charm. Even the most haughty of women are disarmed by a friendly dog. Dogs are very influential in that way, which is another reason I like them.

Toffie handed Dreisbach an envelope that was marked, "Fun Money," and allowed Henry to kiss her face. Imagine! Having so much money that you can divide it into little paper envelopes based on mood! If I had labeled money envelopes, they would be: Flower Money, Perfume Money, Navy Suit Money, Restaurant Money, Travel Money, Emergency Money, and Getaway Money.

I could feel our little congress waning and here I felt it was critical that Toffie keep her sunglasses on. Short of blinding her permanently, we had to keep her ignorant to Henry's true coloring. I found women like Toffie—rich women, that is—will do nearly anything out of vanity. Take high heels for example. They look torturous, and yet millions of women wear them every day. Vanity is the great equalizer among Women of Means.

"Ms. Montmaarten! My God! How gorgeous! The light! The hair against those dark glasses. Simply stunning, if I may be so bold."

I do not often compliment women on their looks, because I know few women and I am not interested in their looks. Because of this, I was worried I did not sound very convincing.

"Really, Arthur? You think so?"

"Oh, yes! Mr. Tamassy. Come look! Why, the halo of blonde hair is simply magnificent. A Boticelli! A Da Vinci! A Rembrandt!"

"It's those sunnies, boy. They just add a little mystery to the girl. If I didn't have a Sheila back home on the barbie or whatever, I'd be asking you to dinner tonight, Miss Toffie. Hell to Aleksi!" Dreisbach laughed and tapped Toffie on her backside.

"Oh, but I can't even see a thing in these," she said, reaching to remove them.

"Keep them on!" Insisted Dreisbach. "Keep them on! You have people to see things for you. Everyone in the Southern Hemisphere wears glasses all day long, even all night long. It's true! I read it in the paper just yesterday. Give it a try. We need a bit of shaking-up on this dreary island, don't you think? Ha ha!"

"But how will I get home?"

"A taxi!"

"And how will I feed the dog?"

"He's already eaten!"

"Even at night I should wear these things?"

"Especially at night, Ms. Montmaarten! That's when people want women with mystique the most."

Vanity makes people all too credulous. Toffie Montmaarten stumbled out of the Theatre with Henry in tow. She only tripped once as she walked to a waiting cab. And she never took off her sunglasses, not even for a second.

XXI

A Con, Indeed

Dreisbach and I had a celebratory sherry at the kitchen table. Our spirits high, we schemed other ways to blind rich women into giving us envelopes of cash. It seemed that Toffie hadn't even counted the amount she had allocated for the purchase of the dog. The envelope contained nearly four hundred pounds. We divided it evenly between us. Fun Money, indeed!

The last of the bills had been pocketed when Horace came through the door. It was near dinnertime and I was getting worried. Not worried for Horace's safety, but that he wouldn't remember it was near dinnertime and arrive home without food for me.

Alas, he had arrived empty-handed. Later I would eat two boiled eggs and a parmesan rind, too knackered even to dine out in celebration of our windfall.

"Hullo, Horace. How'd your date go with the auction lady?"

"Never showed up!I waited for hours. Nothing."

"How very queer," I said. "And you are sure you were at the right house?"

"I only own one."

"Quite. Hm. Maybe it was a scam and she chickened out. Or maybe they got the value of whatever you sold them wrong. Either way, I'm sure you're exhausted. Come have a drink."

"It's just maddening is all. I had things to do today and instead I waited around the house for a stranger to show up."

"Oh, Horace. Wait until you have a job! You'll learn all about being on someone else's schedule."

Horace enjoyed a nip of sherry with us and we talked about nothing important. Horace did not like Dreisbach and he did not really care for the dogs either, so he broached neither of those subjects. I wondered if he would even notice Henry was missing. Probably not. Horace was becoming rather self-absorbed.

At that kitchen table, with the small light and the grimy countertop, I saw that the last few weeks had aged Horace terribly. While I have often described him as an oaf, he was looking much worse than I had ever seen him looking before. He had graduated from an oaf to a has-been. His eyes had creases where they hadn't before and his lips looked dry, no matter how thoroughly he licked them before and after his every sip of sherry. It had been a while since I had sat across from Horace and enjoyed a drink without scheming and plotting.

At last, Horace yawned and I placed my hand on his shoulder. I had grown quite tender towards Horace, worried for my friend's health. Plus, it would have been a pity to have Horace take ill, right when we needed his car the most.

"Get some rest, old man."

* * * * * *

On Thursday we had our appointment with Fanny Maybrick, and my only hope was that she had not spoken to Toffie Montmaarten about her purple dog. We needed Fanny to have faith in Mr. Tamassy. Our entire enterprise hinged on Toffie's vanity.

Thursday morning I had also received a telegram alerting me to an impromptu Newton-Wiggs meeting to be held that same day. The meeting was at four, which gave us plenty of time to make the sale and then I would escort Fanny with me to the Office. On the way, I would make sure to compliment Fanny's ear off about her new dog. How clever she was, how lucky she was. Anything I could do to fill her head with confidence, in the chance that the NWS meeting had been called regarding Toffie's purple dog. We needed Fanny to believe us and not her. It was strictly business.

Dreisbach once again became Mr. Tamassy, but it became clear that, in the short time he had been playing this character, the role began to bore him. Either that or he feared he could not pull of another convincing performance. His latest suggestion for Mr. Tamassy's backstory involved amnesia; he would forget where he came from, and perhaps his accent would change. Maybe he awoke only speaking French. (Elementary French, one presumes.) Perhaps he could even wear a bandage around his head for additional ornamentation?

I drew upon my expertise in reverse psychology. All the way to the park, I told Dreisbach how jealous I was of his Australian accent and his creativity. How it was an enormous injustice he wasn't more successful and that us Englishman just didn't understand his Continental flair. This seemed to work, as it was most definitely Mr. Tamassy who walked up to Fanny; Dreisbach had been left somewhere on the pavement a block or two behind.

Willowy and sad, there stood Frances Maybrick von Uttler-Smith-Jones-Carter-Unsworth. I have said once before that I believe rings to be a great signal of influence and Fanny's topped them all. Having been married so many times, she had many beautiful wedding and engagement rings adorning her fingers. She had to stack two or three to a hand, some wriggling their way well above the knuckle. She was devilishly rich, which made her very attractive to me. She was also extremely depressive, which made her slightly repulsive to me. I would never know if Fanny had married so many times for love, for money, or to trick herself into believing she was not lonely.

This only convinced me that Rue was the right choice for Fanny, who desperately needed a companion. She had no children of her own and, from what I recall, a huge house in Kensington. All that room and no one to chase around the halls, I thought. No wonder she was depressed.

Fanny waved a small wave and looked like it drained a great store of energy for her to smile in our direction. I waved back and Dreisbach (Tamassy) tilted his hat in her direction. He was wearing a trilby. I had never seen it before in my life and it made him look like a pulp detective more than a distinguished Australian dog breeder.

"Ms. Maybrick! Hullo hullo! So good to see you on this lovely Spring day!"

"Mr. Tamassy, and you! How do you do, Arthur? All well? Ready for our meeting later today?"

"Oh, quite, Fanny. Though I am not sure what this meeting is about. I got the telegram just as you, I'm sure."

"It can't be anything serious. My guess is they're looking ahead to Summer for fundraising. There seems to be an issue with the Penáges' endowment, which means we're a little strapped. It was in the newsletter. Didn't you get it?"

For a depressive, Fanny did like to talk a lot, but only about the most boring things. My mind had already begun to wander when she mentioned fundraising. We had hardly caught our breath from the Parade!

I decided to veer the conversation back to Rue, who sported a lovely set of wigs on her tiny Spaniel scalp.

"Oh, we can discuss this business on our way to the meeting. Let's introduce you to your new pet!"

Fanny crouched and I crouched and Rue walked timidly up to Fanny. Dreisbach did not crouch, which meant both Fanny and I were eye-level with Dreisbach's crotch. I blushed, but Fanny was busying herself with introductions.

"Well, hello there, lovely. And what is your name?"

Rue, being a dog, did not answer. I am glad she could not speak, as I had a feeling Rue was an honest girl and would not be able to keep our scheme a secret from Fanny. I interjected.

"She doesn't have one! Well, we were calling her Lady, being so regal and all, but she doesn't answer to it. She might be a little stupid, you see."

I hated calling Rue stupid right to her face, but I also needed to nip any further questions about Rue's past life in the bud.

"I've decided to call her Constance," she said. "After the lake in which my late husband, Ferdinand von Uttler, drowned. I did love him quite a lot, you know."

"A very pretty name," Dreisbach answered, patting her on her shoulder tenderly.

"It'll be Con for short."

Too right, I thought.

"A lovely tribute to your husband," I said. "I knew many von Uttlers during the War. They all died, though, so no way to ask if they knew me. Anyway, I believe we agreed upon one-hundred-and-eighty, yes?" Good old Dreisbach, always corralling the conversation back to money.

"Yes, quite. But I apologize, I left my wallet at home. I was hoping to have my maid drop it off at the Newton-Wiggs office and Arthur can deliver the amount later."

"No trouble at all. You, my sweet gal, were the only thing on my diary for the day. Don't worry yourself. You and Arthur attend the meeting and I will take Constance here to your home and pick up the cash myself. How does that sound to you?"

"Mr. Tamassy, I don't want to trouble you. If you can wait a few hours, Arthur, I'm sure, would be happy to give you money."

"Nonsense, I need a stretch anyway. Not used to being cooped up in a city for so long. Missing a bit of activity. Just write down your address (terrible memory since I got decked by a kangaroo a few years back) and I'll drop your little girl right off."

Dreisbach produced a small pencil and a slip of paper from his jacket. He handed them to Fanny, who used her knee as a writing desk.

"Ms. Maybrick, one other thing, go ahead and put a note to your maid that I'll be getting the cash and all. We don't want her thinking I'm a criminal."

Dreisbach turned to me and winked. And in a low whisper only I could hear, he added, "Gave her a pencil so I can change the amount. Three hundred?"

I patted his the shoulder and then Rue's head, tugging slightly on the wig while I did so to make sure it was secure. Fanny handed Dreisbach the paper, Dreisbach kissed Fanny on the hand and we parted towards different park exits.

"Hooroo!" Dreisbach called, waving his trilby in one hand and carrying Rue by the waist in the other.

"Odd man," Fanny said with a monotone. She once again looked very sad.

"Yes, but he's very good at what he does."

I'm happy Fanny did not ask me to expand on this. Dreisbach was very good at swindling hundreds of pounds from depressive widows, but he was only slightly good at pretending to be Australian.

I filled the silence with another, quieter, "Yep..." and let it trail off into the wind like a dandelion clock.

Being a generally positive fellow, I was extremely uncomfortable being alone with Fanny Maybrich. It is not that she was unlikeable, it was simply that she did not possess anything to like. Other than her wealth, she was very boring. When I pointed to a man sleeping in an alley, she did not laugh. When I told her I thought Hannah Grey-Downs would be very pretty if she lost weight, she did not agree. When I told her I would sometimes stay awake at night, scared witless at the thought of Jane Raitland becoming the Mrs. Desmond Winnicott, Lady Ham-sur-Rye. Fanny only half-raised an eyebrow, which I had trouble interpreting. Perhaps she found my fear ridiculous, or salacious even. In my experience, a half-raised eyebrow can only tell one so much.

My problem on that walk was not that I wanted to share so many personal details with Fanny, but that I was running out of things to say and I did not want to walk in silence. My other problem was that I was beginning to mix up my truths and my lies about myself, so that I had to default to my opinions of others. Perhaps Fanny did not reply because she was preoccupied thinking how ugly the name Constance is for a dog. That kind of second-guessing would have kept me silent for a while, too.

A dog's name is extremely personal and should take time. Even though I was the Chair of the Newton-Wiggs Sociéte's Committee, I would not say that I am an expert on All Things Dog. But I knew enough then, as I do now, to know that naming a dog after a the site of a husband's death was not right, perhaps even a bit impolite. Macabre, even.

As I write about my time with Fanny, I must admit that her responses elude me now. The same way one cannot remember the pain of a sore tooth once it has been extracted, my recollection of Fanny's personality conjures only a faint memory of discomfort followed by the relief of it being over.

XXII

The Second Fundraiser

We made it to the NWS Office just in time for the impromptu meeting. I held the door open for Fanny and she slid by without a thank-you. I was tempted to say, "You're welcome," anyway, just to let her know her bad manners were not lost on me. Inside the Newton-Wiggs Sociéte's doors, I was still a Chair and she was not.

I admit that I was walking on eggshells into that shabby meeting room, thinking that Fanny had entrapped me and I would be put on trial for the high crimes of one Mr. Winston Meredith Tamassy. Viscount Spittlewood would, of course, preside over the proceedings, if it were, in fact, a courtroom. Hannah Grey-Downs would no doubt play the prosecution. Jane Raitland, with her farmboy shoulders, would serve as bailiff.

But I was not arrested on the spot. Had the Newton-Wiggs even been deputized to do so? Much to my chagrin, Fanny was correct. It was just a boring old budget meeting, the alarm bells for which were due to Henry Penáges, the heir to the Penáges' fortune, who no longer wanted to supply another penny to what he called, "a frivolous and incestuous pond of chinless and tweed-clad frogs." This was according to Mrs. Grey-Downs.

A bit harsh, I thought, but not entirely wrong.

I identified with Henry Penáges on one level, considering we were both orphans and presumably around the same age. I am sure he would have especially appreciated my exquisite taste and perhaps we would have shared beauty routine secrets if we ever had the chance to meet. I did not have an issue with Henry Penáges, per se, but I was upset that his parsimony resulted in my having to work more than I cared to. He was, as I recall from his parents' funeral, quite handsome when he cried.

The meeting was boring and I spent the hour doodling in the margins of the agenda that had been handed to me by George, our attendant for the day. He smiled toothily, if not self-consciously, when he handed me my paper. I did not return the smile. I swore to never, in a million years, forgive George for speaking so rudely about me to Miss Greenwood.

No amount of kindness would change my mind! I am embarrassed to admit that I can be icy like that.

The only person missing from the meeting was, to my surprise, Toffie Montmaarten. I was worried that perhaps she had finally taken her varnished sunglasses off and had gone to the police with a tale of an Australian man selling her a purple dog. When put down on paper, it does not sound like a convincing story. Perhaps, if Toffie *had* gone to the police, they wouldn't have believed her either. A tale like that can get someone thrown into an asylum. I prayed that was why she was missing from the meeting today. I prayed very hard that she was locked in a padded room somewhere, speaking nonsensically about a purple dog and an antipodean ruffian.

I would be sure to ask Hannah Grey-Downs, who somehow knew all of the goings-on in London. And if the gossip was good enough, I would then pass it onto Desmond, by way of breaking the chill that had formed between us. He looked dashing in a burgundy jacket, which was just a tad too large on his sloping, Venetian shoulders.

By the time I had covered the margins of my agenda, I had drawn four types of flowers and a passable still life of a pigeon eating a banana. I did not take to art easily but I believe these small sketches proved that I had real talent. I was admiring my own work when my name was called. I looked up from the pigeon eating the banana and asked for the question to be repeated.

It was Jane Raitland who had said my name and she once again mumbled her question.

"A little louder, Ms. Raitland. Are you afraid to wake the baby?"

She blushed and Desmond huffed and still I waited for her to repeat her question for the third time.

"Mr. Croots, do you have any ideas for how we can fundraise for the Summer?"

I did not, but I a adept at thinking on my feet, so I took a moment to sip a glass of water, and then another, and then I stroked my chin.

"What about a gala at the theatre?" I said. The idea was barely half-formed by the time it was out of my mouth.

"A gala at the theatre?" Viscount Spittlewood repeated, probably to ensure accurate recording for his minutes.

"Yes...a gala. Yes! I think it's a good idea and not just because I thought of it. Why not? We will dress up. We will sell tickets. We will produce a play or a talent show or even get a few circus performers. Could be something to it."

I did not fully believe in the idea myself, but I also wanted my idea to be the one selected, now that Desmond was looking directly at me.

"A gala at the theatre?"

"A theatre gala?"

"A gala to be held at a theatre?"

As the Committee members mulled over the idea, I knew it had potential. Finally, Hannah Grey-Downs shook her head, which also shook her large bosom, and said, "No, no, no. We can't, Mr. Croots. We can't! It's too expensive. We just made a rather large payment for taxes and the Parade barely covered that!"

"Oh, money! Is that all you people care about?"

"Well," Desmond said with a smile, "we *are* the Fundraising Committee."

"Well, I was hired to be the Chair because I am an expert party planner. The Parade, I'm sorry to say, was not a party. It was a promenade of peacockery. No offense to you, Mrs. Grey-Downs, but you really drop the metaphorical ball. I believe a gala would be something we can all get behind with our talents, by Jove!"

I had rallied the troops, so to speak, and the murmuring continued.

"My very best friend owns a theatre, so it will be free for us to use. I'm sorry I didn't mention that earlier, I didn't think money was of so much importance to everyone here."

We took a vote, my gavel was thumped, and the meeting was adjourned. We would have our fundraising gala at the esteemed Esstabachen Theatre. I was already scheming a way to get Dreisbach to plan the entire thing *and* write a new play for us. Hopefully it would be a co-ed and clothed production this time.

As we filed out of the shabby meeting room, my curiosity as to Toffie's whereabouts still pestered me. Hannah Grey-Downs was digging around in her purse when I walked by.

"Mrs. Grey-Downs, I meant to ask you, do you happen to know where Ms. Montmaarten is today?"

"Oh, she's in a terrible way, our Toffie. Didn't you hear?"

"I'm afraid not. Our social circles don't really overlap." I didn't want to tell her that my social circle consisted solely of an ugly little man, a poor, sad oaf, and four dogs.

"She fell down the stairs two nights ago at her Kensington place, poor thing. I guess she had eye surgery as she was wearing extremely dark sunglasses at night. She broke her leg, but luckily is back home in her own bed now."

"Oh, how awful! Should we send flowers?"

"Already taken care of. Ms. Greenwood is there right now on our behalf."

Oh, I am sure she was, that Ms. Greenwood. Always a saint, I thought.

"Between you and me, Mr. Croots, I have a thought that her boyfriend Aleksi has strained Toffie a bit - mentally, I mean. Did you know that, for some reason, she had dyed her dog *purple*?"

"No!"

"It's true! My cousin, Lady Seychelle heard it from her charwoman. You know how they talk."

"I didn't even know Ms. Montmaarten had a dog!"

"Nor did I, Mr. Croots. Nor did I. It's my belief for us to keep our eyes open around that Aleksi. I believe him to be a criminal. And one wonders if Toffie really *fell* down those steps!"

Mrs. Grey-Downs had an active imagination, but I did not want to openly question her theory. In my experience in entrepreneurship, it was always best to have a fall guy to blame if things got hot. If ever the suspicion lay at my doorstep, I would simply kick it over towards Aleski.

XXIII

A Visit to Ludton House

I did not go immediately back to the Theatre after the NWS meeting had ended. As soon as Hannah Grey-Downs had turned a corner out of my sight, I made my way to Toffie's house, which was on a pastel-colored street in one of the pastel-colored enclaves that still exist in London. Her house was called Ludton House. I knew of the house long before I had known of Ms. Montmaarten. It had burned down thrice. Electrical issues were always blamed. I found it more romantic to think Toffie did it to make a scene. Perhaps her lifestyle was paid for by insurance money. Fraud can be very romantic, in its way.

I had walked at an breakneck pace such as I reserve for occasions when I have pocketed something from a department store or need to relieve myself after a night at the pub. No time could be wasted, what with Ms. Greenwood's poisoned ear now hearing how Toffie had acquired a purple dog in the first place. If only I wasn't wearing my Good Shoes, I could have run even faster.

As I approached Ludton House, its honey-colored creaked open, and there emerged the severe figure of Ms. Greenwood. She held a bundle of groceries and wore a tweed cap more appropriate for a weekend in Scotland. She smiled and waved behind her. Whatever she had learned,

I would have to carefully disabuse her of. And I mustn't add to her suspicion.

"Mr. Croots," she said. "What a surprise!"

"Quite!" I said. "I suppose I could say the same."

"Could you? I thought Mrs. Grey-Downs would have told the Committee that I was dropping off a few items for poor Toffie."

"Well, I guess yes she did say that. I was meaning just how *long* you've been visiting. That's the surprise."

"Well, Mr. Croots, when one has taken a fall like Toffie has... Well, just talking can be a sort of medicine."

"Yes," I said. "We all love talking. Are you leaving now?"

"Unless you'd like to talk to me, too, Mr. Croots. I'm a very good listener."

"Did you happen to listen to anything in particular when you were with Ms. Montmaarten?"

"Quite! But none of it would interest you. You, of course, are a very important figure. I'm sure you have very little time for our gossip."

Oh, how she was tempting me. I see the bait dangling before me but I did not bite. Ms. Greenwood's smile had not left her face. I wanted to grab her groceries and throw them to the pavement. Watching her chase a cantaloupe down this very influential street would have been quite the sight. Instead, I swallowed my own smile and replied.

"Yes. You're right, of course. And speaking of being busy, we are throwing a gala and I'm quite busy with that now. I think it's best if I see Toffie and you run along to your flat now. I'm sure there is no one to help you with your groceries at home, so best to get home to take a rest now. Good evening, Ms. Greenwood."

I turned to the side to let her pass but she had walked the other way. Even when I was at my most polite, she had a way of being her most impolite.

I wished I had not been so slow in getting to Ludton, but my anxieties had gotten the best of me. I should have strolled. I should have paced myself. I should have stopped for a lemonade and planned my questions carefully. Instead, I let Ms. Greenwood's presence scare me into nervousness. *What did she know?* I wondered as I knocked on the honey-colored door.

Aleksi answered. I had been expecting a woman.

Aleski was in an undershirt, as usual. Being of a medium height, I am quite short for a man, and Aleksi is even shorter than me. His arms and shoulders were completely hairless, which was both an interesting and unsightly thing to see in a person. He looked at me defiantly. I was expecting him to speak first. I was not sure how they did it in Eastern Europe, but it made me stammer to be met by a gaze and not a smile.

"A-Aleksi. Hullo, old man. How are you?"

"You're here for Toffie?"

"I'm here to see how she's doing."

"She's laying down. She got a pink dog. She's not bad."

Not one to exaggerate, this Aleski. Having fallen down stairs and buying a purple dog all in one day constituted "not bad" to this man. How I envied his shrugging, hairless incurious shoulders.

"Can I see her?"

"She's laying down."

"Has she mentioned me?"

At this, Aleksi raised his eyebrows. Finally! Some emotion.

"Why?"

"Well, I don't know if you know this, but I am the Chair of a Committee that Toffie is on. So I am very influential. I'm sure she has mentioned me. We met, you know, at the Parade."

"You used my truck."

"Well, not really. I mean to say, that was really someone else's job. It's a very nice truck, if that's what you want to hear."

"I don't care. Why would Toffie ask about you?"

"Aleksi, old man. Is there someone else I can speak with? A woman, maybe? Someone that cleans the house?"

While Aleksi clearly had some small aptitude for the English language, it wasn't clear he was grasping what I was saying. My uncle once had a parrot who acted the same way. I decided to play charades with him on the doorstep of Ludton House. I mimed a person running a vacuum in midair.

"She's laying down."

"Your charwoman is lying down too?"

"Yes."

"Both Toffie and your maid are lying down?"

"It's big house."

"Was she lying down when Ms. Greenwood was visiting a moment again?"

"Yes."

"Then who was Mrs. Greenwood waving at when she left?"

"Me."

"I didn't know you and Ms. Greenwood were so close."

"We aren't."

"But she stayed to chat for a bit?"

"Toffie is asleep. You are done here. I am expecting phone call."

When it comes to foreigners, I am incredibly forgiving. I know that not everyone has a facility with other languages as I do with German and therefore I was very patient with dear Aleksi. But I found him to be rude. Perhaps he did not know what a Chair was. Perhaps in Russia or wherever he was from, they did not have Chairs, or Committees. Perhaps they didn't even have social clubs devoted to the protection and well-being of dogs.

I softened a bit to Aleksi. I, too, would have left a country like that. And perhaps, seeing me there in all of my influence, I had made him jealous. This was a common problem between myself and other people.

I stuttered a quick apology and turned to leave. But I immediately reconsidered and jammed my foot into the door as Aleksi was closing it.

"Sorry, old man. Can I ask you something?"

Aleksi did not answer, just shrugged his hairless shoulders and stared at me, cow-eyed but menacing.

I went on. "Did Toffie *really* dye her dog purple?"

"Toffie fell down the steps. There's no dog here."

"No dog? I thought..."

"No dog. Toffie doesn't remember a dog. I don't see a dog. Could be maid's dog. Not my dog. No dog."

"All right, old man. All right. No dog. You'd know better than I anyway, ha ha."

"Yes. I have phone call now."

"Quite, yes. You said that." I turned to leave.

"Do you know a Tamassy?"

I froze.

"Yes, Aleksi. We all know a Tamassy. We met him at the Parade. Where we used your truck."

"Do you know him?"

"I know him about as much as you do."

"I will see. I would like to talk to that fruit."

He closed the door behind him. Next time I was at the library, I was going to see what "fruit" meant in Russian. I supposed that his grasp of English wasn't as firm as I had thought.

XXIV

Where's Henry?

If I was briskly walking to Ludton House before, then one could say that I was running to the Esstäbchen Theatre now. Usually, given my medium height and my *penchant* for uncomfortable shoes, I avoid running. But this was a special circumstance and even I had to sacrifice both my pride and the comfort of my heels.

I could not exactly put my finger on it, but Aleksi's intervention at the door had worried me. At first I thought perhaps I was simply prejudiced against his Russian heritage, but believe he was neither a Communist nor a spy. For one, he had a clean-shaven face, and all the Communists I knew at the time were grossly unkempt. For another, his name was emblazoned on the side of his lorry. He would have made an inept spy indeed.

No, it was something else entirely—a lot of something else. For one, I was distressed not knowing Henry's whereabouts. I have already described my susceptibility to pre-annoyance, but I am also afflicted with a pre-despair from time to time. This was one such time. Who knows what trouble poor Henry was in? Did they feed him? Was he locked away in a pound? Or worse? The next time I saw Aleksi, would he be sporting an aubergine-colored fur cap?

Toffie's broken leg was no excuse for such animal cruelty. Nor, for that matter, was being Russian. I was only arguing with myself now as I walked back to the Theatre. A flood of tears mixed with the perspiration on my forehead and, before I knew it, my hair, which had been so beautifully combed that morning, was flattened against my forehead.

Finally, I made my way down the alleyway to the Theatre's side entrance, and took a moment to catch my breath. I dabbed a handkerchief against my brow and smoothed my hair. In the reflection of a broken mirror I pushed my hair to the left and then to the right before settling back on the left. I know this does not seem like an appropriate time for vanity, but one must remember that my self-respect was at a rather low ebb. My poor Henry was lost. Having nice hair was a small victory for me.

My eyes shone blue against my red, tear-stained face. I made a mental note to cry more in public for others to notice. I would have made a handsome sight at a tragic, Italian opera or the funeral of someone I liked. I was calmed by the thought.

Once I had calmed down and the stitch in my side subsided, I opened the door into the Theatre kitchen to find Dreisbach examining something between his toes. His makeup had recently been touched up. I could tell because white paint smeared his mug and dear Henry was merrily chewing on a brush at Dreisbach's feet. His sunglasses sat askew and he was using an empty sardine tin as an ashtray. He seemed rather pleased with himself.

All of the confidence I had derived from how handsome I looked while crying evaporated in the presence of Dreisbach. He had a way of looking suspicious when he was at his most proud. Perhaps it was the crease by his eyes or the feminine way he handled his cigarette. Perhaps it was the fact that I could not see his eyes behind his dark glasses. Either way, I was not comfortable in Dreisbach's presence. The cat had gotten the cream and his appeared smug to the point of perversion.

It was then I remembered why Dreisbach was at Fanny Maybrick's to begin with.

You will forgive me for appearing so cruel as to put Henry's whereabouts on hold while I made sure the money from Fanny was accounted for. But I was, of course, a man of business and felt it only right to settle one matter before beginning another. Had I had an agenda of the sort produced by the Viscount Spittlewood, Rue's money would be the first order of business, with Henry as second. Business can be very cruel. But me? Never.

Dreisbach picked something out of his teeth with one of my calling cards. This now, in case you weren't keeping track, accounted for three of my cards being used. I waited until he was finished before asking for the cash. His smile widened as he produced it from his back pocket.

To my displeasure, the bills were warm and slightly damp. I rubbed my hand on Henry's head to dry it. Henry, while sensitive, can also be oblivious.

"And let me show you something else" said Dreisbach, reaching his hand into his front pocket.

"Dreisbach, I'd really rather you didn't," I said, averting my eyes from whatever could be next.

"Look!" he said. So I did. On a small slip of paper was written a timetable of sorts with days of the weeks and times notated in a girlish script.

Being very influential myself, and being the Chair of a Committee at the time, one might assume I was a skilled scheduler. I am embarrassed to say that this is not the truth. It is a mental allergy of mine, I believe. Some people cannot tolerate shellfish without breaking out into a rash. I cannot look at a set of dates and times without wanting medical intervention.

I am beginning to suspect this is why I was always late for my shifts at The Pelican. But who can say?

I did not have to decipher the timetable for long, as Dreisbach, who often brags of his triumphs before anyone even knows he has had one, explained.

"Good ol' Tamassy found himself a pretty sheila at Fanny's house. And would you know, she's quite fond of yours truly and has always dreamed of Australia. So this here paper demonstrates when she's free to have a pint and get to know more about the Outback and whatnot. And one of 'em is even tomorrow night!"

The thought that someone would be keen on Dreisbach was as confusing as my conversation with Aleksi. But I quickly shook off my befuddlement and finished Dreisbach's thoughts for him.

"This must be the times that Fanny is out of town, then, eh?"

"That's right, old man. So maybe on one of my visits, you can join me. I can keep the housekeeper nice and distracted while you grab your dog and maybe a few rings if you happen to find yourself near her dressing room..."

Dreisbach trailed off and went for a sip of whatever was in his mug. I had a feeling it wasn't tea. I had no intention of investigating. Dreisbach was more clever when he had been drinking. And given the circumstances around Henry's disappearance, I wanted Dreisbach to be very clever, very drunk, and perhaps even very brave. On my behalf.

I shifted focus to the second agenda item of the day: Henry.

I dislike repeating myself. I find it to be a clear indication that I am not influential. It is also very annoying. Sometimes, if I am repeating a story, I may have embellished the facts in my first telling and then I am forced to remember them every time I repeat the story. To avoid this, I called Horace into the kitchen to debrief both he and Dreisbach on my conversation with Aleksi.

Even.more annoying than having to repeat a story is and audience's failure to react to a story in the proper way. I began to wonder, running around London and crying, if I had overreacted to Aleksi. Both Horace and Dreisbach stared at me, waiting for what I assume was the climax of the story.

"...and so you see, something happened! I think Henry is dead!"

The evidence for this was, of course, not great, but I believe that getting the right reaction can sometimes, for better or worse, require a little hyperbole.

Horace was the first to speak.

"You said Miss Greenwood was there?"

"Yes," I said. "I'm sure she was the one who helped bury the body!"

"I doubt—"

"Greenwood?" Dreisbach said. "So strange to hear that name twice in one day!"

Dreisbach had by now foregone the mug and was now drinking straight from a whiskey bottle.

"What do you mean?" said Horace, beating me to the punch.

"Greenwood! That's the name of the housekeeper who took a fancy to me!"

"Dreisbach...you're not saying..." I let the pauses speak for me as in my excitement I could do no more talking. The thought of prudish, snobbish Belinda Greenwood being a housekeeper was a delicious thought indeed.

Horace, who has no taste at all and therefore did not find this particular bit of information delicious, shook his head.

"No, no that's not right. There's no way she's a housekeeper."

"Well, unless she sweeps floors for the hell of it, Horace, I do think I know what I saw!" Dreisbach got defensive when he was drunk.

"But there's no way! Don't you think we'd have heard?"

For a normal employee? Perhaps. But Belinda Greenwood was no ordinary employee. I believe her to be duplicitous indeed. How was it that she had been at the residences of both Fanny and Toffie—at the same time that Dreisbach and I, respectively, were also there. And that does not even account for the things she said about me behind closed doors. I, of course, did not mention that to Horace in my retort. I was saving myself the embarrassment. I was worried he would agree with the remarks made by others, that perhaps my clothes were ill-fitting and I was too perfumed for a man.

Instead, I replied, "Yes, perhaps. But maybe she was simply embarrassed. If she cleaned houses as poorly as she cleaned the Newton-Wiggs Société's office, why, I don't think I'd go about telling others it was my best work!"

Dreisbach gaveled his fist on the table in agreement.

Horace shook his head. If we were not in a hurry to find Henry I would have spent more time arguing my case against Miss Greenwood. As it stood, time was growing as limited as my patience.

"Gentleman!" I exclaimed, clapping my hands and calling the meeting back into order. Both Horace and Dreisbach stood at attention. Even dpoor Henry give a jump.

"We're wasting time on Miss Greenwood! We're not seeing the forest through the poorly dressed, mean-spirited and dull trees. How do you propose we find my dog, you two?"

Dreisbach's cigarette sizzled into the oil of the anchovy tin and Horace stared at his feet. Each of us was deep in thought, trying to map out where a sugar heiress and a Russian lorry driver would take a dog.

Our thoughts were cut short by a rapping at the Theatre door. It was Miss Bonnet who quite rudely failed to greet me. She looked right past me, at Dreisbach, and announced to the room, "Sir, can you *please* stop giving out my number for your calls!"

XXV

Onward to Ondwynn

Miss Bonnet was Dreisbach's neighbor. Other than a few bites of chicken I had once liberated from her kitchen counter when she was out, this was my first encounter with her. I found her anger at Dreisbach using her phone line to be quite rude. If I were ever to own a home and therefore a phone line of my own, I would happily let others use it. That is the difference between myself and others, though. I am altruistic and charitable in all hypothetical situations, and others are not.

Miss Bonnet retreated to her flat next door and Dreisbach followed. Horace grabbed a glass of water from the tap while I examined my nails. How curious it was to have nothing to say once one lived with another person. Horace had so little to say to me, it seems, he did not even ask if I, too, would like a glass of water.

I wondered what Miss Bonnet would think of Dreisbach doing an Australian accent while on the phone.

"Do you really think Miss Greenwood is a charwoman?" I asked by way of continuing a part of the conversation that did not require Dreisbach's presence.

"I just don't see how I wouldn't have–how *we* wouldn't have heard about it."

"That woman always did seem to not be all there. Always distracted, never focused on her job, if you ask me."

I was thinking, of course, of the time she refused to get me a scone on my second day as Chair.

"Maybe," I continued. "She was worried she had left the iron on. A woman like her—with no obvious formal education—can be so easily confused."

Horace's forehead wrinkled. My argument was cogent, but Horace, who is naturally contrary to logical thinking, did not seem altogether convinced. He was very suspicious when it came to reason. I believe this is a side effect of not being as influential as me.

"And *Dreisbach?* How didn't she recognize *him?*" was all Horace could muster.

We had run out of time to discuss the employment history of one Belinda Greenwood (and her perverse attraction to Tammasy) by the time Dreisbach walked back in. If the cat had gotten the cream before, it was now drowning in a jug of it.

"Well, well, well. It looks like that Greenwood girl can't get enough of old Dreisbach!" he announced. He grabbed Horace's glass of water, walked to the cabinet, and added some whiskey.

If I had known then what I know now about Horace's irrational aversion to others using his things, I would have warned Dreisbach. This was, of course, when I was still naive enough to believe that Horace was generous.

Dreisbach, whose stage training always made his pauses exceptionally long, did not begin to explain anything else about his telephone conversation with Miss Greenwood.

"Alright, Dreisbach," I said. "Get on with it." I wasn't happy the spotlight was on him instead of me. While I don't consider Dreisbach to be very influential, one can hardly be surprised that I was jealous of the attention he was getting.

"Well, sadly my date with that housekeeper friend of yours..."

"She's hardly our friend."

"...has been canceled for tomorrow night. She and her missus are going away to a sort of *soiree* in the evening, out in Buckinghamshire. I guess your Miss Maybrick needs that friend of yours..."

"She's not our friend, Dreisbach. Really, she's almost an employee of mine, if you think about..."

"...to help with the new dog I sold her today. Lady Seychelle invited a few people to meet *her* new dog, a *purple colored terrier*. Sound familiar?"

"Henry!"

"Unless good ol' Tamassy brought another *minuit frisse* with him, I think we know where your lost dog ended up, old man."

Dreisbach passed the bottle around. I was sure to take the first drink, as I did not want to follow Dreisbach, or Horace for that matter. I got out my lavender notebook, which was new and reserved only for the most important plans, and began to write down a list of supplies and costumes needed for the following evening in Buckinghamshire.

* * * * * *

Riding in a car presents a perfect opportunity for personal reflection. Too bad Horace was my only friend who drove; it limited my opportunities for personal reflection. Horace drove, and I sat in the seat next to him staring out the window.

I do my best thinking while staring out of a window. Sometimes I read road signs and get nauseous, so my best thinking is often interrupted. But today was not one of those times. Not least because it was dark and there were few road signs on the way to Buckinghamshire.

I was jealous of Rue. After just one day she had been invited to a country house. I, on the other hand, had never been invited to any country houses. I was sure her having one eye would be off-putting for others. Or was that part of her charm? Who can say? I was sure I was a better conversationalist than Rue, who could not talk, as she was a dog. Perhaps she appeared more influential because of her outstanding wig. I made a mental note to get on Tully St. Germayn's good side.

I was sitting up front with him. He had handed me a map and asked that I tell him when to turn left and right. That seemed easy enough but it had been an hour since we had left the Esstäbchen and we still hadn't caught sight of the Seychelle's estate, which was called Ondwynn Park. Of course, it was more likely that Horace simply turned left when I had said to go right. He was very stubborn, as you already know, and most likely did not listen to me.

Dreisbach, for his part, was asleep. He said he was getting into character, for he would be Mr. Tamassy tonight, on the chance that Miss Greenwood would see him. I reminded him that Tamassy was not a particularly tired man and therefore he did not have to sleep. Dreisbach's reply, for which I had no retort, was that it was the middle of the night in Australia already. Horace's map did not extend to Australia. I could not see how far away the continent was, so I could neither prove nor disprove Dreisbach's contention.

At last we spotted a green hill in the distance, decorated by the long, elegant arc of a driveway leading to a stately Georgian home perched on top. I instructed Horace to park at the bottom of the hill. It would be best, I thought, for the car to remain hidden. If someone like Fanny Maybrick was invited for this evening's soirée, then one must assume there would be many other cars parked at Ondwynn. It seemed unlikely that Lady Seychelle would want to spend a minute alone with someone like Fanny. It is always best to insulate oneself, socially, against depressives.

The three of us sat in the car while Dreisbach finished his cigarette and Horace mustered the courage to cut the engine and step out of the car. I amused myself by imagining how the three of us looked. Dreisbach, in his interpretation of an Australian scholar. Horace, in a black roll-neck sweater that accentuated his overall girth. And myself, also in black, but in the suit that Miss Greenwood had once called ill-fitting. I felt comfortable in this outfit and it was equipped with generous pockets in the interior of the jacket. I considered this critical on the off chance I had time to look around the Seychelles' dressing room.

Dreisbach's took one last puff of his cigarette and announced that he was ready.

"All right, lads. Let's go get your dog, Harry and Poo!"

"Don't you mean Henry and Rue?" said Horace. He was never one to let a slip pass unremarked upon.

"Oh, yes, we can bring him along too!" Dreisbach said merrily. He hiccuped once and opened the door and we headed up to Ondwynn.

XXVI

Recruited by the Kitchen

It is my belief that Georgians were skilled at building things, but unskilled at rendering things beautiful. Take, for example, a Georgian manor. Many of them look like the houses I would doodle in crayon as a child: a single block with a door, a few windows, and a peaked roof. The Seychelles' Ondwynn was no exception, only larger in scale and with more Daimlers in the driveway than a schoolchild might imagine.

Only two rooms were lit on the first floor, so we did not worry too much about the noise our feet made on the gravel. It was obvious everyone had either retired to the back of the house or, more likely, they had all retired to bed by seven-thirty. Lady Seychelle, I believe, was quite elderly. Remembering the years I had spent at my grandparents', I have concluded that elderly hosts always make their guests go to bed so early. It is an affliction of age and, presumably, bad manners.

My grandparents, you must know, had terrible manners.

Upon further inspection, the light in one of the rooms only flickered gently. *How sad*, I thought, as Horace hoisted me onto the trellis so that I could sneak through an open window, *the only way to trick guests into thinking this house was warm was with candles and a purple dog.*

Dreisbach, who was known to wander away if left unsupervised, called from around the corner while I was still struggling to balance on Horace's shoulders.

"Pssst!" he said—at full volume.

"Dreisbach!" I whispered back. "Just because you make the *pssst* sound doesn't mean you're whispering!"

"It's called a stage whisper, Arthur!"

I could not concentrate on both climbing the trellis and whatever Dreisbach was saying, so I climbed back down Horace's large back to see what the fuss was. I was happy for the distraction anyway as I had left a rather large muddy shoe print on Horace's sweater and did not want to be held responsible for it.

"What is it?"

"The kitchen door is open. You don't have to go through the window!"

"Why didn't you say that before?"

"I tried!"

"You think *stage whispering* is as good as walking over and..."

I could not finish my sentence, which was disappointing. I had a very good lecture in store for Dreisbach on the importance of urgency when one is executing a business maneuver such as breaking into someone's home. Instead, we were interrupted by the kitchen door opening up and two kitchen maids came out with sheers, presumably to harvest herbs for the evening's meal.

Horace hid behind a bush and I hid behind Horace.

The kitchen maids complained loudly in the manner of all kitchen maids who think they are unobserved.

"This is the last night I'm here, Nell. I swear to it. It is."

"Alice, ya don't mean that. Stop this nonsense and help me find the...what'd she want...rosemary was it? It's so dark tonight!"

"This all goes against my Christian upbringing and I'm surprised that *you*, Nell Rhyss, would be so comfortable with this stuff."

"Fancy! Who says I'm comfortable? It's a job and you know how the Lady is. It's a fad. Make believe."

"Make believe my foot. That's the rosemary there. It's make believe until your soul is crying in hell, I'd say."

The maid known as Nell snipped a few sprigs of rosemary and swatted Alice playfully on the behind. They laughed and went indoors. The last thing I could hear before the kitchen door shut behind them caught my attention.

"A séance! Here at Ondwynn? What would the old Lord think? Fancy..."

One should avoid the occult. While I am not particularly religious, and even less superstitious, one can never be too sure. I have not been altogether lucky on the mortal plane. I do not anticipate faring much better elsewhere.

"So how d'you want to do this, Arthur?" asked Horace. The easy move would have been to turn back and say good-bye to my beloved Henry. The fear, of course, was that the dye would eventually fade and Lady Seychelle would lose interest in Henry. Where would he end up next, once his novelty wore off? I could not bear to think of poor Henry on the streets of Buckinghamshire somewhere. A worse fate I could scarcely imagine.

I feared that Dreisbach, who had been exploring Catholicism at this time, would be opposed to continuing on with the plan now that a séance was involved but, quite to the contrary, I found him grinning widely. I was grateful for Dreisbach's malleable convictions. If only others would give up their beliefs so readily as Dreisbach in the face of making a few pounds.

Now that I think of it, perhaps he was still exploring religion after all.

I paused to consider the best method by which to enter the house, take Henry, all the while avoiding the chatty kitchen maids and whatever dark magic was being practiced inside.

Dreisbach lit a cigarette and offered it to me. I do some very good thinking when I am smoking, and it was my hope that a few puffs would inspire me to lead us into a new course of action. I had hardly taken a second drag when I heard the kitchen door swing back open. Sadly, I did not have enough time to hide behind Horace again, who had, along with Dreisbach, scurried back to the safety of the shrubbery.

"Well, *there* he is!" the one called Alice yelled out into the darkness, giving me a fright and causing me to drop my cigarette. I quickly stamped it with my foot, but not before Nell called out from behind Alice.

"His Lordship don't like smoking! Put that away and get in here. The sauces are getting all cold!"

I wondered if my curse in life was to be eternally mistaken for a waiter and not recognized as the very influential person I had become. In fact, I thought as I scanned the kitchen garden for an escape route from Alice's gaze, perhaps Dreisbach's next play could be an all-male retelling of the story of Sisyphus. I would play the lead. The boulder would be a metaphor for the cross I bear.

"I think you have, uh..." I could not think of a response quickly enough. I did not think with great clarity under pressure and did so with even less clarity now that I could no longer smoke the cigarette that Dreisbach had given me.

"Oh, no, I didn't. We been looking for you! Get in there and do your job, just like everyone else here."

"But I'm not the server!" I yelled back.

Alice only laughed, calling for Nell, who came out of the kitchen door, wiping her hands on her apron.

"What's all this?"

"The server says he's not a server no more."

"Fancy! And in that suit!"

"That's what I thought, Nell. I thought the same thing. It looks like there's a little sauce on your collar too there. Ain't no server, is he?"

"Actually, it's a ragu. And, well..."

There was no way out of it without simply telling the two maids that I was there to break into the house and steal a dog. Obviously I could not do that, so I acquiesced, and followed them into the kitchen, leaving Horace and Dreisbach in the shrubbery.

I made a mental note to throw this suit in the garbage as soon as I was back at the Esstäbchen. Between Miss Greenwood and these kitchen maids, I felt impossibly insulted in what I had once considered a very handsome suit indeed.

The boulder, it seemed, was winning. Alice loaded my arms with plates while Nell walked me through the various *béchamels*, *espagnoles*, and *veloutés* she had concocted in the steaming copper pots bubbling away on the Aga. That was the paradox with women like Nell and Alice. Their nails remained permanently dirty and their hair permanently fly-away, and yet they could out-cook any chef in Paris (or so I would assume, having never eaten in the restaurants of Paris).

Here is the trouble with being very influential and also very polite. Being influential means that there was a better-than-average chance that Fanny Maybrick and others would recognize me—f not immediately upon my entering the room, then most definitely when I served them. They would spot my slightly feminine hands hovering above their plate and my cover would be blown. Being so polite, as I am, I could not tell Nell I had no intention of serving her sauces. As I walked out of the kitchen, I looked for a potted plant to pour them into.

But none were to be found in the long hallway that led to the occupied side of the house. This was a shame as Henry was very fond of potted plants and would have been very unhappy here. This only emboldened me to take him back from the Seychelles, who clearly could not care for a plant and therefore obviously could not care for a dog.

Running out of time, I did the only thing I could do in a situation like this without drawing attention to myself. I ran into a nearby lavatory and crawled through a window to escape.

The beauty of an old house like Ondwynn is that it will speak to you—if you listen. Floorboards creak, and stairs do, too. But one must listen closely to know the full layout of its interior. I have excellent hearing, which thankfully supplements my terrible sense of direction. I walked slowly down the hallway, my arms tiring under the weight of Nell's sauces, and stopped at each door until I hear the telltale sign of the lavatory: the creaking, sighing sound of the toilet tank.

I discarded the tray of sauces on the floor, careful to not clink them against the tiles. I am sometimes paranoid when I sneak around and I could not be certain that Nell or Alice weren't prowling the hallway. I double-checked that the door was locked. Something told me neither kitchen maid was particularly bashful when it came to barging into bathrooms.

I opened the lavatory window and called out, in what Dreisbach would call a stage whisper, "Psssst!"

I soon heard a response: "He's over here, Horace!"

XXVII

The Séance

I will admit to worrying that Horace would no longer be a useful friend once he lost his inheritance. But he proved useful. Owing to his general size and strength, he easily pulled me out from the lavatory window and placed me gently back onto *terra firma*. It appeared I was once again saved from the proverbial chains of servitude. I as pleased, but I knew I could not lose sight of the fact that Henry was still very much not in my possession.

A bang on the lavatory door interrupted my reunion with Dreisbach and Horace.

"Hey! Hey! Are you in here? The Lady came back and said they didn't get no sauces! Are you in here? Hey!"

It was Alice, whose vocabulary I recognized as being less evolved than Nell's. I quickly piggy-backed on Horace so my head could reach the window and called back to her, "Yes! Yes! Please don't come in! I'm quite ill! I seem to be very sick!"

"Well, where are the sauces? Being sick don't mean you lost the sauces!"

"I can't remember! Everything was so dark! Please leave me alone! I'll be right out!"

I had no intention of serving the party, of course, but this seemed to appease Alice, who jiggled the door handle once more before retreating. Even through the window, I could hear her flat-footed stomps, no doubt on her way to tell Nell that the nameless server had ruined her beloved sauces.

"Horace," I said as I dismounted him. "You will have to be the server."

"No. No, no, no," he replied.

"Horace, now is not the time to have your own opinion on things! If serving was good enough for me, then it surely is good enough for you!"

"But what about being recognized? I can't, Arthur! Miss Greenwood, Fanny; they know me too!"

"Horace, you weren't the Chair! They probably don't remember you like they would me and I was willing to risk it. Really, Horace!"

"I can't!"

"You must!"

"I won't"

"You will!"

"What about Dreisbach?"

"What about him?"

"You think *you're* more recognizable than *Dreisbach?*"

At the sound of his name, Dreisbach stepped in.

"All right, all right. Let's see. Horace. It has to be you, old man. We made it this far, we can't go back now."

Horace, who was not fond of Dreisbach in the first place, was especially not fond of Dreisbach telling him what to do, opened his mouth. Dreisbach held up a hand and kept going.

"So, what we're going to do is this. I have a little powder in my pocket and a bit of rouge while we're at it. I believe I have some matches, too, that we can burn and use as kohl. I'm going to make you up a bit, old man, and try to disguise you a bit. And if this crowd is the snobbish sort, they won't be looking at the server, so just get in and get out and see where Henry is and that's it."

It was Dreisbach's experience with putting petulant actors in line which made his direction to Horace so convincing. Horace, for his part, did not protest, but simply sat down on the ground and sighed.

Horace, I was finding, was much more bearable in defeat. After Dreisbach had added a little rouge here and a little powder there, Horace became almost unrecognizable. While a bit of maquillage could not hide his overall bulk, the *tromp d'oleil* of Dreisbach's makeup helped to disguise him much better than I had anticipated.

"Well, chap. This is as good as it's going to get!" Dreisbach said with a flourish. I felt very lucky that he did not have a compact on him, as I wanted Horace to avoid seeing his reflection for as long as possible. At least until the cheese course when it would be too late for him to chicken out.

A mightier knock came from the bathroom window and I knew it was Nell's calloused hands.

"What in the hell is going on? Alice said you was sick. I'll make sure you're sick if you don't open this door!"

Horace, powdered white with rosy cheeks, had no time to lose. I mimed for him to climb through the window to replace me and to answer Nell. Both Dreisbach and I had to hunch down to use our backs as a sort of stepping stool for Horace to reach the window and pull himself through. Nell was now hammering the door steadily, hoping, I assume, to break my spirit. She would have been a fearful guard at a women's prison, I thought.

Through the window I could hear Horace lumbering to the door and opening it.

Nell gasped.

"Who the bloody hell are YOU?"

Nell had seen Horace.

"I'm the server," said Horace. He had proven my theory. Bad liars make terrible actors. Horace did not sound convincing.

"But I thought you were... Weren't you just..."

"Allergic reaction, I'm afraid. Was there shellfish in this sauce?"

Receding footsteps told me Nell and Horace were now walking away, presumably to forgo the sauces and bring out the next course. All Horace had to do was look for a purple dog and keep his mouth shut. I feared he would mess it up, as Horace was wont to do. Perhaps we should have simply pooled our money and bribed Alice to bring Henry to us. But who has the time to trifle with a kitchen maid? I was, after all, the Chair of a Committee.

Having never been invited to dinner at a country estate, I did not know how long these meals usually lasted. And having also never been invited to a séance at a country house, I am sure that tacked on an extra hour or two. The watch I had taken from Mr. Cormant was once again incorrect so I had no way of knowing how late it was. Dreisbach and I sat in silence, waiting for any word from Horace. It was the very darkest of nights, so I didn't worry about being caught by Nell or Alice or anyone else who may have been wandering the grounds at Ondwynn.

Dreisbach was recounting a very lurid anecdote from his time in Germany when I heard the lavatory door open and a little tap on the sill to get our attention.

"Arthur!" Horace stage-whispered blindly into the night. I called back, happy to cut Dreisbach off before his story got any more lurid.

"Horace! Did you see Henry and Rue?"

"Yes! The dogs are in the parlour by the dining room. Dinner's over and I just brought out the cigarettes and coffee."

"Did Miss Greenwood see you?"

"Not the one you're thinking. It's another woman with that name. Looks an awful lot like her though, but it isn't Belinda."

He was once again using Miss Greenwood's first name. But now was not the time to be annoyed at Horace.

"Do you think you can grab them?"

"No. Everyone's moving into the parlour for the séance! There's no way I can get to him without everyone seeing."

We struggled to devise a plan for getting Henry and Rue, but the answer was right there in front of us. I remember as a child having to say grace before dinner when I would visit my grandparents. I would close my eyes tightly and believe I was talking directly to the Lord. How different, I thought, is a séance from a prayer? It seemed to me that, if everyone had their eyes tightly closed, we would be able to grab the dogs quite quickly and make a run for it.

This required Horace and I to trade places again, as he was the only one who could drive and therefore it made sense to have the car waiting when we escaped. Horace climbed back out the window and helped both Dreisbach and myself climb back into the lavatory. Dreisbach would keep watch while I grabbed the dogs. Dreisbach was critical to the mission. I hoped it would not go to his head.

A knock came upon the lavatory door again and it was Nell.

"Come on, now! There wasn't any shellfish in that pudding. Get on out here and stop trying to dodge work!"

Dreisbach pushed me up against the wall, hiding me behind him and then opened the door.

"*Excuse me,* madam?" Dreisbach answered in a prudish voice.

Nell let out a small, "OH!"

"Can't a gentleman have a moment of peace? I'm a guest of Lady Satchel, and the other... Oh, I don't have to explain anything to you!"

"Pardon me, sir! We just had a server who..."

"Keep it to yourself, Miss. And if you don't mind, please direct me to the party. I've wasted enough time talking to *you*."

Nell seemed to have her tail between her legs as she instructed Dreisbach (and by extension me) to the parlour. One last apology was given and she retreated to the kitchen.

Dreisbach and I followed her directions and ran down the hall, stopping just short of the open parlour doors where we heard a low rumble of voices along with a few snores from the dogs in attendance.

There was no source of light, save for a few candles and a what came from the fireplace. It really was a shame that so little of the interior of the house was visible. I had never been a guest at a country home and I was curious to see if I had a better sense of style than the Seychelles. I assumed I did.

A single voice was heard above the others as the parlor fell silent: "Spirit! We ask you this evening to grace us with your presence! We ask that you greet us with a sign."

The room seemed to hold its breath. Even the dogs' snores seemed to fall silent in anticipation.

Nothing came.

"Spirit! If you are here, answer! We are friends! The Lord and Lady Seychelle want to speak with you!"

Again, nothing. And still the clairvoyant pushed on.

"Lady Seychelle, do you have a few words?"

Here, a voice piped up. It was a soft voice and seemed to quaver under the pressure of being put on the spot.

"Yes, Madame Duvet. Thank you. This is... Praline Seychelle. How do you do, Spirit? I would like to speak with my beloved. I would like to know if you can tell my beloved..."

Dreisbach and I were so close to one another, listening just at the corner of the door, that I could smell the powder on his face. It irritated my nose and, before I could control it, I sneezed. The sound cut through the parlor and a woman gasped in surprise.

"Speak, Lady Seychelle! The Spirit is with us now!"

"Yes, thank you Madame Duvet. This is Praline and I want to speak with my beloved Mopsy. Please let Mopsy know that this new dog will never replace our love for you and that you have been so badly missed!"

I turned to Dreisbach but he was no longer there. In the candlelight I could see he had crouched down and had cupped his hands over his mouth.

"*Woof! Woof woof!*" Dreisbach barked into the parlour.

"Oh! Mopsy! Mopsy, Mummy misses you! Mopsy, darling! Don't think we will ever stop loving you, my baby Mopsy!"

"*Woof!*"

The guests began to chatter and I pulled Dreisbach back by the collar to avoid being seen.

Madade Duvet called out to the guests, "Silence, please! Do not break the circle! Keep your eyes firmly closed! The Spirit is here and we must not scare it away!"

With that reminder from the clairvoyant, I felt now was as good a time as I would get to grab Rue and Henry and make a run for it. I signaled to Dreisbach that I was going in and he made a quick look around the corner to make sure the coast was clear. He nodded and, sidling against the door, I entered the parlor.

The parlor itself was softly lit and had a sleepy feeling to it, due mostly to the dust motes visible in the light emitting from the candle flames. Thankfully, the heavy rugs that softened my footsteps. The fireplace did not seem to help the overall somnolent feeling. In fact, in front of it, the guests' dogs all snoozed happily. And just at the edge of the carpet lay Henry.

I felt very fortunate for my medium height, as I was able to crouch down behind the large furniture and crawl on my hands and knees toward Henry. The firelight glowed beautifully against his purple fur. Perhaps, I thought, if we make it out of this, I'll continue dyeing him this color.

From my pocket, I pulled a saucier spoon which still had the remnants of Nell's ruined sauce on it. I waved this under Henry's nose and he perked up. I grabbed him by his collar and placed him on the nearby settee while I looked for Rue.

Rue being smaller, it was harder to find her. I looked for her fringed bangs everywhere, including between the legs of a nearby bloodhound, who growled in protest ("Mopsy is angry with you, dear!" came the voice of the clairvoyant). Having a keen eye and a quitter's disposition, I had no choice but to give up once I did not find Rue in the pile of snoring dogs.

It occurred to me then that Rue could be somewhere else, with this other Miss Greenwood, whom Dreisbach had said was invited to care for the new dog. Perhaps Rue had grown very pompous with her new hairstyle and therefore did not want to associate with the riff-raff on the floor.

And so, with my head peeking ever so slightly above the settee, I gazed upon the séance happening on the other side of the parlor.

A dozen people sat around the table with their eyes closed and hands firmly grasped together. The identity of the clairvoyant, Madame Duvet, was all too obvious. She sat at the head of the table in a lopsided turban and an abundance of costume jewelery, rocking in her chair.

Lady Seychelle sniffled next to her, but she did not wipe her tears, presumably afraid to break the circle. A man who looked like a walrus sat to her left, and then the unmistakable hunched posture of Fanny Maybrick. Next to her sat someone who looked like Miss Greenwood, but was much prettier, and who held on her lap a little, panting dog with a wig glued to its head. I was happy Rue's bangs now covered her eyes. If she had seen me, it's unlikely she could have kept as calm as dear Henry had.

I made the impossible decision to leave Rue in the parlor, to cut my losses—for the time being. I led Henry from the room by the scruff of his neck. Dreisbach poked his head out of the door to greet me. He must have freshened his powder while he was waiting, because he was much whiter than when I had left him in the doorway. He frightened me and I let out a small gasp.

In the silence of the séance, that small gasp sounded like it echoed through the parlor.

A Russian voice cut through from Madame Duvet's mumbling and Lady Seychelle's sniffling: "I think there is someone in diss room wiv us."

Aleksi did have a way of showing up. If only I knew the Russian words for "bad penny".

Madade Duvet's invocations grew louder, her head rolled and her jewelry rattled. She answered only when her performance was complete.

"Yes! Do you all feel it? Someone else is in the room tonight! But who? Spirit, we are friends! Introduce yourself!"

Dreisbach answered the call.

"*Oooooo! This is Fanny Maybrick's husband. Ooooo!*"

Now THAT, I thought, *is a stage whisper*.

Madame Duvet took the bait and said to the group, "Please! If there is a Fanny here, please answer this lost soul!"

Fanny raised her head to the ceiling and gave a simple, "Which one?"

Dreisbach, who did not know the extent of Fanny's marital history, but simply that she was a widow, dodged the question, "*There is not much time! I see the light!*"

"Don't go towards the light, Spirit!" said Madame Duvet.

"I only came...to say...I hate dogs....You must...give it back...."

Dreisbach's voice faded as we ran down the hallway with Henry in my arms. Madame Duvet's speechifying rose to a fever pitch and continued. Only when Horace had pulled up the driveway and we were securely inside his car could we no longer hear it.

XXVIII

Rue's Return

It took no longer than until the following morning for Fanny to contact us about returning Rue. During breakfast, at which Henry was given two slices of ham as a celebratory treat, Miss Bonnet once again knocked at the Theatre's door. She was still in a dressing gown and her hand was on her hip in the exasperated stance women of her class. She would have gotten along very well with Nell and Alice.

"If I have *one more person* calling on this line for you, I'm going to scream!"

I was appalled at Miss Bonnet's manners. Could she not see we were celebrating? The second slice of ham for Henry should have been indication enough. Some people, I find, are not very observant.

"My dear Miss Bonnet..." Dreisbach said.

"Oh, no. Don't you go trying that on me! I'm expecting a very important call. Now, on with you. Which one is Arthur? That's the one I'm looking for."

I wiped my mouth and checked the time and then followed Miss Bonnet out the back door. I was not going to give her the satisfaction of urgency. People who are rude always seem to want a reaction. Instead, I complimented the color of her hair, which was a bright orange, and remarked on the money she must be saving by doing her manicures at home.

"The phone's in the..."

"The kitchen. I know."

I was my good fortune that Miss Bonnet was in a terrible mood because she didn't pick up on my error. I had forgotten that I had snuck into her house last time without having been invited in the traditional manner. She simply turned her back and went to the couch to file a nail and, undoubtedly, listen in on my conversation.

I picked up the receiver and knew immediately by the sinking feeling I got when I put it to my ear that it was Fanny Maybrick on the other end.

"Arthur? Is that you? I thought I'd gotten connected to the wrong line. It *did* take forever."

"Sorry. We're... sorting out something here with our, um, secretary. How can I help you today, Fanny?"

"I'm sorry to bother you. I can't get ahold of Mr. Tamassy. You see, I'm rather embarrassed to say that I'm going to have to return Constance immediately. After some information I received last night, I simply can't keep her."

"I'm so sorry to hear this, Fanny. Don't worry. I'll pass the message along to Mr. Tamassy. In the meantime, I'd be happy to take Constance off your hands—if it's urgent that you get rid of her,I mean."

"Arthur, please don't say it like that! It's not that I *want* to. I received a message from... You wouldn't understand. Please, do meet me at the park where we met the other day. Let's say in an hour? If that works for you?"

I agreed and replaced the receiver. I walked back into the foyer of Miss Bonnet's house and before I could leave, Miss Bonnet looked up from her nail file.

"You know, I would quite like a dog, if you're looking to unload one."

"That's very kind of you, Miss Bonnet. But I do think you should clean your house better before entertaining the idea of a dog. Many breeds are allergic to dust, you know."

I walked out, quite satisfied with myself. Perhaps she would learn not to listen to other people's phone calls.

* * * * * *

In an hour's time I was in the park to meet Fanny. It was a beautiful day, sunny and crisp. The perfect weather to walk back to the Esstäbchen. Rue, with her small snout, could not handle high temperatures or very humid weather. I doubt Fanny would ever think of such things. Depressives, I think, only tend to think about themselves.

Around a bend in the nearby footpath came a snorting, bewigged mass, straining against the lead that Fanny had bought her. Fanny was, of course, right behind. She was in all black and presumably oblivious to the nice weather we were having.

"Thank you for meeting me, Arthur. I'm so sorry again for taking up your morning for this. I just... I couldn't keep her any longer."

"It's no trouble at all! I do hope that R–Constance wasn't too much trouble."

"Not at all. She really is a sweet thing. It's just something...personal."

"You don't have to tell me anything, Fanny. I'm sure Mr. Tamassy will understand too. Of course, we all understand that the money provided won't be refunded."

"Oh, yes. Of course."

"Then there shouldn't be an issue. You know, Mr. Tamassy can be *very* litigious, so I will let him know that everything us settled."

"Yes, yes. Now, is there anything else you may need?"

I thought at this point it would be too much to ask Fanny for cab fare home, so we exchanged pleasantries and I asked if she'd like to give Rue a kiss goodbye.

"Oh? Oh, no. I shouldn't. My husband wouldn't approve, I don't think."

I hoped for Rue's sake that she did not hear Fanny's excuse. Rue can be hypersensitive to slights and I would hate for our reunion to be spoiled by Fanny's poor manners. We said our goodbyes quickly and I decided to enjoy the nice weather by sharing a small ice cream with Rue on a nearby bench. This would be our little secret from the other dogs—and from Dreisbach, who would undoubtedly have asked why we did't bring him any.

There was an ice cream parlor adjacent to the park and so I tied Rue to a nearby pole and went to fetch dessert. I had decided that Rue, with her new hair and introduction into the finer things in life, would like strawberry ice cream. It also happens to be my favorite, too. Rue and I complement one another gorgeously. I did miss her dearly and was over the moon to have her back.

I can say this here, as I am nearly positive Rue cannot read, but for all of her grace, Rue is a sloppy eater. When I put her small dish of ice cream down to enjoy, it somehow ended up all over her nose and her beautiful, fringed bangs. I was very happy that Fanny was not there to see this. It would have embarrassed me terribly.

It was while I was savoring the last spoonful of ice cream (they use real strawberries, which makes a difference, I believe) with my eyes closed that the sun was momentarily eclipsed. I opened them to see a short, bald man with a Slavic face looking down at me.

I hadn't been expecting anyone, so I jumped. There was something about Aleksi that made me nervous, so I squeezed Rue's lead tighter in my hand just in case we had to make a run for it.

Aleksi's serious face broke into what can only be described as an attempt at a smile.

"Hello, Arthur. I knew I would find you here."

"W-what do you want?"

"Don't worry. Don't worry. We're friends, you and me."

I calmed down long enough to notice that Aleksi's Russian accent was gone. But I didn't stay calm.

"You know, Aleksi. Horace and Dreisbach will be expecting me. I have friends who... Why, they'll do anything to make sure I remain unharmed!"

"Harm? Who's harming you, Arthur? I just want to chat."

Aleksi sat down next to me and tapped his thighs for Rue to jump up on him. She obliged. Rue is an excellent judge of character and appeared not the least bit frightened. This, in turn, subdued me slightly. But only slightly.

"What shall we chat about?"

"Whatever you're doing. Whatever you got going on with these dog people."

"I'm not sure what you're accusing me of."

"Whatever you're doing. And I don't care what it is. I just want in."

XXIX

Kenneth

As I walked back to the theatre with Aleksi, I pressed him to explain how in the hell he had figured us out. Somehow, though, I became sidetracked by a sudden interest in phrenology.

You see, I am of medium height, so Aleksi would accurately be described as "compact". He was quite a bit shorter than I, which gave me the privilege of gazing upon his bald crown as we walked. I was fascinated by the lumps, bumps, and bruises that lay across the topography of his skull. What story did they tell? Did they identify anything about his moral character? His intelligence?

I was too distracted by the flaws on Alexis's head to hear what he was saying. This resulted in his repeating himself a few times. I believe he found this annoying.

"Like I said," he said. "A con recognizes a con."

"Oh, I think you're confused! Constance was just a name that Fanny had given her. The dog's proper name is Rue!"

"Huh? No, Arthur. *You're* the con."

I have been called many things in my day, but never so casually. And on the street! Where others can hear!

"I beg your pardon?" I said.

"Listen. You already let me come with you to your headquarters. You already trust me. Let's not argue."

I didn't have the heart to tell Aleksi that I did not, in fact, trust him. But he did have a lorry and that moved the needle quite a lot for me. I let him continue.

"I knew there was something odd about you when we first met. I thought you were trying to get on with Toffie and I've been working on her for a few months before you came along. But I saw how, well, off-putting you were to her, and I guess she wasn't your... type? Anyway, I couldn't put my finger on it until you turned up like an unlucky penny at that séance yesterday. But *then* I knew. You're stealing dogs for reward money."

I was offended at Aleksi's assessment of me. For one, I would hardly call any interaction I have ever had with Toffie or anyone else at the Newton-Wiggs Société as "off-putting". This must have been Aleksi's personal jealousy toward me. And I would have argued that calling my attempts to get my dogs back as "stealing" was slanderous. He was fortunate I did not know a lawyer at this time.

I began to tell Aleksi as much, but he simply laughed and shook his bald head.

"Hey, whatever helps you sleep at night, Arthur. Anyway, I was getting tired of Toffie and, to be honest, I think the milk was running out on that cow. The excitement of dating a lorry driver was starting to wear off on Miss High Society and I wanted to find myself a little financial cushion while I could."

We rounded the block and entered the alleyway toward the theatre entrywway, and I stopped short of the door. Rue rooted happily around in an filled trash can and I looked at Aleksi square in the eyes. I tried my absolute hardest to appear influential to a man who, it seems, did not care one fig about influence.

"Listen here, Aleksi, if that *is* your real name."

"It's not. I thought I told you that. It's Kenneth. And yours surely isn't Arthur Croots."

"What? My name is Arthur!"

"Really? I would have picked a new name."

"Like Aleksi is any better."

"It's more believable than Arthur."

"But Arthur *is* my name!"

"Sometimes the truth isn't believable enough for people. You should really change your name."

"Oh, well," I began. I was going to say that very same thing to you." And then I lost my train of thought. "Let me start over," I said.

I cleared my throat and looked Aleksi (now Kenneth) squarely between the eyes.

"Listen here, *Kenneth*, if that *is your real name.*"

"It is my real name," he said. "I just told you that."

I kicked a nearby trash can, which happened to be the one Rue was investigating, and she yelped. The noise attracted Horace, who swung open the door and took one look at Kenneth and said, flatly, "What the hell is he doing here?"

* * * * * *

Only once we were inside and Rue was reunited with her doggy compatriots and the whisky had been poured could we all take a breath and talk. Dreisbach was of the belief that more was always merrier, but Horace was not inclined to be so hospitable. I would go as far as to say that Horace was downright rude to Kenneth.

I was not particularly a fan of Kenneth, myself, nor was I particularly trustworthy of someone who identified as a "con man", but one must engage in these situations with an open mind. Perhaps if we heard him out we could turn our little business into a larger enterprise? And if we thought that Kenneth was too untrustworthy, well, then we could blackmail him with all the information he was telling us. It really was a very innocent chat. But Horace was too worrisome to see the potential.

He stewed and harrumphed and rolled his eyes. Dreisbach, on the other hand, was happy to ask where Kenneth's family was from and did he detect a bit of Welsh in his accent? And what was his exercise routine that he had such strong arms?

I wanted to take Horace in the next room and ask him to consider the potential someone like Kenneth held for us. What would Toffie's address book look like? We would no longer have to flip through old issues of *The Tatler* or attend any more NWS meetings! But I was far less comfortable leaving Dreisbach alone with a man than I was bringing a self-admitted con man into our home.

I mediated the conversation the best I could. It was not that I did not see the value of Kenneth (and his lorry), but I had to be politic. I was sympathetic toward Horace. Before Kenneth's arrival, Horace was the only one who knew how to drive, and perhaps he was jealous of this newfound, road-ready friend of ours.

He did not see the full picture. He only thought of himself. Horace was a narcissist.

Over buttered toast, prepared by Dreisbach (in a smart apron now, with touched-up face paint) it was settled. Kenneth would join us for a sort of trial run. We did not have any current leads on whom we could sell a dog to, but it was nice that Horace had kept his big, bearded mouth shut. We now had another member of the team, one who could, perhaps, take a few notes from Toffie's handbag if I needed a new suit or food for the dogs.

And of course, now that Horace was poor, the topic of money came right up. I have always believed that money should be discussed in private, on a one-to-one basis, like religion, or when something is stuck in someone's teeth. Horace seemed to have lost his manners along with his inheritance.

There was, of course, the question of whose share Kenneth's cut would come out of. I thought it fair that we all take a cut: seven-eighths of a fourth would be shared vy Horace and Dreisbach, and I would generously pick up the other eighth. Dreisbach (busy asking Kenneth to flex his bicep, now), didn't seem to mind this arrangement. But Horace had an issue with it. I thought it best to go over the details of Kenneth's commission another time. As you know by now, I am a very shrewd businessman, and knew better than to negotiate in front of our newest team member. That would appear weak, which I am not.

Dreisbach's eyelids fluttered as he poured a third round of whiskeys. "So," he said. "Is there someone else in the picture we should know about?"

"There's Toffie, of course. But she's rather incapacitated now that you chaps blinded her and she broke her leg."

I found this reductive, and was prepared to say so, but Dreisbach spoke first.

"She was such a silly woman! Her ego is her worst..."

"Don't I know it! Why do you think I've been keeping it up for the last few months? Easy cash. Every couple of days I just tell her how beautiful she is or whatever she wants to hear and she hands over wads of cash."

"Then why are you giving it up?" Horace asked. *Finally!* I thought. *A reasonable question from this otherwise unreasonable man!*

Kenneth grunted and downed his whisky. "Easy," he said. "I can't stand the bitch!"

Dreisbach laughed admiringly at Kenneth's honesty. Actors always seem to appreciate honesty in others, since they are professional liars themselves.

"And not just that I can't stand her. I was reading her mail the other day and saw that she was writing to her sister that she wants to have a baby with me. I even know *when* she's planning on trying it with me—on a trip to America. She's surprising me with two tickets aboard the *Mathilde* later this month. That's my cue to exit. I don't want to be stuck with Toffie for eighteen more years. No, thank you."

I could quite see why Kenneth wanted out. Toffie's money was Kenneth's, for now, but that would change with a child. It would most definitely be split unfairly. Perhaps even seven-eighths to the brat and one-eighth to Kenneth. Dreadful.

But, as I always do with strays, I took Kenneth into our little enterprise. Just in case he might ever choose to spend a night at Esstäbchen Theatre instead of Ludton House, I explained the rules. I explained that in some regards a Theatre is much more glamorous than a House, but I did not sound very convincing, even to myself. I also said that we did not have money to throw around every time he complimented us, as Toffie did, so it was not worth his energy to try. I did promise that I would not fall in love with him, nor ask for a child with him. But the same could not be promised of one J.W. Dreisbach. I said that as a joke.

XXX

Farewell to Max

The next morning I woke up more refreshed than I had in many weeks. It was not that my body had gotten used to the stack of furs which had become by bed. Rather it was because I felt an overwhelming sense of promise. I knew that success was just around the corner. I felt a deep sense of myself as a natural business man, drawn to success like a dowsing rod to water.

I was completely mistaken, of course. I just did not know it yet.

With the stage play we were putting on for the NWS fast approaching, I thought I would be useful and wake up early to go visit H.H. Hargood & Sons, my loyal, one-eyed stationer. I thought I should lead by example and get new business cards made—with the title of Director and Producer on mine. I didn't know the difference between the two titles titles, so I threw them both in.

Dreisbach, of course, was the Playwright. Horace did not technically have a title, so I called him a Stagehand. (If Kenneth preferred to be Stagehand, Horace would be Box Office Clerk.) I had written a list of job titles down for them to choose from the night before, but had forgotten the list at home and therefore decided not to get anyone else's business cards but my own.

Kenneth had informed us the night before that he was aware of the play being produced at the Esstäbchen and it was partially why he was so keen to confront me in the park. I said I did not know he was so interested in being an actor, since he was elderly and unattractive. He said he did not want to be an actor, but wanted to help with the con. He had assumed we were putting on the show to somehow swindle the audience out of millions.

This was a much better plan than a simple fundraising event for charity. I was jealous that I had not thought of it first.

It was only when Horace had gone to bed that I leaned in to tell Kenneth and Dreisbach that we would find a way to make the play profitable and that Horace would be given the details on a strictly need-to-know basis.

I have a theory that morality can sometimes spring up out of nowhere in people, like a mole or a grey hair. Horace seemed to have been afflicted with just such a spiritual carbuncle. It really was a pity, as I preferred to avoid keeping secrets. As you know, Horace was still my best friend at the time.

If we were going to take Kenneth's advice, the affair had to appear as absolutely legitimate as possible. I had planned to make business cards regardless, but now it was imperative to do so. No one would suspect a man who had very nice business cards of being a criminal.

I reached the familiar sign of Hargood's and opened the large oak door. Anticipating the friendly tinkle of the bell attached to the door, I was crestfallen to be greeted by silence. It was funny, I thought, how gloomy a store can be when something so familiar is missing.

It was only after I had paged through a few diaries that I realized what familiar thing was missing: his green-eyed cat. Though I am not very fond of cats, it was strange to not feel its small presence in the shop. I hoped, for Hargood's sake, that the cat was simply napping in the stockroom and that both he and the cat would appear shortly.

Just as I was about to examine an exquisite pencil, Mr. Hargood walked out, looking very upset indeed. Even his glass eye, which usually was not very expressive, conveyed a deep sadness. He sniffed a few times (and, I must add, did not use a handkerchief) before realizing I was in the shop.

"I'm sorry, but we're closed," he began. And then, "Oh, hello there, Mr. Croots."

I admit I was flattered that, even in his distress, Mr. Hargood remembered my name.

"Is everything okay, Mr. Hargood?"

"Oh, yes. Well. No." He paused here to gather his thoughts before addressing me again. "May I be honest with you, Mr. Croots?"

I typically prefer shopkeepers not be very honest with me, but I made an exception for Mr. Hargood. I find him to be a kind man, but mostly I still needed my business cards made and did not want to come back another day.

"Of course you can, Hargood. What's the matter?"

"Max..." he began.

That was all he could croak out but it was enough. Max was his cat and Max was dead. Being a very compassionate person, I felt incredibly sorry for Mr. Hargood, with his bushy eyebrows and his pinky ring too small for his hand. It seemed Max had been his only friend in the world. I understood how lonely he must have felt.

"Not Max!" I said, trying to mirror the weighty emotions Mr. Hargood was demonstrating. I believe I was convincing, but it was hard to tell because his one good eye was not looking at me, so I had trouble reading his reaction to my acting skills.

"Does this mean you are closing, or..."

Hargood sniffed again without answering. I did not have a handkerchief to offer him and there is never a polite way to tell someone to just blow their nose already. I tolerated it as well as I could. I really did need the business cards.

I took another tack: sympathy.

"Max was such a good cat," I said. "I always did enjoy his meowing and the way the shop smelled like tuna."

"He was quite a character!"

"He did enjoy staring, didn't he?"

"More than any other cat I had met!"

"Was he sick for long?"

"Oh, who's to say? You know how cats are." (I did not, but decided it best to not interrupt). "But this morning he didn't come to wake me up for his breakfast and he hardly ate anything and then... Oh!"

Hargood began to cry. Deep sobs welled from his chest and I was shocked at how openly emotional he was in front of me, who was nearly a stranger, and a very confused customer, at that.

In moments of deep distress, most people look ugly. Luckily for Hargood, who was ugly to begin with, sobbing somehow managed to render him dignified. The water streamed from his good eye while his glass eye remained stoic. A working-class Odin who had lost his familiar. Alas.

I was not sure what made me say what I said at that moment. Was it a purely sympathetic act? Did I feel Hargood had lived up to his potential and become a very influential person? He did look dignified, even as he wiped his nose on his shirtsleeve. Perhaps it was because I needed my business cards so soon. Either way, the words came out of my mouth before I had fully thought them through.

"Hargood," I said. "Why not get a dog?"

Hargood, who had calmed a bit after relating these news of Max's death, looked up at me with a knitted. Brow I thought I had offended him, as I know cat people are very particular and loyal to cats. His face then broke into a smile.

"Oh!" he said. "I did always want a dog. But that Max of mine hated the idea. He was jealous of his daddy, you see."

"Max did have that look about him."

"Did he ever! Always quick to scowl when someone got too close to his dad!"

"Yes, well. I don't think you'll have that issue with the dog I have in mind for you, Mr. Hargood. In fact, she's very social. Not at all the jealous type."

"How kind of you to think of me. But it really is too soon."

"Nonsense!"I told him. "Always best to replace a loved one as soon as you can. Why, when my mother died, I went to live with my aunt for three months right after the funeral. It helped tremendously. In fact, to this day, I still get my mother and Aunt Rosemary confused. I just remember good memories of *both* at once."

I could see the wheels turning in Hargood's head. I assumed he was thinking of how awful the first night alone would be without his beloved Max. Cats, I understand, are very loud and noisy at night. Hargood would have gotten used to the sound, I am sure. I am also sure that the dripping faucet, his own breathing, and the noisy neighbors would sound all that much louder in Max's absence.

"And," I said, before Hargood could say no. "This particular dog has a lot in common with you. She has the same visual impairment as you."

I closed one eye and pointed to it so he took my meaning. I am very good in delicate situations such as this.

"Your dog has astigmatism?"

"What? Don't be stupid, old man! She's got one eye like you!"

It really is amazing how people can be blind to their own flaws. Hargood had totally forgotten he had one eye, for example. And Horace, who used to be so kind, had turned sour. But he had no idea. He had not paid for a single meal in weeks.

I didn't know if Hargood was upset that I had pointed out his missing eye, or that I had called him stupid. Either way, he did not answer immediately. As shrewd businessman, I have always viewed initial silence as an effective negotiation tactic. So I offered Rue at a very reasonable price of twenty pounds.

Hargood shook his head.

"That's very kind of you, Arthur. But that's far too much for a dog. I got Max for free, found him right on the street, and he was just as good as any expensive breed."

I found it incredibly hard to believe that any stray cat could be seen as "just as good" as my sweet Rue. I pressed him a bit.

"I understand, Mr. Hargood. I do. You're in mourning. But twenty pounds doesn't seem like a whole lot when one considers how much love a dog can bring into your life. And who better to love you for your differences than one who can relate?"

Hargood thought this over and gave a contemplative, "Hm."

"A dog will do you well, I think. Getting you out of the house. Meeting your neighbors. Going for walks. I always felt that it wasn't healthy, just you and your cat, cooped up here. A dog like Rue has *magnetism.* People are drawn to her, and not just because of her missing eye! Why, you may even strike up a conversation with a stranger who would one day be your wife!"

Hargood laughed and I knew I had him. The easiest way to make any money is to exploit someone's loneliness. What an empath am I, discovering this path of magnanimity, this calling to help others.

Hargood was adamant he could not afford the twenty pounds, which surprised me as he surely could have pawned his pinky ring for a few quid. I did not press, though, as I did not want him to think I needed the money. I wanted him to believe I was a humble advocate for healing. I was, I assure you. But there was also the money.

We agreed that the best way to pay for Rue would be to give me credit at the stationery store. This meant I could choose from any of the cardstocks in Hargood's little catalogue, even the ones which I had coveted but could never afford. I decided on a dove grey cardstock with the words DIRECTEUR in a grand, gold-foil script. It would make a handsome presentation to the attendees of the gala at the Esstäbchen. I would even mail one to Miss Greenwood to make her jealous.

I was in such a good mood, I decided to get Horace a set of business cards, too. His read "Assistant to the Director", which I felt was an honorable title indeed.

At last my stationery was ordered. Hargood, a consummate professional, seemed to have been distracted with my inquiries on paper quality and coloured inks long enough to forget about dead old Max. I promised to deliver Rue later, after I had eaten lunch.

This would also give me time to find my manicure scissors and cut off the remainder of the wig that I had glued to Rue the week prior.

XXXI

Crêpe Paper and A Glass Eye

It is a truth universally acknowledged that people will ruin your mood the moment they can. This is especially true when one is in a good mood from being charitable. This is why I rarely help others; I know my good mood will soon be soured.

This was the case when I came back to the Theatre and Dreisbach was yelling at Horace. While the two have never seen eye-to-eye (Horace is much taller than Dreisbach, for one thing), they had rarely exchanged more than the most basic pleasantries. "Can you pass the milk?" for instance. Or, "Did anyone feed the dogs?" Or, "If anyone is looking for me, tell them I moved to Panama."

It really did annoy me that I did not even get to brag about my generous gift of beautiful Rue to ugly, lonely, one-eyed, old Hargood. I thought for sure Horace would like to hear about how kind I was, seeing as how lately I had the feeling he thought I was a criminal. But I could tell he was not in the mood to be impressed by my kindness and in fact was very frigid towards me when I walked into the Theatre.

"What the hell do you mean, coming into my room and taking my watch?"

"Horace, calm *down*. I was only going to *see* if any pawn shop would even be interested in taking it. I wasn't going to actually sell it without telling you first!"

"I don't want my stuff touched! How would you like it if I came into your room and took your things?"

"Well, to be fair, old man, you and Arthur and four dogs *did* come into my room and you *have* been taking my stuff quite regularly. Rent-free, I might add!"

I thought it best to interject now, as the topic of money should be off-limits among friends, and even more so among enemies. People like Dreisbach and Horace always go tit for tat. Nothing is ever really out of kindness and therefore forgotten in a fight. Instead, every gift or kind act is remembered and used against the other later. I detested this. In fact, if I owned a watch or a theatre, I would never hold it against someone else, I assure you.

"Gentleman! Please!" I said. "Let's calm down and talk things through. What's going on?"

At this, both men turned to me and began speaking at once.

"Dreisbach stole my..."

"I can't possibly..."

"...and now how am I supposed to – "

"...I can't write a play under these..."

Each wanted to paint himself as victim and the other as antagonist, but I could also see that, if I were to listen to both sides, that I would not be able to tell the others about Mr. Hargood and Rue and how kind a person I was. Instead of listening, I simply nodded until both had paused to catch their respective breaths. I held up my hand and said, quite judiciously, "I have heard enough."

Horace, who often mistakes our history as friends as an invitation to ignore me, opened his mouth to protest more against Dreisbach.

"Ah, ah, Horace," I said. "I told you both I have heard enough."

This shut him up, so I continued.

"The problem here seems to be a lack of money, which has made us all a little desperate. I know, Dreisbach, that you have a lot on your plate right now with the Newton-Wiggs gala, and we should *all* be a little more sensitive to that."

I looked at Horace.

"And I also know how particular Horace is with his stuff, seeing as how he is poor now and can't afford nice things, so do *try* to avoid stealing from him, won't you, Dreisbach?"

It seemed like a fair compromise and I think both men were chagrinned at how easily a man like me, who is skilled at business and adept at affecting compromise, could boil their troubles down to a few sentences. Horace grumbled and Dreisbach muttered but neither protested. I took this as an agreement between them and could now credit myself with another successful mediation. But I didn't stop there.

"Now, Dreisbach," I said. "Can you explain why you needed the money from Horace's watch? Don't you still have a few pounds from the last sale?"

"Well, I can't be expected to pay the actors in *dogs*, now can I, Arthur? And set design and costuming and lightbulbs and catering..."

"I see your point," I said. "But can't you just... Don't you have people who do that kind of thing for free?"

"This is theatre, Arthur! It's not some state school production put on by slack-jawed farmboys! I was put in charge of this show and I demand the best when my reputation is on the line!"

Horace snorted.

"Is something funny?"

"Your reputation? Weren't you arrested last year for indece..."

"And how is *that* germane?"

"I'm just wondering how your reputation could be intact when a year ago you were found in the park with your..."

"I'll have you know, the papers used my *old name*. No one here knows who the hell Johann Wilhelm Dreyfuss is!"

"Well," I said, trying to calm them down again. "To be fair, no one knows who J. W. Dreisbach is either. But I do take your point. We simply don't have enough money to afford what I think you have in mind."

"Exactly! Which is why I was going to sell Horace's watch!"

I really could see Dreisbach's point and had a hard time understanding why Horace wouldn't just let him sell the bloody thing, but felt it best to not take sides since Horace could drive and the answer to Dreisbach's dilemma was right in front of us.

"How about instead of taking *each other's* expensive items, we take other people's?"

I was met with two quizzical stares instead of the look of excitement I was expecting. So I elaborated. We would use Horace's car to load up some of the houses I was most familiar with to take items which could be used for the production. The Cormants, Ms. Rublack, they could be our own private prop warehouses. I promised I would even find Dreisbach his own watch to sell if we had the time. That seemed to please him.

Horace, on the other hand, frowned. I was used to this frown, the one he wore when he'd staked out the moral high ground for himself, so I was pre-annoyed before he even opened his mouth to speak.

But then he did open his mouth to speak. And I became even more annoyed.

"Arthur, this has got to stop!" He said. "I... You... We... We can't be doing this any more. We need to stop this and find another way. We can't be stealing from people. Aleksi... Dreisbach... Us... Breaking into people's homes. Toffie. Broken legs... How are we any different than criminals?"

I was surprised at Horace's accusations since he was very much a part of what we were doing. I believe moral superiority is the leading cause of short-term memory loss and should be studied by scientists. Instead of telling Horace as much, I gathered my thoughts before responding. But then I suppose I took too long, and Horace took my silence as an admission of guilt.

"See?" he said. "You can't even think of a lie that will make sense anymore. I'm sorry, Arthur, but I have to stop this now. I have to try and live a better life. I'm going to collect my things and see if I can find a place to stay for a few days. I need to at least try, Arthur. I'm sorry."

Horace walked past me to his bedroom, which was actually just a part of the backstage partitioned off with a Chinese curtain. We did not look at one another. I am a very influential person, but even I know that one cannot change someone else's mind when it is made up.

XXXII

A Night at the Theatre

Horace really did leave the Theatre and did not come back. It was a surprise to both Dreisbach and myself, and Kenneth, too, when we told him. It is often hard for me to take threats seriously, as I often make them solely for attention, so I thought by the following morning Horace would be back at the breakfast table. But he was not. And the show must go on, as they say. So we hadn't the time nor the energy to miss Horace much in the time leading up to the play.

Even though my title was Director, it seemed that Dreisbach was in control. Usually this would have bothered me, but I was feeling rather magnanimous without Horace's ill mood to distract me from my kind and generous heart. I let Dreisbach take the reins on this project and in return I had a lot of time to sit and nap and walk the dogs, three of my favorite pastimes.

We decided to move forward with the plan to gather supplies from people's houses instead of trying to buy props and set decoration. Bollocks, we said, to Horace's newfound morality!

The play was an all-male retelling of Jason and the Argonauts and many of what was needed for the play were, in fact, household items easily found in most middle-class homes. Bedsheets could certainly pass as togas (or whatever Greeks wore). The Argo could be built from an upturned table and the remainder of the paper fans left behind from the days the theatre was a Chinese restaurant. Various papers, costumes, and oriental rugs could be cut, sewn, and painted to give them new life on the stage.

It was this realization that led me to ask Kenneth if his moving truck would be available that night. I showed the script to both him and Dreisbach, posting out where I had underlined various scenes and, in the margins, wrote the following:

RUBLACK
CORMANT
NEWTON-WIGGS

Yes. Without Horace around to dampen the creative atmosphere of the playwriting process, I was able to think of a brilliant way to not only produce the play that followed Dreisbach's vision, but to also prevent me having to work. In short, we would break into a few homes that evening and take the necessary supplies to create the props, costumes, and scenery. And we would bring Jason and his Argonauts to life.

I am not usually boastful, but it was hard to deny that my idea had reenergized us. Kenneth, who had driven his truck to the Esstäbchen, said that we could go that evening. I, wanting to take advantage of Horace's absence, agreed. Dreisbach, who had drunk a bottle of wine at lunch, had nothing to say other than stressing to us the importance of finding a golden fleece. "It *has* to be magnificent," he said. "The entire play will be ruined without it!"

The thought of the play being ruined set Dreisbach sobbing. We decided it best that we handle things just the two of use. Kenneth grabbed one arm and I grabbed the other and we put him to bed.

We would start with the house furthest away and work out way back home to the theatre. I thought this was a very smart plan and was happy to know that Kenneth agreed. Kenneth called the theatre "home base," which lent an air of conspiracy to our endeavor. I was starting to like Kenneth. I wished he could grow hair, though, so he might be a bit less ugly.

We dressed in black and I rode in the passenger seat of his lorry as we made our way to my former flat. I was sure that we could sneak in unnoticed and take what we needed. Ms. Rublack was usually puttering in the front of her flat, which left the kitchen exposed. I remembered a china set and a tablecloth in her pantry that would do nicely for the feast scene. They were of questionable quality, which I thought fit in well with craftwork available in Iolcus of ancient times. If I recall, many of Ms. Rublack's dishes were chipped. Authenticity, I thought.

It is a strange thing to sit in an automobile and navigate to locations one has only ever walked to on foot. Walking a wello-known route becomes instinctual—when to turn left at the bakery and right at the park. Or the shortcut down the alley, or the street one avoids because of an embarrassing incident that happened at a pub. But how does one translate this into giving directions from the passenger seat?

My inability to give proper directions annoyed Kenneth, but it was his fault, not mine. Obviously. How could he expect me to know every single street in London? A lorry is much taller than me, and I am of medium-height, so a lot of what I saw from my seat was unrecognizable to me. Why did he drive such a large thing? It was like riding an elephant.

Of course, I did not tell this to Kenneth, as I did not want to annoy him more with my questions or my very reasonable explanations. I felt it best to keep quiet and let him meander through London until something looked familiar. It was not until we had passed the same statue three times that Kenneth slammed his hands against the wheel and pulled over.

"Do you know where the hell we are going?"

Well, I wanted to answer, *of course I do. I just did not know how to get there*. It was in this moment that I realized how much I enjoyed Horace's quiet demeanor and general lack of anger. He also was very good at reading a map, so I feel he would have been better in this situation than Kenneth.

I decided that the best course of action was for me to get out of the lorry and to get my bearings by walking. Because I am of medium height and occasionally walk quickly, I told him I would walk very slowly so he could follow behind in his van. I wondered if Kenneth was simply used to his Aleksi persona, or if his Aleksi persona was the *real* him. Either way, he had become taciturn. I jumped out and waved for him to follow me.

My plan worked well, as I'd expected it would. I was finally able to see that we had been going north when we should have been going south. And we had been going east, when really I believe west was a better way to get to the Cormants'. Kenneth had somehow gotten turned around. I had been wrong to think that, since he could drive, he would have a good sense of direction. It would take ages to walk to the Cormants' (I was walking slowly so Kenneth could follow), and by the time we got there I would be out of breath and sweaty and not at all in a suitable mood to remove items from their house.

Once again, something like this would never have happened with Horace. But who can spend their time focusing on the "What if's" of life?

I focused on cursing Kenneth in my head. What a bald idiot! I thought. What a buffoon! How could he have gotten us so lost?

What a bald idiot! was, I think, my favorite thought of the night. If I were to rank them in order.

As I was ranting, I walked past an officer of the law and did not even realize it. I tend to avoid constables, bobbies, crossing guards and the like as much as possible. They are a curious and chatty breed of people and I am neither curious nor chatty, especially when I am on the way to break into someone's home.

"'Ey! 'Old up there!"

It was the unmistakable voice of one who had the slightest bit of power over someone else. I quickened my pace, hoping he would think I was influential and too busy to stop for him and his Cockney accent.

"I said slow down!"

I maintained my pace.

Panting, the officer eventually caught with to me and I turned to greet him. My gaze drifted over his shoulder and saw that Kenneth had pulled to the curb and turned off the lorry's lights. My eyes went back to the officer.

"How do you do?" I said, as coldly and impatiently as possible.

"All roight, there. All roight. I just wented tah warn yah. I think that lorry back there was followin' yah."

"Oh? You don't say..."

"I been watchin' it for the last block. He was goin' s'slow and then I see when yah turned, it turned as well. I wanted tah warn yah, see'in as how I can't do much but... warn yah and all."

"Oh, well. Thank you so much. I'm sure the driver is just lost. But I do appreciate your thoughtfulness."

"Oh, I don't know about that! Lost m'foot! These guys will wait until yerra down a dead street at night and then BAM!"

I did not ask him to elaborate on what "BAM!" meant, but instead apologized for being in such a rush and said I needed to go. I held out my hand for him to shake to punctuate our goodbye.

"Just looking out fer yah. Be safe this evening, ma'am."

He tipped his hat and turned away, humming a tune that was popular on the radio that week. I looked down at my hairless, feminine hands and told myself that I really should stop using the perfumed lotions.

When the constable's back was well turned, I threw my hands in the air and waved in large arcs for Kenneth to see me. I then waved left dramatically with both arms to signal that I would be going left if he were to look for me. I felt it best to revise the plan once again and to now make it back to "home base" empty-handed. I knew Dreisbach would be disappointed, but his disappointment would be more tolerable than more attention from the police.

Across the road, now hidden from the prying eyes of the officer, Kenneth slowed the lorry long enough for me to hop in. We drove off at a normal pace, looking for a residential road to park and discuss our course of action.

When we'd settled, Kenneth simply turned his head and said, "Well?"

While I do like to be recognized for my razor-sharp planning skills, I thought his tone was a little cold. Perhaps Kennth was more Russian than he was letting on. Perhaps Aleksi wasn't an act at all. Either way, I looked back and him and said, "Well?"

"Where are we going?" he asked.

Yes, that was the million dollar question, wasn't it? Where did we go from there? I said I thought it would be too risky to go forward with our plan that evening and that we should go home and convince Dreisbach to put on one of those avant-garde modernist plays people liked nowadays with no set decoration or actors. Kenneth, who had no sense of the theatre, simply nodded his head and started the engine.

We had only driven two blocks when there, in front of us, was the familiar oak door of H.H. Hargood & Sons. I asked Kenneth to pull over immediately and let me out.

Kenneth, who probably had never used a high-quality stationer before, seemed confused.

"A change of plans!" I explained.

I remembered that Hargood, in his grief, had not replaced the broken bell that hung from his shop door. This, of course, left him susceptible to someone easily breaking into his shop. By looking through the windows at Hargood's flat above the shop, I could see that the lights were out and he was, most likely, already asleep.

I explained to Kenneth that, instead of stealing props, it would be best to make our own with paper and inks which I would take from the stationery store. It may not have been the original plan, but it was *a* plan. Perhaps we could perfect the art of papier-mâché before the opening night. I always did love a project, said. Kenneth reacted by lighting a cigarette.

Best of all, I could also get Rue back.

In front of H.H. Hargood & Sons' door, I took out the small manicure set that I had tucked into my jacket pocket. From it I produced a nail file and took off my left shoe. With the file inserted into the door lock, I hit the handle of the file with the heel of my shoe until the lock broke internally. Yes, it did ruin my nail file, I am sorry to say.

But my options were limited and Dreisbach would not let me use his manicure set.

Inside, I waited for my eyes to adjust to the dark. When this did not work, I remembered that Hargood often lit candles for ambiance and kept a set of matches behind the till. I lit a red taper and wrapped a bit of blotting paper around the base to protect my hand from wax. I wish Horace *was* with me on this trip, as he could see how moral I was in not even attempting to take money from Hargood's till. I may have been a criminal in Horace's eyes, but I was no thief!

I emptied a wastebasket onto the floor, began collecting items I thought Dreisbach might find useful, and placing them in the basket. I took crêpe paper, colored inks, a collection of wax stamps, and the wax itself. I found a few canvases and ribbon in a corner dedicated to arts. I took a fountain pen for myself and a few good graphite pencils for sketching scenery. I even took five inkwells, which I thought could pass for fine china if the audience did not look too closely.

I felt that, if Hargood or Rue had not woken yet with the noise I had already made, then I was safe to open drawers. Behind the till I found loads of cardstock and an impressive pair of scissors that I thought could make an excellent stage dagger. I added these to the wastebasket. I also included a few sheets of tissue paper, which would be crumbled up and painted yellow and folded into a vest to act as a Golden Fleece.

And finally, there on a shelf where Mr. Hargood sat to greet customers, were two stacks of business cards. One read DIRECTEUR in gold lettering and another read: ASSISTANT TO THE DIRECTOR in black lettering. I took them both. I felt that I was doing Hargood a favor by taking the business cards now. I was sure he would be too distracted with his shop and missing Rue to remember to call and tell me to pick up the business cards later.

I felt I had redeemed myself by turning a failed mission into a great success.

I took the wastebasket outside and handed my spoils to Kenneth through the driver's window. I then told him to hold on one more second, as there was something else I had to grab.

A curtain divided Hargood's public and private realms and I had never breached that threshold. There is something very intimate about walking around someone's home while they are sleeping and it made me very uncomfortable to spend too much time there when he could have woken at any moment. But, then again, when would I have a more opportune time to get Rue back?

At the top of the landing, I was greeted by two distinct snores: an old man snore and the snore of my beautiful Rue. Hargood's was a rough,low growl; Rue's was whiny and pitched. But both were loud, making it easy to guess where they were in the black unknown of Hargood's second-floor flat.

I remembered that Hargood did not have his left eye, so I made sure that I stayed on that side of him to avoid being seen right away. This was easy, as the bedroom entrance faced his left side. Rue, on the other hand, was sleeping at the foot of the bed, leaving her easy to reach. But unfortunately, Rue was a very deep sleeper. I did not want to just grab her and run, as she would probably be surprised and bark, which would have definitely woken Hargood up.

I had a stellar idea: I would simply trick Rue into coming into the hallway. She would already be awake. I would would grab her there and we could go.

I grabbed the bit of blotting paper which had been used for the taper and began crinkling it gently between my fingers. I did this a few times slowly, and then added a bit more paper to make it louder. It sounded like a sandwich wrapper, which was the plan. Rue, who had a very healthy appetite, would recognize the sound and come investigate the unwrapping of the sandwich.

While I do believe dogs are clever animals, they are not the smartest. Their instincts are predictable, leaving them easily manipulated. Even Rue, who was markedly more clever than my other dogs, was no different.

Up popped her head and she began to sniff about in the air. She cocked her head to one side and then the other, considering the crinkling sound carefully before finally deciding to leave her warm bed and have a midnight snack.

I was hunched over on the landing and just out of sight from Hargood (that is, if he were to turn his head and use his good eye). I continued crinkling the paper until she was safely in the hallway. In the little bit of available light in Hargood's upstairs flat, I saw my Rue, tired but as beautiful as ever. She looked at me and smelled my hand and wagged her little tail in recognition.

"Come on, darling," I said. "Let's go home."

XXXIII

On the Lam

The play was a disaster. The whole night was a disaster. It was the end of everything—Dreisbach's career as a playwright, my career as the Chair of a Committee, and my life in London. It was the night that left me trapped on a ship with my ex-best friend, Horace, and my four dogs, sailing for America and God-knows-what.

The set decorations were nice, though. Dreisbach and I did a splendid job, indeed. We created entire feasts from *papier-mâché* and even coaxed Kenneth to steal a mink stole from Toffie, which we promptly dyed yellow. The golden fleece! The scenery was painted on huge, canvas sheets. Dreisbach did not seem to know where Thessaly was located, though. He painted a few pyramids in the background. We did not have enough paint to fix his mistake.

Otherwise, we were quite pleased with ourselves. I was not pleased, though, with Dreisbach's actors.

I had left most of the decision-making to Dreisbach, including casting. I was unsure how actors were paid, so I left those negotiations to him. It seems he had no intention of paying actors, so we were left with a motley group of street urchins, the independently wealthy, and a few teenagers who had nothing better to do in their gap year. They were all men (obviously) and none of them looked at all handsome in the togas we fashioned from spare linens from the storage room.

One actor complained that his costume smelled of mildew. I asked that Dreisbach fire him immediately and to give his lines to someone more grateful for his role.

When it became clear that many, perhaps all, of them were ungrateful for the opportunity we'd extended them, I agreed to step in as Director. I had to. There were many notable people on the guest list.

In fact, I had asked Hannah Grey-Downs, whom I had left in charge of the invitations, to send over the final list. I was surprised not only to see the Marchioness of Dunhillerin, but also her twin sons, Hamlin and Jock. Their appearance would make the social papers. It would have been wonderful press for us, indeed, had things not gone awry.

There was also a hodge-podge of art world types and dog enthusiasts. There were the Pryce-Reese's and the Smith-Johanns (who, as you already know, became rich by inventing a new type of cheddar that was a big hit at the Ritz). I ran down the list to see if anyone I personally knew would be in attendance, so I would be sure to wave and make them feel very special at my acknowledgement. Only one name turned up. Well, I should say it was two names, on one line. Together.

Jane Raitland and Desmond Winnicott, Baron Ham-sur-Rye.

I cursed Hannah Grey-Downs and her guestlist. I felt sick to think of Jane and Desmond in love. Jane was a country mouse who somehow ended up in the city. Desmond, with his nice eyebrows and permanent tan, must have seen that! Perhaps it was why children liked to poke snakes with sticks. A morbid fascination with something they are fundamentally disgusted by. Yes, that had to have been it, I thought, as I crumbled up the paper and told one of the street waifs to stand up straighter and to project his voice when he was on stage.

I was as naturally skilled at telling others how to be good actors as I was at tying knots and speaking German. If the police had not shown up during the first act, I believe that night would have been the start of a smashing career in theatre.

In the first act, before the Greek chorus even had time to explain why the cast was all-male, or why there were pyramids in the scenery, it happened. The lights were low and at first none of us knew what was happening. I assumed that Henry, who can be quite loud when he is nervous, had simply knocked over a box for attention. But then there was a shout, a bang, a door opening and closing, a woman's scream. It all happened so fast. I knew that running was my only option.

It is a funny feeling, knowing you are done for. That the efforts to try and live a good life were not enough. That somewhere there will be others who see the lengths you went to for your dogs was, in their eyes, "criminal". But for me, it was simply a way to survive. How could I, a man with so many talents, be expected to live forever taking dinner orders and refilling water glasses? How could I, a man of influence, live in a bed-sitting room with no one to greet me when I arrived home? That life, to me, was intolerable. And as I yelled for Dreisbach to kill the stage lights, I felt as if I was being punished simply for wanting more.

Dreisbach pulled the levers and the theatre went black. There were more screams and a "Damn it!" from the audience. I hoped people would think this was an interpretative, immersive play and would stay seated. At least long enough for me to sneak into the coat check area to pocket a few pounds.

I ran to the small closet where I had put the dogs to keep them out of guests' way and took a moment to get my bearings. I would, of course, grab Dreisbach's wallet on my way out, which he usually kept on the kitchen table. I could then run out of the alley and get a head start. But it was then I knew that I had no choice but to say my goodbyes to my beloved Henry, Rue, and Milly. There was no way I could take them with me. I had no money for food. No place for us to sleep. I did not even have rope to use as leads. All of this had been for them and now, crouched down in a storage closet that, at one time, held boxes of napkins and takeaway containers, I was saying my goodbyes.

"Arthur!"

The door opened behind me, and even in the blackness of the theatre I could make out Horace's fuzzy but imposing form. I welcomed seeing him, but I was annoyed that I did not have the chance to give him the cold shoulder, as I had intended to when I would see him next. But now was not the time to teach Horace a lesson. Now, I was only concerned about not getting arrested.

"Arthur, we need to go. The police are after you."

"Yes, I'm quite aware – Frances, don't shake, darling – I'm quite – Rue, *please*, stop kissing for one moment."

"We need to *leave*."

"What the hell do you think I'm trying to do?"

"They're going to find you soon, Arthur. Will you *please* come with me."

It was then I realized that I would not leave alone, down an alley and with Dreisbach's wallet. Rather I would leave with Horace and my four dogs. Crowded on the floor, trying to wrangle the dogs into a semblance of calm, I asked Horace to shut the door behind him and to only open it if he heard me knock.

The audience was rumbling now and I could hear a constable demanding for someone to turn on the lights. A torch shone behind the curtains and its beam was just over my shoulder, allowing me to slip quietly behind a massive box and out of sight. I crawled slowly to my bedroom, and grabbed a pile of laundry which included my Good Shirt, my second-best shirt, a hat, my black suit that Miss Greenwood did not like, and my passport. It was a snap to bundle everything together into my arms, as I did not own many things at the time.

I own even fewer now.

My dressing gown hung on a nail. I took the belt to use as a lead. This was all I had with me when I left the Esstäbchen Theatre, and London, for good.

It seemed that the all-male cast confused the police officers, as they were attempting to round up the actors on stage and interrogate them one-by-one in front of the audience. This afforded me enough time to make my way back to the small storage closet where I knocked gently, three times. Horace did not answer, so I knocked louder and stage-whispered, "Horace! Open this damn door!"

He opened it immediately.

"Sorry," he said. "We never decided if you'd do a special knock or not. I wasn't sure if it was you."

I did not bother to argue with Horace. (Who else would be knocking so politely on a small storage closet?) I began tying the dressing gown belt around the midsection of the four dogs. It was the only way to grab ahold of them in one go and when I was done I was proud of the knot I had tied. If only Dreisbach had found a need for a Cerberus-type creature in his play. How my dogs would have shone in that role?

"Here, take them," I said.

"You can't be serious! We can't take four dogs."

"The hell we can't! They're the reason we're in this mess and I can't... I can't... I can't leave them, Horace! And besides, it's not like they're looking for you out there. Just help me get them out of here safely and you can leave for good this time."

"What do you mean, Arthur? They're looking for both of us."

"What do *you* mean?"

"I was in line for the play, and... What can I say? I wanted to see what nightmare came out of Dreisbach's mind this time. I saw a man speaking with the police. Older. Glass eye. He was confirming some details he had in a little notepad. I heard *both* our names, Arthur. Seems we got connected to a robbery. It had to be from Ondwynn and the dog. But I don't know how that man found out!"

"It wasn't that," I said. "It was these damned business cards. That old man is Hargood. He connected the dogs because I took our business cards with us on the way out after breaking in and taking a few things."

"What do you mean 'our business cards?'"

"It really was meant to be a gift, Horace. But now you ruined the surprise. But who has time to be mad about where someone stole what and from whom? Just grab these dogs and we have to go!"

As I said these words, the lights in the theatre came on and we were left to make an even quicker getaway. I thought for sure we had a couple more minutes, as I have met quite a few policemen in my day and rarely have I judged one capable of turning on a light switch.

"Horace, we have to leave now. Take the dogs and we have to go now. Did you bring your car?"

"Yes, I've been living out of it for the last few days, trying to figure out what to do next with myself."

"Good. Then you already have your belongings there. I need you to make a run for it now, Horace. I need you to take the dogs and meet me outside the alley with the car running and ready to go."

"Arthur, I don't think..."

"Horace, do you trust me?"

"No. Well..."

"Well" Bloody hell, man! Let me put it another way. Do you want to go to jail?"

"No."

"Then grab the dogs and go. I'll be there in a moment."

Out Horace went into the hallway. The officers had not yet reached this part of the backstage and I believe Horace was saved thanks to the labyrinth of Chinese curtains that populated the back of the theatre. In the distance I heard Dreisbach shout, "That way, officers! The scoundrels are escaping out the front door!"

Dreisbach was an ugly little man with his little perversions and terrible *maquillage*, but he was a true friend. Perhaps (now that Horace is no longer my friend), he was the best I'd ever had.

I ran through the small kitchen and out into the alley. In a way, I was happy to find it was raining, which added a cinematic quality to our escape. On my way down the alley, I grabbed a slab of wood and found Kenneth's moving van in its spot. Climbing up on my toes and looking around me quickly, I broke the driver's side window with the plank.

There, inside the sun visor, were two tickets. Kenneth had previously said that he and Toffie were going to take a trip and I had gambled the last ounce of luck I had on seeing if they were still here where he had once said he'd left them. I snatched and slid them into the inner pocket of my suit jacket. We would visit the ticketing office in the morning to exchange for passage on the *Mathilde* the next day, which is how we ended up in an interior portside room instead of the suite Toffie had originally booked.

I ran back to the alleyway door and jammed the plank of wood against the knob to lock it from the outside. On the street I was greeted by a nervous-looking Horace driving his car and the oblivious smiles of Milly, Celia, Henry, and Rue through the backseat window. I had given up so much of my life to ensure my dogs and I were happy, and seeing their tongues out and tails wagging, I regretted none of it.

I opened the passenger-side door and climbed into the car. Henry jumped into my lap licked my hand. Horace accelerated into the London traffic and in the rear distance I could see the police officers departing the Esstäbchen Theatre, scratching their heads.

I told Horace to make his way out of the city and we would worry about how to get to Southampton when it was safe to do so, as I was generally useless with a map and, presumably, even less so at night, when I am exhausted.

After twenty minutes or so in the car we had all settled down a bit. Henry was asleep in my lap and Horace was no longer white-knuckling the steering wheel.

"I think we'll be okay, Horace. I think the worst of it is behind us now."

"You think so?"

"I know it, old man. You tend to forget, but I am a very influential person and think my skill set wasn't valued in London like it will be in New York."

Horace did not respond immediately and I was worried he did not agree that we would thrive in New York. It annoyed me to think that he was not confident in my abilities to influence others (especially Americans, who are the easiest of all people to influence), but when we stopped at a turn in the road, he looked over at me.

"I believe you, Arthur," he said "It'll work out somehow. But you must promise me this one thing: no more goddamn dogs."

I said nothing. As you know, I am a man of my word, and I had absolutely no intention of keeping that promise.

Epilogue

As you can plainly see now, the reason I am aboard the *Mathilde* heading towards New York is the fault of Mr. Hargood. If there is one takeaway from this journal of mine, it is that one must never trust an English stationer. They are, it seems, a very vindictive breed of professionals. Instead, one should order business cards from France or perhaps even Belgium.

It has been three days since I began to write down the events that led to our escape from London and still Horace and I have not made up. In fact, he complains nightly that he is cold and that I should not have used his sheets to make the rope I have been using to climb up to the Romanian count's deck. I tell him that I would happily provide him with my blankets, but the dogs like to sleep on my bed and, really, the blankets are for them, not me. Every morning we reach an impasse in resolving this issue.

I do hope that the generosity of New York rubs off on Horace. He could surely learn how to be a more charitable person. He has not even asked about Milly's seasickness and instead spends most days in the casino. If he is winning, he has kept it a secret. The next time he falls asleep, I will be sure to check his wallet.

I do not know what awaits us in New York and I can only hope that we will blend into the crowd of tourists which flock to Manhattan like migratory birds. In the meantime, I have found a bobby pin in the dining room, which I plan to use to pick the lock on the Count's door. If Horace does not plan to share his winnings with me, then I must think of how I will fund my new life in New York with my four dogs. I am sure Count Găvăneşti will have a pair of cufflinks or a fountain pen which I can pawn.

But for now, I am tucked in the corner of the Count's balcony, peeping through the window. I must wait for the red ember of the Count's cigarette to grow cold so I know he has fallen asleep. I will then unlock his balcony door and see what there is I can find.

By tomorrow morning we will be in New York and I will need all the help I can get.

Printed in the USA
CPSIA information can be obtained
at www.ICGtesting.com
CBHW021905200424
7153CB00001B/1/J